LONDON
London, J. A.
Darkness before dawn /
33090022457479

No longer property
Long Beach Public L

MAIN 07/13

"Is the blood supply adequate?" I ask.

"No."

Of course not . . .

"How much more is needed?" I ask.

"At least double," Valentine says.

Double! I fight not to let my shock show. "I'm sorry, Lord Valentine, but that will be extremely difficult."

"Then I cannot guarantee the safety of your city or its citizens." His eyes are dark. So dark I can't tell if they're staring straight into mine or at my neck. It's a threat. "I hope, for your sake, that the citizens of Denver find their charitable side," he says in that icy, dead tone. I hear the door open.

"You're late," Valentine snaps.

"My apologies, Father," a deep voice says.

My breath backs up in my lungs and I manage somehow to remain still. I know that voice. But it can't be. It can't.

LONG BEACH PUBLIC LIBRARY
101 PACIFIC AVE.
LONG BEACH, CA 90822

Darkness Before Dawn

J. A. LONDON

HARPER TEEN

An Imprint of HarperCollinsPublishers

HarperTeen is an imprint of HarperCollins Publishers.

Darkness Before Dawn
Copyright © 2012 by Jan Nowasky and Alex Nowasky
All rights reserved. Printed in the United States of America.
No part of this book may be used or reproduced in any manner whatsoever
without written permission except in the case of brief quotations embod-
ied in critical articles and reviews. For information address HarperCollins
Children's Books, a division of HarperCollins Publishers, 10 East 53rd
Street, New York, NY 10022.
www.epicreads.com

Library of Congress Cataloging-in-Publication Data
London, J. A.
    Darkness before dawn / by J.A. London. — 1st ed.
        p.   cm.
    Summary: When seventeen-year-old Dawn Montgomery, daughter of
the slain delegates to ruling vampire Lord Valentine, becomes the new delegate she finds herself falling in love with Valentine's kindhearted son, and
risks her life when she is drawn into their dangerous political game.
    ISBN 978-0-06-202065-9
    [1. Vampires—Fiction. 2. Orphans—Fiction.] I. Title.
PZ7.L8422Dar—2012   2011024250
[Fic]—dc23   CIP
                                                                  AC

Typography by Michelle Gengaro-Kokmen
13 14 15 16   CG/RRDH   10 9 8 7 6 5 4 3
❖
First Edition

33090022457479

For Kari and Zareen, whose insights into the story
and characters were invaluable

Prologue

As the carriage rolled across the desolate plains, the assassin slid his gaze over to his traveling companions. Husband and wife. Joined by love and a dedication that would soon cost them everything.

"It's unusual for Lord Valentine to send an escort along for our journey back to Denver," the wife said, studying him.

"Attacks have increased lately," he replied, his tone as dead and uncaring as he was.

"We are appreciative of the consideration," the husband added. "The Great Vampire Lord doesn't often show such favor."

"You were always his favorites," he said, already speaking of the couple in the past tense.

The moon was high and clear, its blue light piercing

through the windows. The horses were traveling at a full gallop, their hooves pounding against the ground in perfect rhythm.

"Lord Valentine was pleased with the latest blood supply figures," the wife said, a nervous tic in her voice, as she perhaps recognized that not all was right.

"Of course," he assured her, although quantities and numbers were irrelevant to him. He marveled at their innocence. "I would like to ask you a question," he said, looking directly at the husband. "Does your daughter have any idea about her true heritage?"

The man was taken aback. It was the last thing he expected to hear.

"Dawn lives in ignorance," he said. "And it is my dearest wish that she stay that way forever."

"A shame," the assassin murmured.

"What is he talking about?" the woman asked, concern etched across her face.

She doesn't know, the assassin realized. *Her husband has kept the truth from her. I'll never understand these humans.*

"It's nothing, love," the husband said, his attempt at a comforting tone so butchered it was comical.

"Oh, it's everything," the assassin replied.

"The past was buried long ago. There's no reason to dig it up."

The assassin looked at them both and was satisfied. Those would be their last words on this earth.

No pain was felt. It happened too fast. All was over before they could even scream.

Chapter 1

Standing on my balcony, I watch the sun paint its descent across the sky. Soon the monsters will come out to play. They like the night. They feed on it.

Sometimes they feed on us.

From here, I can see the twenty-foot-high concrete wall that surrounds Denver. It was built shortly after the thirty-year war that pitted humans against vampires came to an end. It keeps out most of the monsters. Most of them.

Tomorrow night the Agency—which is responsible for protecting the city—will send me out beyond the wall. Alone for the first time as the official delegate to one of the most powerful vampires in the world: Lord Valentine.

Just like my parents. For two long years they met with Lord Valentine twice a month to discuss vampire-human relations, negotiate the blood supply, appeal to his mercy—what little he has of it. Before them, other delegates served, but none lasted as long; none pleased Valentine the way that they did. While my father was the official delegate, my mother wouldn't let him carry the burden alone. They loved each other so much. I try not to resent that she placed her love for my father above her love for me. She knew the dangers, knew I could be left an orphan. Still, she traveled at my father's side. Then one night, three months ago, they didn't come home. Their burned carriage was found abandoned by the road, the ground around it soaked in blood.

Valentine sent condolences and an assurance that those responsible—rogue vampires traveling through the area—had been dealt with. Later I learned that he tied the accused to crucifixes outside the wall, forced them to greet the sun. Because vampires heal quickly, it must have been a long, excruciating death as they slowly turned to ash until all that remained was their fangs. For some reason, those never burn.

My parents' memorial service had barely ended when Valentine notified the Agency that he wanted *me* to take over as delegate. No one asked why he chose me. When someone has the power to destroy all you hold dear if he's not happy, you do whatever it takes to keep him satisfied. Even if it kills you inside. Even if most of what you hold dear has already been taken. But sometimes I *do* wonder: Why me? I'm only seventeen, the youngest delegate ever appointed.

The Agency assigned Rachel Goodwin to serve as my

guardian. She moved into my family's apartment to watch over and guide me. She's also my mentor, teaching me all the ins and outs of being a delegate and dealing with vampires—etiquette, protocol, and the manners that Valentine expects those who meet with him to exhibit. For two months now I've been meeting Lord Valentine with Rachel by my side. She did most of the talking; I was just there to observe her interactions with Valentine. But following our last meeting, the Lord Vampire told her that she was no longer needed and that I was ready to go solo. The Agency didn't argue, but then, they seldom do. That's my job.

"Okay, I've got the address." With green eyes gleaming, my best friend, Tegan Romano, snaps her cell phone shut and jerks me back to the present as she joins me on the balcony. She gives me the location of the party. It's in an area of the city that still reflects the devastation from the war.

I think about texting it to Michael, even though I know he's taking his advanced defense class tonight.

"Don't even think about texting him," Tegan says, as though she's reading my mind. "Tonight is girls' night."

But I'd feel better having Michael there. Michael Colt has already been accepted into the Night Watchmen's elite bodyguard training division. Right now, he's just marking time until graduation next spring.

"You're not cheating on him if all you do is dance," she adds.

"It's not that. I just . . . miss him." With my delegate preparations and his bodyguard training, we've had so little time for each other lately.

"You can see him tomorrow. Besides, he's busy tonight anyway, right? Otherwise he'd be here and you wouldn't be stuck with me."

"I'm not *stuck* with you."

"So come on. Since you two got so ridiculously serious, you hardly ever hang out with me anymore."

"We hang out."

"And I'm the third wheel."

Not usually. She almost always has a guy with her. Just no one she's head-over-heels crazy about like I am with Michael. It's kinda funny. Michael and I grew up together, were always friends, and then about four months ago, on a dare at a party, we kissed. I think the sparks we ignited surprised both of us. We've been an item ever since.

As Tegan and I step back into the apartment, the radio gives the evening announcement: "Sunset will be at seven fifteen p.m. and twenty-three seconds. At the sound of the third beep, the official time will be six thirty-five p.m." *Beep. Beep. Beep.*

Out of habit, we check our watches and cell phones to make sure the hour and minutes are correct. Accuracy can determine life and death most nights, as we race the dark home, huddle in our rooms to await dawn. But not tonight.

Tegan's mother knows she's spending the night, but she expects us to stay here under Rachel's watchful gaze.

Turning off the radio, I'm glad that Rachel's working late at the Agency right now. She'd never approve of what Tegan and I are doing. The party is being held at a house near the wall.

"This party is going to rock," Tegan says.

"How did you even hear about it?" I ask as I snatch my leather jacket from where I'd draped it over the couch earlier and slip it on. My favorite part is the fur-lined collar; it keeps my neck warm, makes it feel protected. My black hair is curling riotously past my shoulders. I decided not to tame it. Tonight I want to be as wild as my hair.

"Oh, you know," she says evasively. "A friend of a friend who knows a guy . . ."

She knows lots of guys. They all want to know her. She's petite, with short blond hair that frames her pixie face and makes her startling green eyes stand out.

I stop at the door. "Do they go to our school?"

"No. The one on the other side of the city. What does it matter?"

Warning bells go off in my head. "What do you know about these people?"

"They're *vampires*," she says sarcastically, not happy that I'm questioning things.

"That's not funny."

"Well, what do you think? You've gotten so paranoid since—"

She stops, looks embarrassed. I know what she was going to say. Since my parents were killed. "I'm not paranoid. I'm just being cautious."

"These people are okay." She shrugs. "I'm going. Be a chicken if you want and stay here."

She opens the door. I can't let her go alone. No. That's just an excuse, a weak justification. The truth is: I want to go.

"Hold up." I grab one of several metal stakes that sit in a ceramic vase like a hideous flower arrangement and wedge it inside my leather boot. I never leave home without one after the sun sets.

I close and lock the door behind me. She wraps her arm around mine, and we walk in sync to the elevator. "We're going to have so much fun," Tegan assures me.

I try to believe it. I want to believe. A final night of fun before I face my destiny.

The few precious cities left in the world are each controlled by an Old Family patriarch or a trusted member of his family. Lord Valentine is one of the oldest. He was the first to make the presence of vampires known. Although it's been nearly fifty years since they stepped from myth into reality, the history books explain how it played out. They became overnight celebrities. From nighttime talk shows to the lowliest paparazzi, everyone wanted a piece. The number one question wasn't how many people they'd killed or even how many vampires existed in the world. It was about fashion and traveling and how they saw humans. We had vampires in our midst and all we wanted to know was their opinions about us. We were so egocentric and oblivious, eager for entertainment. We're not so entertained now.

I can almost understand why we were so naïve. After all, they must not have seemed that different from us: They have heartbeats, they breathe, their skin is warm. But the similarities only served to distract us from seeing the monsters hiding within—until it was too late.

Outside, Tegan and I head to the nearest trolley stop.

Since the war ended, the only decent transportation in this city is the trolleys. Connected to the tracks and electrical lines above them that shoot out sparks, they carry people toward their destination. Always on time. Always efficient. Tonight it's crowded and we have to stand. Tegan's so close to the door that her leg sticks out and she playfully touches the ground every few minutes until the conductor yells at her to stop.

There aren't many cars these days. People are left to walk the streets or take the trolleys, which are the lifeblood of this city. And if they're the blood, the Works is the heart. No matter how many times I pass by it, I'm still captivated by its sprawling mass of steel pipes reaching out to the sky; only a handful of other buildings match its height. Out of the top plumes the constant blue smoke created from the processing and burning of coal, which fuels the massive generator that provides electricity. Rub your finger across any wall in the city and it comes back black. The closer you are to the Works, the more power you get and the more regular it is. The area near the wall where we're heading puts up with daily rolling blackouts.

We head away from the center of the city. Plastering the walls along our route are the propaganda posters set up by the Agency to encourage citizens to donate blood.

A tube going from an arm into a glass mug: HAVE YOU GIVEN YOUR PINT TODAY?

An unrealistic image of a woman giving blood while tucking her daughter into bed: KEEP THEM FED SO YOUR CHIL-DREN CAN REST THEIR HEADS.

A veteran from the war in a wheelchair: THEY GAVE THEIR BLOOD; NOW GIVE YOURS.

As part of the VampHu Treaty that ended the war, humans in the cities supply blood to the vampires on the outside. In return the vampires don't attack the cities. Donating blood is voluntary; no one is *forced* to do it. At first, people were so scared of the vampires, the tragedies of war still recent memories, that they fled to the nearest donation site in the hope of keeping their new vampire masters fat and jolly. But after only a few years people are now full of excuses: *I'm too busy; I have to make dinner; I have schoolwork.* They assume others will do it for them. Our once-steady supply is beginning to slip. Every month we receive less. Which makes my new position as delegate much more challenging.

The sun dips below the horizon, turning the city from deep orange to light blue to dark purple, and finally to black. Everyone around us begins to fidget, checking watches as if in disbelief. They begin calling home, their signals bouncing off the one and only cell tower in the middle of the city. *I'm okay*, they say. *I got off late. I know. I know. I'll be home soon.* The trolley is too slow for some, and they simply get off and make a dash for it.

That's a dangerous game to play, but some protection is out tonight: I spy a Night Watchman slipping out of an alley. They're easy to spot. Dressed all in black, they wear a balaclava or hood to hide their identity, and a distinctive medallion to distinguish them as an official elite guard of the city, a piece of metal so intricately designed that it's impossible to copy. While most people scurry indoors once the sun sets, the Watchmen come out to hunt for the rogue vampires that sneak past the wall into the city.

And Michael will be a Watchman soon. . . .

I try not to think about the dangers he'll face. I've lost my parents and my brother. My brother, Brady, was only twenty when he died. I don't know if I can survive losing someone else I care about so much. I shake off the thoughts. Tonight is about having fun.

As we travel farther out, the streets stop having names; the buildings stop having signs. After twenty more minutes of rumbling along, taking in the row houses and the homeless people staggering just outside of them, Tegan says, "This is our stop."

We hop off while the trolley is still moving slowly, and I follow her. Bad things can happen to those who wander out here. The rebuilding efforts haven't extended this far yet. It's a part of town that most parents forbid their kids to visit. They think we're too young, can't take care of ourselves. Because it's not a heavily populated part of the city, no guards are out here patrolling the streets. I know that makes it dangerous. But sometimes we just want to prove that we're not afraid of the dark.

Even when we are.

Chapter 2

We wander through the neighborhood, searching for the right street. The cool thing about being this far from the center of the city is that in place of massive apartment towers are actual houses. Sure, they're on shaky foundations and they're just one storm away from being knocked over, but they're houses nonetheless.

"Here it is," Tegan says.

The house we're in front of has more lights on inside than any other on the block, which isn't saying much. Music is spilling into the street. Through the windows, I see the shadowy silhouettes of guys and girls having a great time. At the door, a large bouncer, six and a half feet tall and built like a train, holds out his hand to stop our progress. He has several crucifixes dangling from chains around his neck, despite the fact that they were proven to be ineffective against vampires long ago. I've even seen vampires wearing them.

"Fang check," he says, and Tegan shoots him a wide grin. He lifts up her lip, examines her teeth, then waves her in.

"Fang check," he says to me, and I endure the same process, his burly fingers rough against my mouth. "Have fun, ladies."

It's a silly ritual. Vampires can keep their fangs retracted, and when they do, they look just like us. But I guess whatever makes people feel safe . . .

Inside the music is deafening. Five guys and a girl are on a makeshift stage set up in the huge living room. Drums. Bass. Guitar. Synthesizer. Mic. They've got everything. The boys are attacking the instruments like their lives depend on it, but it's the girl who catches my eye. She's my age, but she has utterly mesmerizing tattoos covering one arm. She's singing with one of the guys, but it's her voice that comes through. It's grungy, like she's been smoking since she was born. Her hair is butchered, cut just above her chin.

That's who I want to be. I want to be her. I want to be able to do anything I want, instead of what I'm forced to do. I don't want to have to wear particular clothes or keep my hair a certain length because the Lord Vampire insists. I want to have no responsibilities. No worries.

Tegan grabs my arm and pulls me through the crowd. In the kitchen an older guy is handing out beer in small cups. It doesn't taste very good, but still I chug it, then grab another and drink it as well. I want a buzz, anything to keep me from thinking about the dangers I'll face tomorrow night. No one here cares that we're only seventeen. It's one of the reasons that Tegan chose this party. The other is that no one knows us. For someone like me, anonymity is rare.

"Where are you two from?" a guy asks us. He's tall, with shaggy blond hair. Based on the smile Tegan is flashing at him, I can tell she thinks he's cute, but he's not really my type.

"Downtown," she says, referring to the center of the city. The very safe, recently rebuilt center.

He laughs. "A couple of good girls, huh?"

"Not all good." She winks; he grins.

"You ever been this close to the wall?"

"No, and we're so scared," Tegan says, holding on to me and faking a shiver.

"Don't worry, I'll protect you." He pulls his right pants leg up to reveal a wooden stake strapped to his calf.

Tegan looks like she's impressed, but she's carrying one as well. And, like me, she knows how to use it. Neither of us believes in relying on someone else for protection.

The guy looks at me, gives a little jerky nod. "Cool ink."

"Thanks." I know he's referring to the crucifixes tattooed on my neck. One on each side, right where a vampire's fangs would go. My brother had a pair as well. Not that they did him any good. I tell myself that now isn't the time to be thinking about it. The nightmares devour my sleep; I can't let them consume my waking moments, too.

The guy signals the one pouring the drinks to get two more.

"Some of the premium stuff," he says, handing each of us a cup. "It might sit better with you. After all, you're probably used to fine downtown drinks. Not that other garbage."

We take them. Tegan, as if she has something to prove, swallows it in one gulp. "Awesome stuff. I could use another."

"Sure thing," he says, before stopping and staring at me, my drink still in hand, untouched. "Hey, you look familiar."

My heart jumps, slams against my ribs. I'm going to be in big trouble if he recognizes me. My face has been plastered all over the news and newspapers lately. Luckily, it's an official delegate photo—partial profile, hair up, makeup designed to make me look older, a blouse with a high collar covering my tattoos, and a dark jacket. "Just one of those faces, I guess."

I think Tegan picks up on my nervousness, because she starts pushing me toward the door. "Maybe we'll see you on the dance floor," she says to Shaggy Guy.

She grabs my arm and drags me out of the kitchen before I even have a chance to drink the premium stuff, and I toss my still-full cup into an open trash can. Dancing is hard enough for me, but drinking while rocking to the beat—forget it.

"Don't worry. No one is going to figure out who you are," she whispers near my ear.

"I hope you're right."

"I'm always right."

In the living room, she pulls me toward the dance floor, already swaying her hips, getting into the rhythm. Then she grins broadly as two guys approach. It's just that easy for her. The little game is played, each one jockeying for position, deciding whether they want her or me.

Tegan whispers into their ears and then cuts to the chase, yelling to me over the music, "This is Chris"—she points to a guy with flaming red hair and a solar system of freckles covering his face—"and Marc." His black hair falls across his brow, nearly hiding his eyes. "Pick one."

Like they're door prizes.

After downing the beer so fast, I feel as though everything is moving slowly. I don't want to make any decisions. Tonight was supposed to be decision-free. Turns out it is. Before I can answer, Tegan takes off with Chris, and Marc grabs my hand and pulls me deeper into the crowd. Then he releases his hold and starts gyrating. I tell myself that I need this. Some fun, a little craziness. Everyone is looking for a good time, because nothing is simple anymore. Maybe it never was.

The music thumps, changes tunes, and we're just dancing. I move my head from side to side, letting my long hair whip back and forth. I forget about my responsibilities. Forget about what awaits me tomorrow night. Forget everything except the rhythm of the beat.

One song shifts into another. I get lost in the moment and, in the process, lose sight of Tegan. It doesn't worry me until I realize several songs have passed since I saw her. My body is damp from dancing, the crowd is suffocating me, and suddenly I feel like there's no escape from this wall of bodies. I need some air. I need some space. I need Tegan.

"I'll be right back," I shout into Marc's ear. But he doesn't care. He just turns and starts dancing with someone else.

Wading through the forest of dancers, I circle the room. Tegan's nowhere to be seen. I go back to the kitchen. She's not at the beer counter, and neither are the two guys who were talking with us earlier. My instincts warn me that something's not right, and I always listen to those.

I move back into the living room and hear a commotion on the stairs leading to the next floor. Quickly I start up them, pushing past a couple caught in a lip-lock. Tegan's gold-glittered boots become visible. I see her struggling to climb up the steps. She's being helped by the guy with blond, shaggy hair. The one who gave us "special drinks." The pieces fall into place when Tegan starts laughing maniacally and has trouble standing. Her top-quality beer was laced with something designed to make her more . . . agreeable. Not all the monsters have fangs.

The guy keeps pulling her up, whispering into her ear, and rage fills me. I storm up the steps and push him as hard as I can.

He crashes to the floor. "Hey, bitch!"

He pops back to his feet, trying to stare me down, but I'm not in the mood to be intimidated. Tegan wraps her arm around the banister, using it as a crutch to remain standing. "Dawn?" My name gets tangled on her tongue. "I was . . . to play a game with . . . um . . . What's your name?"

She looks disoriented, eyes glazed over, her head wobbling like it's too big for her neck.

"Come on, Tegan, we're going." I wrap my hand around her arm. The guy reaches for his stake, but I'm faster. Mine is out, the tip pressed against his chest before he even touches his.

"These work equally well on people," I say.

His eyes widen. He raises his hands, backs up.

"I know who you are now," he says, his voice laced with disgust. "Dawn Montgomery. The city's new delegate."

"So you also know that I can have the Agency here in five minutes and you're busted. But all I want is to leave with my friend."

"Sure. Go ahead. Just don't come back."

"Why would I want to?"

Quickly pulling Tegan to her feet, I put her arm around my shoulders and hold her by the waist. I carefully guide her down the stairs. I give Shaggy Guy one final glance and see the anger in his eyes, but know that it can't possibly match mine. "Bastard!" I throw back at him.

"Was that his name?" Tegan murmurs.

"Yeah." I shoulder our way through the moshing crowd. It's a struggle to keep us on our feet. Tegan's dragging me down.

"You can't sleep yet," I tell her.

I take Tegan outside, hoping some fresh air will clear her head.

"Is she all right?" the doorman asks, before fang-checking another partygoer.

"I don't know," I say.

"Well, don't bring her back in. The last thing we need is a girl ODing on the dance floor."

"Someone spiked her drink!"

"Whatever . . ."

That's the thing about people in this city: No one cares. Was it always this way? If so, what were we fighting for during the war?

"Are we going home already?" Tegan asks.

"Yeah, just hold on."

As we stumble past a crowd of people heading toward the door, the wind blows across our damp bodies, cooling us. The air is dirty out here, but at least there's plenty of it to breathe in. Holding Tegan close, I walk down the cracked sidewalk until the party is just a whisper, then a murmur, then nothing at all. I turn around and can't even see the lights. When I was inside, I thought the whole city could hear that music. But no, it barely reaches a single block.

I lower Tegan to a bench alongside the trolley tracks and drop down next to her. She presses her head against my shoulder.

"I don't feel so good," she mutters.

"Just hold on until we get to my place and you can sleep it off." Or maybe I should take her to the hospital. She's breathing, but so listless that I'm getting more worried. I shove my stake back into my boot and pull out my phone to call Michael. Or even Rachel. But there's no signal.

Dammit. With only one tower, service is sporadic, even more so this far from the city's center. I think about walking a short distance away to try to find a signal, but I don't want to leave Tegan by herself. The trolley should be here soon. It can get us downtown, and from there we can catch another one to the emergency clinic.

The streetlight above me flickers, and I pray it doesn't go out. I'm beginning to realize how alone we are out here. Not a single soul around, every shop closed or abandoned. The few row houses surrounding us are blacked out, the families either asleep or not even in.

I stifle a yawn. All I want is to lie down on the bench and go to sleep. Drinking two beers so fast was a bad idea. Coming out to this part of town with Tegan was an even worse idea. What were we thinking? That we'd stay at the party until sunrise? That we wouldn't be caught out on the streets alone at night when the monsters come out to play?

The hairs on the back of my neck rise and I twist around, reaching down for my stake, but no one's there. No one could be; it's just a wall with a tattered Agency poster begging for blood donations covered in graffiti: *Suck on this!* and *No more blood!* and *Stakes, not blood!* Fangs have been drawn on the calm woman's soft smile, and a crude imitation of a stake is piercing her chest. Not everyone appreciates what the Agency is doing. Looking around this run-down part of town, I guess I can't blame them.

Ding, ding, ding.

I turn back gratefully as the trolley rides up to us. When I put Tegan's arm around my shoulders and lift her, she makes a barely audible protest. The trolley glides to a stop. I drag her to the rear door and struggle to get her on board. Once inside I shove her into the corner seat. The trolley starts moving forward with a jerk. I lose my balance, toppling beside her.

Straightening, I glance around. The conductor doesn't look back at us, just stares ahead at the tracks like they might suddenly make a break for it and he'll have to catch them. Three other guys sit in the trolley, with their heads bent forward, obviously asleep. Probably tramps hoping to ride the entire line before getting kicked off. It's safer to sleep on the trolley than on the street.

We pass through an area with all the lights turned off, and, with the clouds hiding the moon, it's like we're going through a tunnel.

When we emerge into a better-lit district, one of the men seems closer to me. Surely it's just my imagination. Or maybe my perception is skewed since I had the beer. The entire car seems smaller.

Pulling up the collar on my jacket, I slump further down on the seat. I nudge Tegan. Her eyes are closed; her head has listed to one side. She looks like a rag doll, totally relaxed. Too relaxed.

I nudge her again. "Tegan?"

She doesn't react. I'm trying not to panic. Hopefully I can get a signal now. I reach into my pocket for my cell phone just as we pass between two tall warehouses, the passage so narrow it seems like it was once a single building, but the track was laid down and sliced it in two. The only light comes from a series of bulbs on a single line, crisscrossing from one wall to the next like festival lights put up at the last minute.

We slow down. I remember there's a sharp turn at the end of this. The conductor must be preparing for it.

But then we stop.

The three men snap their heads up at once, instantly alert, twist around, and stare straight at me. I start to shout at the conductor to get us moving again, but as I watch, his head slowly turns until I think it's going to do a full one-eighty. As if on cue, they all smile. Their huge fangs glisten with saliva.

Vampires!

Chapter 3

My fight-or-flight instinct is urging me to get the hell out, but I can't leave Tegan. They'd feed on her for days, maybe weeks, before letting her finally die—or worse, turning her into a monster like them. I can't lose her, not after my parents, not after Brady. I'd rather risk my life protecting her than add to the memories that already haunt me. I quickly stand, getting in front of my best friend. But before I can get my stake out, one of them grabs my shoulder and throws me toward the center of the trolley. I land sprawled over one of the hard benches that face the windows. I see Tegan sliding down to the floor like her muscles and bones have turned into jelly. I have to believe she's safer under the seat and with all their attention focused on me.

One of the vamps lunges for me, but I kick him back so

hard he smashes into one of the tiny windows and it shat-
ters.

My adrenaline rushes through me. No matter what
happens next it'll all be a blur. I won't even think. Just act.
Let my training and instinct take over. That's the only way
I'll get out of this alive. If I let myself think, I'll panic.

I yank out my stake and scramble to my feet. I waste no
time going after the nearest one. If I can kill one of them, it
might be enough to scare off the others. The odds aren't in
my favor, and the desire to run overwhelms me, but I stay
strong. I'm Tegan's only chance.

The conductor reaches out to grab my neck and I make
a stab for his heart, but he twists around too fast and the
stake cuts deep into his arm. He gives a horrific howl.
When he reaches for his wound, I fall back on a nearby seat
and kick straight up, catching him under the chin, sending
him flying back onto a bench.

I dodge past the two who are down. My target is the
one who is kneeling, reaching beneath the seat, clawing
desperately at Tegan. If I can just get the stake into him—

From behind me, one of them kicks the back of my
knee and I go down. The floor comes up too fast for me to
brace myself, and my forehead does all the work, taking
the brunt of the impact, smashing into the hard surface
with a thunderclap that echoes around me. By a miracle I
remain conscious.

The attacker grabs my ankle and pulls me across the
floor. He spins me over and straddles me, putting all his
weight on my hips. The others start gathering around. At

least Tegan is safe for the moment. I grip my stake, ready to stab the vamp on top of me, when he leans down for my neck. I see the bloodlust in his feral eyes. His ugly face is thin and scarred, and his fangs are frighteningly large.

His mouth opens wide, ready for the plunge, when one of the other vamps releases a bloodcurdling shriek. From the floor, the only thing I see is him disappearing through the rear door. Another scream echoes from outside. Then deafening silence.

I feel a spark of hope. Maybe a night patrol has arrived to help us. But we're not out of danger yet.

The vampire on me has grown still, too distracted by his accomplice's cries, maybe too confused or scared to finish me off. This is my chance. I imagine him as no different from the dummies I practice staking in school. Using every ounce of strength, I ram the metal stake into him. But because of the angle, I miss his heart. He jumps off me, my weapon still in him. He's groaning in pain, but still very much undead. And worse, he's taken my best weapon from me. But I still have my fists, my training, and, more important, my will to stay alive. I stand up too quickly and pain explodes through my head, reminding me without mercy of the fall I just took. The edge of my vision darkens.

I hear another scream and suddenly only two vampires are in the trolley. With both vamps distracted, gazes darting between each other and the door, I try to get to Tegan. Somehow I have to get her off this trolley. But my body refuses my commands. I'm frozen in place when a stranger steps onto the trolley. It's too dark to make out the details,

only that he's dressed in black, blends in with the night.
He's not wearing a balaclava or the Night Watchmen's
medallion, but since he's already quickly dispensed with
two vamps, I have to assume he's one of the city's elite. Off
duty, maybe.

Out of desperation, the uninjured vamp attacks the
stranger, but he slumps over quickly, a stake through his
chest; I don't have time to register how it happened. I can't
find my strength, and my vision is fuzzy, the image in front
of me turning black. The last vampire left yanks my stake
from his chest. Before I can react, he wrenches me in front
of him and holds the stake up to my throat.

"Don't come any closer," he says, his voice high-pitched
with fear. "I'll kill her."

But the stranger just takes another step, and I feel the
point of the stake pressing against my neck. Maybe the
stranger doesn't care. Maybe he's not a knight in shining
armor.

"I mean it! I'll . . ." But the vampire doesn't finish his
sentence. The stranger moves quickly. It's probably the
result of the blow to the head I took, but he becomes almost
a blur, leaping over the seats, yanking the vampire away
from me. I sink to the floor. I hear a distant scream, a gur-
gle. Then nothing.

I want to sleep, but I force myself to fend off the fog
in my brain. I begin slowly crawling toward Tegan. The
stranger is suddenly standing over me. He lifts me up with
amazing strength. For a heartbeat that seems to last an
eternity, I'm mesmerized by his presence. He looks to be

a little older than I am. His long black hair hangs to just below his strong jaw and falls in a way that makes his blue eyes stand out from the shadows.

Suddenly he shakes his head as though he, too, had been caught up in something he didn't understand. He releases his hold on me and steps back. "Come on," he says, his voice calm, serious. "I'll get your friend. You follow me. Others will be on their way."

He edges past me, our bodies brushing, creating an awareness that baffles me. I register the firmness of his muscles, his power. He maneuvers Tegan out from beneath the seat and lifts her into his arms as though she were a small child. He turns around and steps out of the trolley. I'm still in shock. I give myself a mental and physical shake. I have to follow Tegan. I hop off the trolley.

"Who are you?" I demand to know.

"Later. This way," he says, taking us out of the narrow passage and onto the main street.

I hear things: the thumping of vampires above us, moving from building to building. Their shadows dance in front of us, monstrous in size, so close to the lights that hang down.

"How many are there?" I ask.

"I don't know," he says. "But I can't take them all."

The fight I just endured takes its final toll and I stumble. I fall to one knee, curse, push myself up. The stranger shifts Tegan, draping her over his shoulder. Then he grabs my hand and we begin running.

We rush down a dark alleyway that I'm convinced

is safe only because he leads us. A sharp turn and then another, and we're in the deep corridors of the city. Tall, bricked walls like mazes hide the old parts, the blocks and buildings that stood erect before the war.

"Here," he says, stopping in front of an old abandoned movie theater.

The stranger, with Tegan still hanging over one shoulder, pulls out a key and undoes the padlock. The chains it held fall and coil onto the ground like great metal snakes. He swings the door open and ushers me inside. It's dark in there, but what choice do I have? This stranger risked his life for us, and in this moment, I have to trust him.

The stranger comes in behind me and hands me the key. "Bring in the chains and lock things up from this side."

I do as he says, hints of outside light allowing me to work in this dark entryway. When I turn around, he's already walking away, a tiny flashlight suddenly illuminating an eerie path.

"We're safe in here," he says.

Slipping the key into my jeans pocket for now, I follow him down a hall and up a narrow flight of stairs. He opens a door. I hear a click, and a small room is flooded with light. He eases Tegan down onto a cot. He feels her brow, checks her breathing. I tell him quickly about the party, how someone spiked her drink.

"She'll be fine," he says. "Probably won't remember any of this tomorrow, which might be for the best. She just needs to sleep it off. As long as we keep her cool, there's nothing to worry about."

Taking in the surroundings, I can see that the room is well maintained despite the theater being so ancient. Shelves hold metal canisters that are unfamiliar to me. Posters line the walls, old and nostalgic, not printed today but from days gone by. Some weird machine that looks like a giant camera sits on a table, staring out a small window in the wall.

"Where are we?" I ask.

"The projection room," he says.

"A what?"

"They used to project movies onto a screen from here." He gestures to the machine.

"Oh." There aren't any working movie theaters anymore. They're just relics like this one. I might enjoy exploring it if I weren't shaking so badly. The adrenaline has subsided and left me with a terrible feeling of anxiety, as if all the danger I was in is only now registering. I keep seeing the vampire standing over me, Tegan sprawled on the floor, me helpless to do anything about it. I was completely at their mercy. A lot of good all my training did. When faced with the reality of a vampire attack, I was pretty incompetent.

Will I be as inept tomorrow night, when I'm tested by Valentine? Will I fail to protect the citizens?

"You're trembling," he says. "Here, this'll help." He opens a small refrigerator, reaches in, then tosses me a can.

I stare at it. Carbonated drinks are rare. Expensive. "Where did you get this?"

"Found a stash in a storeroom. You scavenge around, you can find all kinds of treasures."

He doesn't look like a scavenger. His black jeans and sweater aren't frayed and worn. He has too much confidence. I'm trying to trust him. He hasn't given me any reason not to, but still . . . I shake it off. Tegan's right. Since my parents were killed, I tend to get paranoid. "I'm sorry, but I don't even know your name."

"Victor. Drink up." As though to encourage me, he opens a can for himself. I hear the hiss of carbonation being released. I watch his throat muscles work as he takes a long drink. It reminds me that my throat—and Tegan's—are unmarked by fangs because of him.

"Thanks, Victor. I owe you. I can't imagine what those vampires would've done if you hadn't come along."

"Sure, you can," he says. "You *are* Dawn Montgomery, after all."

My heart leaps in my chest. "Is that why you saved me? Because I'm the city's delegate?"

"I wasn't sure until just now, when I saw you in the light," Victor says. "All I knew was that two girls were in danger and I acted. It's that simple."

"Not so simple. You were really good. Are you a Night Watchman?"

"Not in this lifetime," he says. "Just a guy who happened to be at the right place at the right time."

Yeah, right. Night Watchmen are notoriously discreet. They don't boast. They don't swap stories. The fear is that if they're identified, vampires might try to take them out.

Or Lord Valentine will request an audience with them. He doesn't approve of the elite group of vampire hunters, fearing that if they grow in number they might try to dethrone him. "Well, whatever you are, thanks again."

Victor simply shrugs and nods toward my can, still unopened. I pop the top, hear the fizz, and take a sip. It's so good! The sugar hits my system. It doesn't seem like it should, but it does calm me. I hadn't realized how shaken I was. Almost turning into a late-night snack will do that to a girl.

Victor arranges two chairs near the bed. I sink onto one and he drops onto the other.

"The Agency's going to kill me," I say.

"They don't have to find out," he says. "I'll take you home as soon as it's safe again."

"Did the vampires chase us the whole way here?"

"I think we managed to elude them once we hit the alleyways. They've been getting desperate lately. It used to be one, maybe two vamps roaming the streets. But now they're traveling in packs, getting bolder."

"Well, I'll talk to Lord Valentine about that tomorrow," I say, feeling a swell of pride in my chest for the first time since I became a delegate. Maybe I'm just trying to impress Victor, since I failed so miserably on the trolley.

"I've heard Valentine is a tough vampire to deal with," he says.

"He's . . . intimidating. And clever. I don't trust him. Tomorrow night will be the first time I face him alone. That's why I went to this stupid party in the first place. I just wanted to have some fun and forget all my responsibilities for a while."

"Not sure I agree with your choice of playground." He gives me a wry grin, and I feel my cheeks warming with embarrassment.

"Yeah, that was pretty stupid. I just . . . I don't know. Sometimes I just wish everything was different."

"Can't blame you for that, I guess. When the VampHu Treaty was signed I'm not sure anyone expected the vampires to be quite so controlling."

I shrug. The Vampire Human Treaty shackled us to these cities, imposed our quarantine. I've read the VampHu Treaty, all six hundred pages. I've memorized the key laws; I can recite the preamble by heart. Part of the job description. And part of the legacy my father left me. He was a vampire historian, a leader in a very young field. It gave him an uncanny understanding of vampires that made him excel as an intelligence officer during the war, and integral to the peace negotiations afterward. He even wrote portions of the treaty. Which has made our family name, Montgomery, a household one. For better or worse. Probably the reason Valentine eventually asked for him as a delegate.

All I can say now is, "They won."

"I'm not sure they really did. So many are starving for blood." He shakes his head. "Sorry. I hate politics. Just seems like there has to be a better way for us all to live together. Guess that's where you come in. I can't believe they selected someone so young to serve as a delegate."

"No one can, but Valentine requested me. And what he wants, he gets."

"Brutal."

"Yeah. But at least I'm following in the footsteps of my parents."

"I'm sorry they were killed."

It's strange. While the whole city knew my parents were murdered, most people don't mention it. And truthfully, I prefer it that way. It's definitely better than the mechanical condolences I get from people I barely know who feel obligated to say something. But the way Victor said it—I could tell he meant it. And, for whatever reason, that opens up the hurt I desperately try to keep at bay. Tears sting my eyes. The whole horrible night seems to be pressing in on me. "Can we talk about something else? Like you, maybe. Who are you?"

He leans forward. He's near enough that I can see his eyes are really two shades of blue: a lighter shade surrounded by a darker circle, like the surface of the ocean giving way to the depths below. "Maybe you got hit harder than I thought and have a concussion. I already answered that question."

"No, you told me your name. You didn't tell me *who* you are. I mean, do you live here? Or is this just where you bring damsels in distress that you've saved? I know you don't go to my school." I would have noticed him. *Every* girl would have noticed him. I feel guilty at the thought. I have Michael. I shouldn't be noticing other guys.

"I haven't gone to school in a long time," Victor says.

Truancy is a huge problem in the city, but he seems too smart for that.

"So what do you do?" I ask.

"Just waiting to inherit the family business."

"Which is?"

Tegan moans. I look over at her. Her eyes flutter open, then close again. I go over to the cot and touch her forehead. She's clammy. She moans again. "Are you sure she's okay?"

He moves to the foot of the bed and studies her. "Pretty sure."

I snap my head around to stare at him. "Pretty sure?"

"I'm not a doctor. Give her some of your drink. I'm going to check outside, see if it's safe, so I can get you home."

"Yeah, okay, that's probably a good idea."

I slip my arm beneath Tegan's shoulders, lift her up, and press the can to her lips. She's so pale. I wish now that I'd hit Shaggy Guy harder. I'm surprised when she actually sips some of the soda. She smacks her lips, and I give her some more. She's stirring, fighting to keep her eyes open. But once again, she loses the battle. I decide that I need to call Rachel. Even though I'll pay for it with her icy glare later, I can have her send someone to pick us up. I reach for my cell phone—only to discover it's not in my pocket. "Crap."

"What is it?"

Victor is standing in the doorway. I didn't see him return. I try not to be bothered by how stealthy he can be—it's an asset for a Night Watchman, after all. "I think I dropped my cell phone in the trolley. I was just about to call my guardian and have her send someone to pick us up."

"I'd rather you not tell anyone about this place. Or me. It will only . . . complicate matters. Okay?"

"You *are* a Night Watchman, aren't you?"

"My anonymity, this haven . . . they're important."

I eye him for a moment. I've met an actual Night Watchman. I'm sure of it. I don't know why he wasn't wearing his hood to conceal his identity or his medallion, but maybe the first vamp ripped them off in the fight. His skills, his secrecy, his desire for anonymity are typical characteristics of those who guard the night. Then I realize that it doesn't matter that I have no confirmation of what he is. All that matters is that he was responsible for saving us. "Your secret's safe."

I see the appreciation in his eyes. Against my will, I experience a small thrill, and heat races through my body. I remind myself firmly of Michael. It's time to go home. "Are there vampires out there?" I ask.

"No, we're good to go." He lifts Tegan into his arms and carries her down the stairs. I follow. At the bottom, he heads in a direction different from the one we took coming in. Tiny lights line the floor. We go down one hallway, then another.

Using a hip, he presses on a bar and shoves open the door. "Go on."

I slip past him into an alley. When he steps out, the door slams behind him. "It locks automatically," he says, as though I asked.

I just wish it hadn't made so much noise. I look around

nervously. That's when I notice the car. Black, like midnight. Hard to spot in the shadows.

Victor strides past me toward it. "Get the passenger door, will you?"

"You're kidding me," I say, rushing after him. "You have a car? That works?"

Since the war ended, most cars have become little more than stationary set pieces. Even if the parts can be found to keep them running, gasoline is a rare commodity. The Agency has them, but the fuel is rationed, so they're seldom used. That he has one means he's either superrich or the Agency is providing it—in which case he has to have a powerful role within the Night Watchmen. He doesn't look old enough to be a lieutenant, to have a group of Watchmen beneath him. But then, I'm hardly old enough to negotiate with a vampire lord. Since the war, it's like the world has gone totally off its axis. The only rules that exist are those for survival.

As I get nearer, I see a galloping horse on the grille and realize it's a Mustang. Michael would kill to have one of these. He's always talking about cars, even though he'll probably never own one. I open the door.

"Sorry, but it'll probably be better if you get in the back," Victor says.

"Yeah, of course." He explains how to draw the seat forward, and I clamber into the back. He sets Tegan onto the passenger seat and buckles her in. Her head lolls to the side. I'm really trying not to worry about her. Victor slams the door closed, comes around, and slides into the driver's seat.

Turning on the engine, he heads out. The streets are empty as he expertly maneuvers around debris. I'm not surprised that he's skilled at driving. I'm starting to think that there's nothing he can't do.

As we get closer to downtown, more lights hold back the shadows, and a few people are out. I'm not sure if they're being brave, or—like me—just being stupid. I can't believe Tegan and I were so reckless. She yawns, moans, stretches.

"Is she waking up?" I ask.

"Yeah, I think so."

Accelerating, Victor turns down a street, whips into an alley. We're lost for a minute in the blackness. Then we're back on a dimly lit street. A few minutes later, he's pulling to a stop within heavy shadows. I can see my apartment building. Good idea not to park where the guard in the lobby could see us.

I hear movement in the front seat. A gasp. "Who the hell are you?"

I reach around the seat, squeeze Tegan's shoulder to reassure her. "It's okay. We got into some trouble at the party, and he helped us."

"God, I think I'm going to be sick. How do I get out of here?"

Victor reaches across, pulls the handle, and shoves open the door. Tegan tries to tumble out, but the strap of the seat belt holds her captive. Victor releases it, and she's scrambling out and staggering even farther into the shadows. It would be funny any other night.

Victor gets out of the car to help me exit. He extends his

hand toward me and I take it. It's warm and strong, and he pulls me out with no effort. I can see Tegan hunched over; can hear her gagging as she upchucks. Lovely.

"She'll be okay," Victor says.

"Yeah, I think so. Probably should have made her throw up earlier. I've never dealt with something like this before."

"I'll wait here until you get inside."

"Thanks." I feel like I should say more. Hug him even, for saving us.

Tegan waddles back over to us. "God, that was awful." She squints at Victor and asks again, "Who are you?"

"Victor."

"He's a friend," I say.

"Sounds like a story I need to hear."

"Not really. Come on. It's not safe out here." I wrap my arm around her waist. "Thanks again, Victor. I owe you."

"*We* owe you," Tegan says, shifting into flirt mode. She's definitely feeling better.

Slightly irritated, I drag her away. I just spent the last few hours taking care of her after she got too friendly with the wrong people. And she's acting like nothing happened.

Inside the lobby, the guard raises his eyebrows at us. I give him a sickly smile and we head to the elevator. We get off on the twelfth floor; the apartment I now share with Rachel is at the far end of the hall.

Once we're through the door, I'm surprised to find that Rachel isn't here. Surprised and relieved. She probably left me a message on my cell phone. I don't want to think about how I'm going to explain losing it. Cell phones are so rare it can take months, even years to get one.

Tegan follows me into my bedroom and grabs the duffel bag she brought over earlier. "I've got dibs on the shower first."

She disappears into the bathroom, closing the door behind her. I hear the water running and cross over to the doors that open onto a balcony. The great thing about our apartment is that the living room and both bedrooms have a balcony. I step outside and look down on the street, where Victor parked. His car is gone. He's gone.

I'm not sure how I'll keep his secrets from my best friend. But at the same time, this night has felt so surreal that when I wake up in the morning I might convince myself it was all one giant dream. That Victor and the trolley and the theater never existed.

I remember the key. Reaching into my pocket, I close my fingers around it. I have proof tonight happened.

Then a fissure of unease spikes through me with an unexpected realization.

I never told Victor where I live.

Chapter 4

Tegan and I got lucky. Extremely lucky. The sun is spilling through the window when Rachel knocks on my bedroom door. Tegan barely stirs, but I sit up and invite Rachel in. She's in her mid-twenties, pretty, and one of the few people who know more about vampires than I do.

"Just wanted to check in on you," she says.

"Are you just now getting home?" Or maybe she's about to head out again. Her brown hair is clipped up. A two-piece dark blue suit over her petite body can't hide the fact that she spends a lot of time in the gym. She has the most boring brown eyes, but she still looks better than I ever could.

"Yeah." I can see now how tired she looks. "Some kids decided to throw a party out near the wall. A couple of them got abducted, so I had to check it out."

My stomach clenches, and I swallow hard. "Really."

"I'll share the details later, so you can discuss the situation with Valentine. I'm going to bed before I fall flat on my face."

"Yeah, okay, sure. I'm glad you're safe."

She gives me a teasing grin. "Yeah, I'm glad I'm safe, too."

She closes the door, and I plop back on the bed, unsettled by her news.

"Was it the party we were at?" Tegan whispers in a small voice.

I glance over at her. In spite of the fact that her hair is sticking up at all angles, she doesn't look the way I'd expect after a night that could have ended very badly. "Maybe."

"God. We were lucky." She shoves herself into a sitting position, grabs a pillow, and hugs it to her chest. "So tell me what happened last night. I remember dancing, then I was in a car. What happened in between?"

"Well, you probably can't remember because that bastard spiked your drink with something. I caught up to you heading upstairs with him and hauled you away."

"Spiked my drink? Are you serious?" she asks.

I nod. "Mine was probably spiked, too. I just didn't get a chance to drink it."

"Jerks. I'm sorry, Dawn. You were right: The wall is dangerous."

It feels good to hear that, but I'd rather erase the whole night than have my ego stroked. I think. I don't know if I'd want to forget about Victor.

"Okay, now tell me what you know about the hot guy with the car. Was he at the party?"

"No, we ran into him after we left." I squeeze her arm. "There were some vampires. Victor saved us." And even though I promised—"I'm pretty sure he's a Night Watchman."

Her eyes widen. "I knew it," she says, and I don't feel so bad about spilling an obvious secret. "Between the car, being out at night, and not to mention those sizzling looks, I just figured he had to be a Watchman."

"Yeah, I'm not really sure good looks are a requirement when they're screening applicants. Anyway, you can't ever tell anyone about him."

She grins. "Of course not. Any idea where I can find him, though? To thank him."

Right. She's thinking boyfriend material. I guess I can't blame her. After all, I have Michael—

I groan.

"What?" Tegan asks.

"Michael. I lost my phone. What if he—"

Her phone starts ringing. She scrambles out of bed and scrounges around in the clothes she was wearing last night until she finds it in a pocket. She looks at the display. "Speak of the devil." Then she answers. "Hey, Michael. What's up?"

I get out of bed, walk over to her, and hold out my hand for the phone.

"He says he's been trying to get in touch with you," she

says as she slaps it into my palm, then says in a low voice, "Please don't tell him about me. He already thinks I'm a bad influence on you."

"As if I would. What kind of friend would I be?" I lift the phone to my ear. "Hi."

"Why haven't you returned my texts or calls?" Michael demands to know. "Are you mad about last night, because I couldn't make time to come with you?"

"No." A little. "I lost my cell phone."

"How?"

"At a party." A lie. "Long story." Truth.

Silence stretches between us; then finally he says, "I'm sorry, Dawn. I know it seems like we haven't spent much time together lately—"

"Because we haven't."

"It's not all on me," he says, and I hear the irritation in his voice.

"I know." He hasn't been the only one preparing for the future. Two weeks after my parents died, the Agency began training me for my role as delegate, and it's been nonstop ever since. They've never had an opportunity like me. They can forge the perfect agent from the ground up, finishing my education about all things vampire that my parents started years ago.

"Since it's Sunday, no school, you wanna try to get together later?" he asks.

"Yeah, sure. Where?"

"Daylight Grill. This afternoon. Get some carbs in you before facing Valentine."

In spite of everything, I grin. Any other guy might bring a girl chocolate. But Michael is all about a healthy, strong body. "Okay. See you."

Hanging up, I toss the phone back to Tegan and flop down on my bed. "I don't want Michael to find out what happened last night."

"Works for me, since I don't want *anyone* to know. We were pretty stupid. I just . . . I just wanted us to have a memorable night together before, you know, tonight."

"It was definitely memorable." Then I realize what she's truly saying. I sit up and face her. "I'm going to be okay."

"But what if you're not? I mean, your parents—"

"Now who's being paranoid?" I tease.

She gives me a halfhearted grin, and I can see that she's really worried. I wrap my arms around her and hug her tightly. "Nothing bad is going to happen tonight."

A shiver creeps through me. Those were the same words my mother said to me every time she and Dad left for Valentine Manor.

The Daylight Grill sits along the popular Day Street. Huge lampposts line the avenue, chasing away the shadows at night, trying to maintain a sunny atmosphere twenty-four/seven. Indoors, the oversize windows let the light in, but the farther one gets away from them, the darker it becomes. All shades of gray lie in between, giving the place an intimate feeling.

Michael and I are sitting in a booth, facing each other. Sometimes I still have a hard time believing he is my boyfriend. Tall and athletic, he's the hot guy in school, the one every girl crushes on. He wears T-shirts that mold over his broad shoulders and reveal his amazing biceps. But it isn't just his toned body, tanned from hours of training in the sun, that turns girls on. His eyes are a deep brown, not dull, but rich and dark. His blond hair is buzzed short, "the most utilitarian style," as he describes it. He exudes power and confidence.

Very much like Victor.

I consider asking Michael if he's met Victor during his training. But I don't want to explain how I ran across him, because that would lead to revealing how terribly stupid Tegan and I were last night. Michael doesn't know the party we went to was near the wall. And I want to keep it that way.

After finishing off a bowl of pasta and meatballs, we're sharing a slice of cheesecake.

"Wish I were going with you tonight," he says. "I don't like that Valentine gets to make all the rules."

"What choice do we have?" I ask, skimming my finger along the condensation gathered around my glass of lemonade. The Daylight Grill makes the best lemonade. "He controls all the vamps in this area. Keeps them from invading the city."

"He's doing a lousy job. Did you hear about that trolley car that was found abandoned on the tracks last night? Dead vamps in and out."

My stomach knots up. "Anyone know what happened?"

"A Night Watchman got to them, obviously." A gleam

nes into his eyes. "I can't wait until I can be out on the streets, hunting with the Watchmen. Right now it's all training scenarios. Last night we pretended to raid a warehouse and had to find the other Night Watchmen hiding inside, pretending to be vampires. It was like a deadly game of hide-and-seek."

"I bet you kicked butt."

He grins. "I didn't do too badly. It was my idea to search the rafters, found two 'vampires' up there. The trainer said vamps will hide anywhere, especially when the Watchmen come knocking."

"Sounds like you had fun."

"Well, it's all to hone our skills. But I proved my worth. Which is why I should go with you tonight. I'm telling you, Dawn, I'm ready."

He might be, but I'm not willing to put him in danger. Still, if I admit that, he'll take it as a lack of faith in his abilities. So I fudge a little.

"I'll be fine. The coach carries Valentine's crest." The crimson head of a snarling wolf in the center of a V. "Vampires know that if they attack they'll have to deal with Valentine himself."

"That's not always enough protection." He falls silent and I know he's thinking about my parents. "The Agency has cars. Why can't you ride in one of those to Valentine Manor?"

He knows why. We've been through this a hundred times. Valentine insists that delegates travel by his coach. It's the only way he'll vouch for their safety. But

I understand Michael's frustration. "Obviously Valentine has control issues."

"He needs to see a shrink."

We both smile at that, even though it's not really funny.

Michael sobers. "I could hide in the coach—"

I reach across the table and place my hand over his. "He'd kill you if he discovered you."

"I'm good, Dawn. Really good."

"And he's surrounded by minions. Please, Michael. I'll be fine."

He threads his fingers through mine. "I'll single-hand-edly start another war with the vamps if Valentine hurts you."

Maybe it's wrong for me to experience a thrill of excitement over his words. I don't want another war, but it warms my heart to know I mean so much to him. Humans started the first war in an attempt to eradicate the bloodsuckers from among us, calling it a war for "human survival in the face of an unprecedented enemy." But after thirty years of fighting creatures that are nearly impossible to destroy, we surrendered. We gave up almost everything for an awkward sort of peace.

The sun is beginning to set when he walks me back to my apartment building.

"I have a couple of hours before I have to leave," I tell him. "Want to come up?"

"You bet."

Once we're inside the apartment, Rachel greets us.

"Michael's going to hang out for a while," I say.

"Don't forget how long it takes to get ready," she reminds me.

Valentine insists that I wear clothes from another century. Victorian. The corset alone takes thirty minutes to fasten, and I have to use an old-fashioned buttonhook on the stupid shoes.

"I won't," I assure her.

"Okay. I'm going to finish up some paperwork for the Agency. Then you and I will need to go over some things for tonight."

"Not a problem."

"See you in a bit then." She goes into her bedroom and closes the door.

"I didn't think she was ever going to leave," Michael says as he stretches out on the couch and gently tugs me down to join him, so I'm halfway sprawled over his long body.

"She's just worried."

"She's not the only one."

"Then I guess I need to distract you." Easing up, I kiss him. He threads his fingers through my hair, holds me in place as he deepens the kiss.

He smells so good. Like lemon. I've been carrying lemon drops in my briefcase to eat on the way, just so I can feel like he's with me.

Drawing back, he studies my face as though he's trying to memorize every line and curve, as though he's afraid he'll never see them again.

"I'm crazy about you. You know that, don't you?" he asks.

I run one of my hands over his hair, feel the spikes tickle my palm. "I know. I'm nuts about you, too."

"Someday we'll have more time to be together, when we're not so busy learning how to save the world."

"Meanwhile we have moments like this," I remind him.

"Yeah, we definitely have moments."

Then he kisses me again. I want this moment to go on forever, just Michael and me, lost in a world where nothing exists except each other. Where passion consumes us. The kiss becomes more, becomes everything, feeding our desire for each other. I never want to leave him.

On the other side of the apartment, Rachel's door moans as it opens. Michael—always alert to his surroundings—ends the kiss. With his large hand cupping the back of my head, he nestles my face against his solid chest. I hear the rapid thudding of his heart. Even though I know I need to, I can't seem to move away.

"Dawn," Rachel says quietly, "you need to get ready."

Michael's hold on me tightens, as though he can stop the passage of time, the clocks from counting off the seconds, the world from revolving.

But beyond the wall, Valentine waits. Nothing Michael does can change that. All I can do is hope that this won't be the last time we're together.

Chapter 5

It's dangerous out here, beyond the city walls. Starving vampires lurk in the shadows. The countryside is vast, desolate, and destroyed. I'm only seventeen, but even I remember the bombs falling in the distance. Dropped by us in desperation to win. So much ash rose from the burning ground it blocked the sun for years. I remember the sight of my first sunrise without a barrier of haze. I was thirteen.

"Ten minutes, Miss Montgomery," Winston, my driver, shouts from atop the carriage.

"Please, just call me Dawn."

"Yes, Miss Montgomery."

In the distance, Valentine Manor—with its three towers and far too many windows for a creature allergic to the sun—looms. A visitor first seeing the castlelike structure would think it was some medieval noble's estate airlifted from Britain. They say it took only two weeks to build. Lord Valentine has that many Lesser vampires serving beneath him.

Most vampires, like those who attacked me on the trolley, never see the inside of mansions like this. They never have lavish parties or court young girls. Only the Old Families hold that kind of power, enjoy the fruits of wealth. Most vamps go hungry every night. They work like crazy in the hopes of extra blood rations. But the Old Family vampires are often cruel, and I wonder sometimes if there would be fewer rogue vampire attacks if Lord Valentine would take better care of his minions.

Of course, blood rations wouldn't be a problem at all if people would stop believing the false promises of a better life and willingly embracing the opportunity to be turned. I don't understand why they don't get that turned vampires are called "Lessers" for a reason. They're not seen—or treated—as equals.

The road curves around in front of the massive building. Thick fog settles outside my windows. We stop and Winston's shadowy silhouette appears in the mist. His hair is thin and gray, too long for his short face. He opens the door and holds my gloved hand as I step down; my other fist clutches the handle of my briefcase. We walk past the two horses that brought us here. Large and strong. Uneasy at the smell of vampires in the night.

"I'll be waiting," Winston says, and swings up onto the small bench at the top of the black carriage.

"Thank you, Winston," I say, already shifting into

ultrapolite mode. I've had Victorian etiquette drilled into me, because Valentine expects a certain tone during the meeting.

For some reason, Valentine likes the ancient rituals. He insists that delegates wear Victorian-era clothing. Which is why I'm in a long black dress with a high collar and a corset that cinches in way too tightly, making it hard to breathe. My hair is piled on my head in a complicated style with a few dangling curls. My feet, bound in pointy shoes that look like miniature torture devices, click across the thick stones. I go up the steps. Time to announce my arrival. I let the iron knocker fall; the growling wolf's head bangs into the door, sending its ominous echoes across the silent fields that surround the manor. Except for the one building and stables, it's desolate and haunting out here. To calm my nerves, I take a deep breath, hold it for a count of three. A little trick my mother taught me. I can do this; I've been trained to do this.

The door opens with a creak and I'm once again face-to-face with a vampire: the fangs, the pale skin, the feral eyes. I can't help it; my heart skips a beat when his black gaze dips to my neck. Beneath the high collar of my dress my pulse pounds. He can probably hear it.

"Good evening, Miss Montgomery. The Lord is waiting for you in the dining hall."

"Then I shall not keep him." I've rehearsed the stiff line over and over to get the inflection—or lack of one—just right.

The chilled night air follows me inside. No electricity

runs through Valentine Manor. Instead, hundreds of gas and oil lamps give off a unique, haunting glow. Vampires can have anything they want now, and this is what they choose. I don't understand their aversion to technology's advancements.

We walk past a sweeping marbled staircase. Along the walls hang portraits of Valentine family members, past and present. Once they pass through puberty, born vampires show the effects of aging much slower than we do. Twenty of their years to every one of ours is the closest estimate we have. Then at a certain point, the aging process stops. Immortality awaits.

Or so we believe. Vampires reveal to us only what they want us to know, so we have a lot of unanswered questions.

The vampire leading me is one of the Valentines' most trusted servants, turned by Lord Valentine himself. I wonder who he was in his previous human life. I wonder if he even remembers. He could be hundreds of years old. Lesser vampires never age beyond what they were when they were turned. This one is tall, with long hair that drapes across his shoulders. He's dressed to the nines in a suit and vest, a gold pocket watch hanging from it. His pasty skin makes me wonder whether he was ill when Valentine turned him. Some humans ask to be turned rather than face death. Eternal life is a tempting purchase. But at what price?

One I'd never pay. Nothing is worth becoming a monster.

Thick wooden doors line either side of the hallway we walk along. Ones I've never seen opened. Probably rooms made of pure gold, or at least worth that much. There is no end to an Old Family's wealth.

We head toward a pair of French doors twice my height. Flanking either side are massive sculptures pulled from Greek ships that sunk millennia ago. Marbled and weathered, they are gods in human form that stood the test of time. Despite their majesty and the history chiseled into every crack and vein, they're outdone by the vampires who live longer. Human gods have been replaced by more tangible ones.

The servant opens the doors wide. The dining hall is the size of a small house, the single table stretching from one wall to the other. A parody of grand living. At the far end sits Lord Valentine, his massive chair carved out of a single oak tree, turned away from the table so it's more of a throne than a piece of dining furniture. Its thick, rounded legs end in talons. In his coal black suit, the vampire himself is far more impressive. Well over six feet. Broad shoulders. The large ancestral ring is wrapped around his right forefinger. In spite of everything I was taught about the protections offered to delegates, and all the reassurances that my host would not select me as a tasty midnight morsel, I'm suddenly scared. I wonder if my parents were, too.

"Miss Montgomery has arrived, m'lord," the servant says, bowing his way out the door and closing it quietly. Leaving just the two of us. The behemoth I'm staring at could kill me before I even screamed, and wouldn't think twice about doing it if I disappoint him. Diplomatic immunity may save me from the vampires outside, but not from the rogues inside the city—or, more important, the one within this room.

With hints of gray, his long hair is pulled back into a conservative ponytail, held in place with a braided strip of leather. He exudes power. A tidal wave resting in every subtle movement. With a motion of his hand he can topple empires.

"Please have a seat," Lord Valentine says, his deep voice filling the room. His hand, holding a golden goblet—full of blood, no doubt—indicates the chair across from him.

I take my seat, folding my skirt beneath me. His gravity is overwhelming. I place my briefcase on the table, careful not to scratch the wooden surface.

"I'm pleased, Dawn. You've exceeded my expectations," he says.

I jerk my head up, but he's not looking at me. His gaze is lost somewhere in the dark corners of the room. I'm tempted to tell him that I don't care if I please him. Exceeding his expectations is an empty compliment. But I'm not here as Dawn Montgomery. I'm here as a delegate. So instead, I just say, "M'lord?"

"You embraced your destiny. You became a full delegate in a shorter time than most."

"I had an advantage. I learned a lot from my parents."

"And there is a great deal more you have yet to learn," Valentine says, "things that your father failed to share with you. You are very special, Dawn, in ways you can't fathom."

His arrogance infuriates me. He doesn't know what my father taught me—or failed to teach me. He's pointing out my weaknesses with backhanded compliments. He's trying to unsettle me, and I expect nothing less from him on this crucial night. But I'm ready. My parents taught me that he talks in riddles and circles. They taught me how to stay calm, to stay focused. To change the subject . . .

"I would like to discuss the recent abductions from the city," I say, unsnapping the hinges on my briefcase and pulling out some paperwork that lists the names and includes photos of those who have gone missing. Just as I did when Rachel gave me the information, I hesitate at the top photo. Shaggy Guy is staring back at me. Swallowing hard, trying not to think about how much danger Tegan and I were truly in, I slide over copies of all the information. Valentine doesn't move to take it. "Over the past week, four of our citizens have been abducted."

Valentine slowly places his goblet on the table. "Do you believe my underlings are responsible?" he asks, his hands clasped at his lips, eyes not on mine.

"We have witnesses who saw the abductions who say vampires are responsible. We know that a great lord such as yourself would not condone such actions, but we also realize that Lesser vampires are not always in your control."

"They are always in *my* control," he reminds me with a stern voice that can silence cities. Silence lives.

"Of course," I say. I fight the urge to apologize. He might see it as a weakness. I have to show him I'm strong. But if I don't comment, he might see it as rude and snap my neck. I'm thinking too much. *Just get the first night over with*; that's what Rachel said. She taught me everything I know about protocol. Tonight is a test for her as well. If I fail, my blood is on her hands. "Then who do you believe is responsible for the abductions?"

"Those who are foolish enough to step outside the city at night have only themselves to blame. The VampHu makes them fair game for the Lessers."

People younger than twenty-one aren't allowed beyond the walls at night. But anyone older than that is not detained by the guards at the heavily armored gates. They know the risks. After what Tegan and I did last night, it's a little harder for me not to be sympathetic at the notion of wanting more freedom, but it's so much more danger-ous beyond the wall. Out there people are hunted down by roaming vamps. Sometimes vampires drain them immedi-ately. Sometimes they take them captive and feed on them over time. Since the war, VampHu prohibits vampires from turning humans, and most vampires obey that little rule. They finally figured out that the more vampires there are, the less human blood there is to go around.

"But these are happening within the city," I say, real-izing this challenge may end my life. I think about the four who attacked me. I could tell him about them, but that will only complicate matters and show my stupidity and defenselessness.

"Are you implying that we've broken the VampHu Treaty?" he asks. "That's a very, very serious accusation."

The heads of the fourteen Old Families would convene to pass judgment if I filed an official complaint. As far as I know, no one ever has. "No, m'lord."

"Rogue vampires are to blame. They travel from city to city, looking for weak walls and even weaker humans. They killed your parents, did they not? So do not blame the great House of Valentine for your reckless behavior. Your citizens make themselves victims. I will hear no more of this."

I'm angry that he's blowing off our legitimate concerns. But I can also sense the fury rolling off him because I dared to question his authority. I'm surprised he's allowed me to continue breathing. I look through my agenda at other topics to address. This one is obviously over.

"Is the blood supply adequate?" I ask.

"No."

Of course not . . .

"How much more is needed?" I ask.

"At least double," he says.

Double! Has he gone insane in his old age? I fight not to let my shock show. No emotions. I can't show him any emotions or he'll take advantage of the situation.

"I'm sorry, Lord Valentine, but that will be extremely difficult."

"Then I cannot guarantee the safety of your city or its citizens," he says, finally turning toward me. His eyes are dark. So dark I can't tell if they're staring straight into mine or at my neck. It's a threat. Not an empty one either. This conversation, my life, could be over before my next heartbeat.

"I'll see if I can increase the supply," I say to placate him for now, until I can talk with Rachel.

"I hope, for your sake, that the citizens of Denver find their charitable side," he says in that icy, dead tone.

My heart jumps when I hear the door open. I assume it's the servant coming to escort me out, but I dare not look; it's bad form. I'm just relieved the meeting is over.

"You're late," Valentine snaps.

"My apologies, Father," a deep voice says. "I only just got your summons."

My breath backs up in my lungs and I manage somehow to remain still. I know that voice. But it can't be. It can't.

I hear the quiet footfalls. I see movement out of the corner of my eye. Suddenly he's standing there. Beside Valentine.

My savior from last night. Victor.

He's not a heralded Night Watchman. He's a damn vampire!

Chapter 6

"Dawn, I don't believe you've met my son, Victor Valentine. Victor, allow me to introduce Miss Dawn Montgomery, our new delegate."

I feel as though I've dropped into the seventh level of hell. It's taking everything I have not to display any sign of recognition. To keep my face impassive. To reveal absolutely nothing at all. What games are being played here?

Victor bows slightly. "Good evening, Miss Montgomery." His manner has changed. He's more like his father, more refined and formal. It doesn't fit him.

He's wearing a black shirt beneath a dark blue silk suit, and the corner of a red handkerchief—decorated with two embroidered Vs—peers out of the pocket over his heart. He's definitely projecting Old Family. It explains so much.

The car. The carbonated drink. He's filthy rich. It also explains why he was so insistent that I not tell anyone about him or the theater. He's a vampire, living in the city. Maybe spying for dear old Dad.

I want to strike out at him for deceiving me, for talking with me as though we had things in common. For making a fool of me. He had to know that I assumed he was human. Instead he's a bloodsucker.

But I'm pretty sure none of my thoughts, my sudden hatred of him, is showing on my face, because Lord Valentine continues as though nothing is amiss.

"We were discussing the blood situation," he says. "Miss Montgomery assures me that the supply can easily be doubled."

That has me snapping my attention from son to father. I did no such thing! But I'd be a fool to contradict Valentine.

"I'm sure that will be much appreciated," Victor says. "We have many starving vampires."

Like the ones last night? I want to ask. But I don't. I hold my tongue.

Valentine swirls his goblet, the blood dancing in it. "As you can see, Miss Montgomery, my son understands the value of blood." I hear pride in his voice and something more. The blood he's referring to isn't only that which comes from humans. He's talking about bloodlines. The blood of family.

Victor takes a seat beside his father. I can't tell what he's thinking. Then a sudden thought pops into my head. Maybe Valentine summoning Victor is part of tonight's test. Maybe he knows that I've met his son before. I hate the games vampires play.

"Now, Dawn, where were we?" Valentine asks.

I don't realize I've been holding my breath. I'm not looking at Victor, but I can feel his gaze boring into me. I despise that he's witnessing my first night alone, without Rachel. I need her to guide me through this. I need . . .

No. I don't need anyone. I just need to remember who *I* am. I'm smart. Brave. I'm a delegate. The city's only connection to Valentine. I think about people on the street. To Valentine, they are merely sacks of blood. But to me, they have hearts and souls, and each one is depending on me right now.

"The blood supply can be increased," I say. "But it will take time."

Valentine gives a small, calculating smile. "I have all the time in the world."

Beheading, stake through the heart, sun, engulfing fire—we've discovered those things can kill a vampire. I'd give anything to have one of those means at my disposal right now. I'd go for Victor first.

I quickly discard the thought. I need to focus on the powerful vampire in front of me. But that's a little difficult to do, because I'm distracted by Victor's presence. I have to wonder whether he's using his powers to influence me. It's never been proven, but it's long been suspected that vampires can control us with their thoughts. Can bend us to their will. Some call it being vampire struck. I imagine it's nothing but hundreds of years of practice in the art of subtle manipulation.

Victor may have toyed with me last night, may be messing with me right now, but when I get back to Denver, I can mess with him. I'll tell Rachel about him, about the theater. His sanctuary in the city will be destroyed. Maybe I should wait until he's in it.

But then I remember how he saved me, and I feel a stab of guilt. How much do I owe him? Loyalty? To keep his secret? I don't know. But neither do I trust his motives for coming to our rescue. Vampires never do anything without an expectation of gain.

"Miss Montgomery?"

I snap my attention back to Valentine, only then realizing that I've been staring at Victor. "Yes, m'lord?"

"I see my son intrigues you."

"No, I . . . I've just never met a young vampire before."

"Four hundred years. Hardly young by your standards, but you are correct that he is young by ours."

"Did he fight in the war?"

"It's rude to talk about me as though I'm not here," Victor says, and I can hear the irritation that so often marks his father's voice.

I turn to him. "Did you fight in the war?"

"I'm not sure what bearing that information has on the blood supply."

Valentine chuckles, and I realize we're entertaining him. The last thing I want to do. I angle my chin defiantly. "In your absence your father and I discussed the abductions that happened last week. Maybe you know something about them." I shove my folder of photos toward him.

To my surprise, unlike his father, he doesn't ignore them. He opens the folder and turns the pictures over slowly, one by one. Then he lifts his gaze to mine. "I'm sorry. I don't."

"They were attacked in the city. We know there are vampires within the walls. They're fair game if we find them," I say, giving an emphasis and meaning to my words. You're *fair game*.

"I'm well aware of the conditions of VampHu, of the dangers that vampires found within the city face," he says.

"Your Night Watchmen are apparently useless," Valentine suddenly barks, "and I stated earlier that I was finished discussing the abductions."

"I thought I should enlighten your son about them— since he was tardy."

Victor narrows his eyes at me, but Valentine chuckles again. I give my attention back to Valentine. "Other than the blood supply, is there anything else that displeases you, m'lord?"

"That you do not trust the house of Valentine."

I don't trust any vampire. I want to remove the black gloves he makes me wear and scrub at the skin that Victor touched last night when we were running through the alleys. I want to forget every word we shared. His smile, his concern. None of it was true. It was all a ploy. Vampires lure us in and then destroy us.

"Perhaps if you were more lenient in your requests, m'lord, the citizens' trust could be more easily gained."

"What exactly do I demand, Miss Montgomery, that is such a burden?"

Victor appears more interested in my answer than Valentine.

"More blood than is reasonable. If we charted the minimum amount that a vampire needs to survive and then got a census of the number of vampires in the area, we could get an accurate projection of the amount of blood that is truly needed."

"Charts and censuses won't be necessary. My word is all you need. And I have told you exactly what is required. Double."

"Based on what, m'lord? We don't even know how many vampires we're supplying."

"Are you trying to calculate the number so you can plan an uprising against me? Has the Agency sent you to determine the extent of my following? If they feel that my position has weakened, they will quickly find that they are in error."

"No, m'lord," I hastily answer, "but if we could make the citizens feel more secure, that the terms of the treaty hold and they are safe within the city walls, perhaps they'd be more willing to give."

"Knowing the numbers would not reassure them. To the victor go the spoils. Humans never should have started a war with us. Your defeat was inevitable. It is only through our kindness that we have not made you all slaves. Perhaps you should remind the citizens that our generosity is easily withdrawn."

This meeting has taken a turn for the worse—ever since Victor strode into the room. Why do I feel a need to prove that he may have fooled me last night, but I'm not someone to be messed with?

"We're not the enemy, Dawn," Victor says.

"Tell that to their families," I say, pointing to the photos on the table.

He bows his head slightly, as though conceding the point.

"I believe we are done," Valentine suddenly announces.

When the servant arrives to retrieve me, Valentine remains sitting. I give him a small curtsy and he nods his head very gentlemanly. The Old Family vampires are conservative creatures. Despite the fact that they kill us for blood, they're still elegant. Polite and courteous. Appreciative of a lady who behaves like one.

Victor rises to his feet. "It was a pleasure, Miss Montgomery."

I want to respond, *For you maybe*. Instead I keep my tone as cordial as possible. "I look forward to our next meeting."

It'll take place at your theater and I'll have an army of Night Watchmen with me.

With my back stiff and my head held high, I follow the servant from the room.

Outside, Winston hands me up into the carriage. Receding fog drifts past us as we clatter along. Back to home and safety.

At the city's main gate, we go through the ritual of having our Agency IDs checked while they search the coach for any hidden vampires. Bowls of blood are strategically placed—the thought being that vampires won't have the strength to keep their fangs retracted long enough to get through the checkpoint.

Winston and I are cleared to go on our way into the city.

It's still dark when we arrive at my apartment building. As the driver helps me out of the coach, I breathe a sigh of relief. "Well, we survived, Winston."

"Yes, we did, Miss Montgomery."

"Please call me Dawn."

"Yes, Miss Montgomery. Sweet dreams." He climbs back onto the coach and, with a flick of his wrist, sends the horses cantering down the street. He's a strange old guy, but they say no one is faster with a stake. Wish he'd been my parents' driver—but like them, their driver was killed.

I feel a growing sense of relief as I take the elevator to my floor.

Before I've even slipped my key into the lock, the door swings open. Rachel looks like she's aged ten years.

"Oh, thank God you're back. How'd it go?" Before I can answer, she grabs my arm and drags me into the apartment.

"What do you know about Valentine's son? Victor?" I ask, as I drop my briefcase on a table and start unbuttoning the bodice of my dress. "He was there tonight."

"Instead of Valentine?"

"No, with him."

"Why?"

As soon as I'm out of my bodice, she starts unlacing the back of my corset. It's a ritual that began when she accompanied me to Valentine Manor. I feel my rib cage expand as the laces are undone, and take a deep breath before answering. "I don't know. Mind games, maybe."

I know I need to tell her about the trouble that Tegan and I got into and how Victor saved us because Victor being Valentine's son has changed everything. He's not a secret I can keep any longer. But I can't just blurt it out. I need to come up with a strategy that will lessen the amount of trouble I'll be in. "I need to get the feel of Valentine Manor off me and then we'll talk, okay?"

She smiles, and in that moment she's just my guardian, looking out for me, not working for the Agency. "Sure. Relax for a while. The important thing is that you survived. You hungry? I'll fix you something to eat."

Food is her answer to everything. "Starved."

In my bedroom I strip off my clothes and pile them in a corner. With each item, I'm shedding the mantle of delegate. I walk to the bathroom, removing pins as I go until my unruly black hair falls down around my shoulders. It matches the real Dawn. I fantasize about one day showing Valentine who he's been messing with. I'll do it with a stake in my hand.

Around my throat is a choker of tightly linked metal chains. Bite protection. It was hidden beneath the high collar of my black dress. I twist and turn the complicated mechanism to unlock it in the back. The band clinks as I lay it over a towel rack. I can breathe a little easier.

I catch my reflection in the mirror above the sink. My blue eyes are dull, weary with the weight of what I have to tell Rachel, and from the postadrenaline crash of my first solo visit. I feel dirty after my encounter with Valentine. In the shower, I let the hot water pour over my body, shedding another layer of delegate. The splashing noise relaxes me. Until I shut my eyes. Then I see Victor's face, his incredible blue eyes as he studies me. Was he tense, wondering if I'd tell his father everything? But if he didn't want me to, why respond to the summons? He had to know I'd be there. So why come at all? Why risk exposing his true self to me? Maybe Rachel will have a better idea of what it could all mean.

I shut off the water and towel dry. I slip on some flannel pants and a tank top from the Race for the Blood 5K run my parents organized and cosponsored. I'd volunteered to help with the registration. No one showed up. No big surprise.

When I pad out into my bedroom, I discover that I'm not alone.

On my bed sits a vampire. One I hoped to never see again. One I just finished rinsing off my skin.

Victor.

Chapter 7

Victor immediately stands and holds up his hands. He's not wearing the suit anymore. He's in a black T-shirt and jeans. Once again blending in with the night. Or he would be if he wasn't in my blue bedroom. He sorta sticks out here. "I'm not here to hurt you, Dawn."

Right. His tone is reassuring, but since I saw him beside his father, everything about him is suspect. Not only is he a vampire, he's Old Family, which means he's manipulative, deceitful, cunning. He's nothing like I thought he was.

I don't have to ask how he got in here. The French doors leading out onto my bedroom balcony are slightly ajar. With a vampire's strength and uncanny agility, he could have easily scaled the building, leaping from balcony to balcony. And he didn't need to wait on an invitation to enter. At this moment, I really wish that wasn't just a myth.

I bolt for my dresser, open a drawer, yank out a metal stake, and spin around. But Victor moves too fast, displaying the blinding speed possessed only by the powerful Old Family vampires, those born with fangs, those who don't know what it means to be human. I barely have time to raise the stake before he grabs both my wrists and manacles them behind my back with one hand while the other covers my mouth, as we slam into the wall.

I'm immobilized, completely helpless. I hate him for that. For overpowering me so easily.

I realize that last night he moved more slowly, deliberately striving to disguise what he was. Even now, with his mouth closed, his fangs hidden, he's too human. He leans in and I feel the press of his body against mine. His warm breath skims over my cheek, circles around the shell of my ear. "If you make any more noise, Rachel is going to come in here. It won't be pretty."

Fear assaults me. My stomach sinks to the floor. I know what his veiled threat means. He'll kill her.

He eases back, and once again I look into his blue eyes. Last night they'd intrigued me. Now I'm repulsed. His gaze drops to the rapidly pounding pulse at my throat. We stay like that for what seems an eternity. Normally I wouldn't let him touch me without a fight, but he's right: With all the noise I'd make defending myself, Rachel would come in here—

I can't lose someone else I love. And I do love Rachel. She's been a part of my life ever since my parents first went to work for the Agency. She was a friend to the family long before I needed a guardian. I don't want to be responsible for her death. My brother died protecting me. I don't know that I could survive any more guilt.

A knock sounds on the door, and I jerk, my heart speeding up.

"Dawn? I heard a noise. Is everything okay in there?" Rachel asks. Her voice is sweet, innocent. She's completely unaware of the monster in my room.

Victor's gaze burns into mine. "Your choice," he says quietly, and slowly removes his hand from my mouth.

I swallow hard. "Just me being a klutz. I dropped something. I'll be there in a few minutes, Rachel."

"Hurry. Food will be on the table in ten. Don't want it to get cold."

I hear her footsteps retreating and briefly wonder why I didn't hear them arriving. Something to do with my focus being on Victor. Victor. I may not be able to fight him, but I'm not going to die docilely. I set my jaw and glare at him, daring him—

"You think I'm here for your blood," he says quietly.

"Why the hell else would you be here?"

"To forge a friendship."

Is he joking? "Yeah, well, that's not going to happen. You're a damned vampire. Why didn't you tell me who—what—you were? You let me believe that you were a Night Watchman. That you were . . . *human*. But you're a monster, just like your father."

"Don't ever say that. I'm not like him."

"It's in the blood."

"You think you know everything about vampires, but there is so much you don't understand."

"I understand you've destroyed everything I care about. I know I loathe you."

If vampires had feelings, I would have thought that I'd hurt his. He gently takes the stake out of my hand, as if he were taking a present, then releases his hold on me completely. I quickly slide away from him and cross my arms over my chest.

"Has Tegan recovered from the other night?" he asks. Okay, I wasn't expecting him to care about that. But, of course, he doesn't. He just wants to keep track of all the players on the board.

"Yeah," I say. "She doesn't remember much. And I haven't told her anything. She's not a threat to you." I don't want him trying to get her next.

"I never thought she was," he says.

His arrogance increases my hatred of him. Unsaid is that he doesn't see me as a threat either. And I want to be. So badly.

"Why are you really here?" I ask.

"Because I *know* how much you hate my kind," he says, anger and frustration mixed together. "I figured the first thing you'd do now that you know about me is tell the Agency about the theater. I wanted to ask you to honor your promise not to."

I shake my head.

"Dawn, there are good vampires out there. We're not

all like those monsters who attacked you, and we're not all like my father."

"Prove it. Turn yourself in to the Agency. Work for them."

"That's impossible. I won't have them monitoring my every step. They'd lock me up and use me only at their convenience."

"So?"

"I wouldn't be able to wander the night."

"Your problem, not mine."

"It would've been your problem when you were attacked on the trolley," he says. "Had I been locked up in an Agency tower somewhere, then where would you be now?"

An image flashes through my mind: me being fed on by vampires. No, a single vampire. Nameless, faceless, shapeless. But he sounds just like the one in front of me. I force it out of my head.

"Why *did* you rescue me?" I ask.

"I told you: right place, right time."

As soon as I saw Victor standing next to his father, I thought this was all a game, and his intentions were to manipulate me. I figured his father sent Victor after me, maybe even arranged that attack on the trolley so his son could rush in and save the day. That sounds *exactly* like something Valentine would do. No, Victor saving my life can't be just a coincidence.

"You expect me to believe that?"

"Would you rather I hadn't?"

"It's just a little unlikely," I say. "The city's delegate being saved by a Valentine vampire? I mean, what are the odds?"

"Good, if you watch the night like I do," he says. "You really think you're the first human I've saved?"

A strange part of me wants to believe him, to think he's different from the monsters in my dreams. But I have seen what monsters can do.

"There have been others?" I ask.

"Of course. Those weren't the first Lessers I've slain, either. The Night Watchmen patrol this city, but I do my fair share, too."

"Why? What do you have to gain from killing your own kind?"

"They aren't my kind!" he says, his voice low but bordering on anger. "They're murderers who think they have the right to feed off any human they please. I'm not like that. Humans have hearts and souls, and have every right to walk the night without fear of being attacked. But we need more blood, Dawn. Vampires have the right to survive, too. Trying to bully it out of the humans—I know that's not the way to do it, but we can't survive without it. Animal blood doesn't cut it for us. You know that."

"Save it for the negotiation table. Or *are* you here to take my blood?"

"If I wanted it, I'd already have it."

I can't deny the truth of his words. He's had so many opportunities: on the trolley, at the theater, right now. He's done nothing to indicate he's a threat to me, but I'm having a hard time looking beyond the fangs. And he did threaten Rachel.

"Dawn?" It's Rachel again.

"Coming!" I look at Victor. "If I don't go, she's going to come in here."

"Just think about what we can do to get more blood."

"We?"

"You're the delegate, but if there's something I can do to help, I will." He purposefully sets my stake down on my dresser and starts walking toward the balcony.

"Victor?" He stops, his back to me. "You knew I would be at the manor tonight. Why did you go there?"

"Because, like you, when I'm summoned by my father, I can't say no. Disobeying him can lead to . . . unpleasant consequences."

A chill goes through me as I try not to imagine what those might be. I feel a twinge of sympathy toward him—which is the last thing I want. He's a vampire. I can't forget that. I move to my dresser and pick up my stake.

"If Rachel had come in here, would you have killed her?"

He turns and his eyes pierce mine. "The only answer you'll believe is yes, so why bother to ask?"

He's right. Even if he said no, I'd think he was lying. He knows me so much better than I know him. I'm at a disadvantage. One I'll stay at, because I have no desire to become familiar with him.

"I have to tell the Agency about you," I say. "I'm sorry, but I can't let an Old Family vampire walk the streets without alerting them."

"What will you tell them?"

"About the attack. The rescue. The theater."

"I can just move. They'd never find me."

"Still, I have to."

"I saved your life that night. If I've earned a measure of trust, no matter how small, then keep the theater a secret. If you have to tell them a Valentine is within their walls, I understand. But don't tell them you know where. If you do, any deaths that happen as a result will be on you."

I don't like the implied threat, but I think about Victor staking those vampires, how quickly he saved my life. He saved Tegan, too. He took us into his home. I think about the warm feeling that ran through me as we talked, and how good it felt knowing he was protecting us from the night. All these pictures and emotions rush through me, and I can't believe what I'm about to say.

"Okay. The theater stays between us. For now. But if I suspect you're killing humans . . ."

"Thank you, Dawn." He takes two steps, stops, and looks back. "A bit of advice: When you're dealing with my father, let him see the Dawn Montgomery who's facing me now. He doesn't realize how strong you are. I didn't either." He appears uncomfortable admitting that. "I—he—thought you were just a puppet. Learning differently will unsettle him. Give you an edge."

"Why would you give me advice?"

"Maybe I don't like my father any more than you do."

Before I can think of a response, he steps out onto the balcony and closes the door behind him. I rush across the room and open the doors wide. He's gone.

But I have a feeling I haven't seen the last of him.

Chapter 8

I walk into the kitchen to find Rachel staring at a small TV on the counter. The few available channels show news or some very, very low-budget soap operas. They're recorded in small studios using ancient equipment that barely works. One of the stations shows reruns of old television series made before the war. I wish a comedy were on the screen now, but unfortunately, it's Roland Hursch, the wealthiest man in the city, and the most antivampire. He's ranting outside of a blood site, protesting against those going in to donate.

"This is our enslavement! This is our curse!" he shouts, holding up two empty blood bags. "We give to those monsters, and for what? They still violate VampHu; they still find their way into our city; they still abduct our citizens and drain them dry. It's time we stand up against the

Agency; it's time we make our voices heard. It's time for Dawn Montgomery to step down as delegate, and let someone with actual experience, actual knowledge, take charge at the negotiating table with Valentine."

I must have made a sound, because Rachel suddenly jerks around. "Sorry." She clicks off the TV.

"That's okay. It's not anything I haven't heard before," I say as I reach into the fridge for some orange juice and pour myself a glass. I try not to wonder whether Roland Hursch is right. Abductions are on the rise; blood donations are down. What good am I to the city? Then I remember what Victor said—that I'm stronger than he realized. . . .

I shake my head. I'm not about to start taking compliments from a vampire to heart. They're notorious liars. Anything to get what they want, Victor included.

"Kids aren't bullying you at school, are they?" Rachel asks, her voice filled with concern.

"Nothing I can't handle." It's not so much political with them as it is jealousy. Working for the Agency, I get a nice apartment, clothes, anything I want. Plus I've acquired a sort of celebrity status—even if most of the press is negative, some kids envy that.

"We can talk to the principal, have bodyguards with you at all times," Rachel says.

"Yeah, like I'd want bodyguards traipsing along behind me in the hallways."

"They'd be incognito. No one would know."

"Rachel, think about where I was earlier. Valentine

Manor. Do you really think I'm bothered by a couple of kids at school painting my locker red?"

"Did they do that?"

"You're missing the point here. I'm okay at school."

She studies me for a moment, then says, "Let's move on then. During your meeting with Valentine, what did his son do, exactly?"

I lean against the kitchen counter and gulp down my juice. My gaze falls on a faded picture held in place on the side of the fridge with a magnet. It was drawn in crayon with a child's hand. My hand. It shows four people, all smiling. My family. The only picture I have with all of us together. I don't know why I keep it. It doesn't even resemble us, really.

"Just observed, mostly." I know I should tell her about Victor rescuing me or being in the city or his visit to my bedroom, but for some reason saying the words is harder than I expected. Not so much because it'll mean confessing what I was really doing that night with Tegan—but because I'm not ready to tell her *everything* about Victor. Which makes no sense. It's certainly not because of a stupid promise I made to a vamp. They're not binding.

"You're right. He's playing some sort of mind game," she says. She sets two plates of pancakes on the island counter. "Dig in."

I sit on the stool and drench my pancakes in syrup.

"So hit the high points of your meeting with Valentine," she orders.

I already did. I mentioned that Victor was there. I'm

having a hard time moving beyond that, moving beyond his being in my bedroom, moving beyond his body pressed up against mine. It was so personal, so intimate. As I lift my fork, I catch a whiff of Victor's scent—tart and spicy—that transferred to my clothes when he was leaning against me. I have to stop thinking about him.

"Uh, well, he wants more blood," I finally say to Rachel.

"I hope you were a bit more articulate when you were with him," she says, her brow furrowed.

"I was. I'm just tired. It's been a long night." But I persevere. I tell her everything that Valentine and I discussed. When I'm finished, she tells me to try to get some sleep. I'll have to give my report to the head of the Agency before I go to school.

It seems forever before I'm falling into bed. The last thing I remember before sleep claims me is staring at the doors to the balcony—securely locked, for what good it will do—and anxiously waiting for the sun to chase away the night.

I wake up as the sun is barely peeking through my bedroom window. I'm glad that no vampires can surprise me now. I clamber out of bed, take another shower, and put on jeans and a red cotton top over a long-sleeved gray one. I pull my hair back into a French braid.

Grabbing my hoodie and messenger bag, I head into the living room. Rachel arches an eyebrow at me in disapproval.

"Why aren't you wearing your suit?" she asks. "You

knew the director wanted you to report on the Valentines this morning."

I shrug. No harm in reminding him how young I am. "I am *not* wearing a suit to school."

"We could stop back by here after the meeting so you could change."

"I don't want to take the time. I'm going to be late enough as it is." I don't mind skipping history class. But there's no way I'm missing my defense class. I have some pent-up frustration I'm desperate to release since Victor's visit. Besides, Michael's in that class, and I'm anxious to see him. I don't know that I've ever missed him so much.

"At least leave the hoodie in the car," Rachel orders.

"No problem."

When we get downstairs, a black sedan is waiting for us.

"Morning, sunshine," Jeff, the driver, says. He serves as our bodyguard whenever Rachel or I move about the city on official Agency business. He's wearing a suit and sunglasses. His strong jaw tells me he's taken more than his fair share of punches. His steady hands tell me he can place a bullet anywhere I care to point.

At first I think he's talking to me, but then I notice Rachel's blush.

"Jeff," she says succinctly.

Whoa! What is this?

He opens the rear door. Rachel climbs in. Jeff winks at me. Now I'm wondering whether it was more than vamp abductions that kept Rachel out all night. I slide onto the seat. He slams the door shut.

"What's with you and Jeff?" I ask quickly before he gets in behind the wheel.

Rachel gives me a stern stare and then turns her attention to some papers. Maybe I'll ask Jeff later.

We head downtown. Once we pass the Works, we take a sharp right and head toward the government district. Street after street is filled with apartment towers: forty-story buildings where the middle and upper classes, both relative terms now, live.

As we drive farther into the government area, the buildings get taller, shinier, until the one at its heart looks like a giant crystal cigarette. Windows all around reflect the sun back down on us. We park in the multistory garage.

"Showtime," Rachel says.

In the director's office a floor-to-ceiling window makes up the entire wall behind his desk. From this height I can see a portion of the high barricade that encircles all of Denver. Guard towers stretch above it periodically, each one with spotlights and soldiers armed with flamethrowers—terrifying weapons that deliver liquid hell to any vampire reckless enough to scale the wall.

Rachel is beside me as we take our seats opposite the director's imposing desk.

"Miss Montgomery," Clive, the director of the Agency, begins. His white hair looks as though he's plowed his fingers through it a hundred times, and his slight frame doesn't seem capable of supporting the weight of responsibility he carries, but I learned early on not to underestimate him. He's protective of the citizens. "How was your meeting with Lord Valentine last night?"

Okay. Here I go. My first official report. I give as accurate an accounting of the meeting as I can.

Unfortunately, Clive is less than impressed with the evening's results. "You have to convince him that he needs less blood, that these abductions are his fault, that he needs to get his damn bloodsuckers out of our city! That's your *job*; that's what your parents did. We had a blood surplus for the first time ever while your parents were delegates. Since their deaths, we've lost it all."

And what of my loss?

"Clive," Rachel says quietly, "it was her first time."

"I knew she wasn't ready," he huffs.

"I am ready," I announce, surprising not only Rachel and Clive with my outburst but myself. I remember what Victor told me. "I'll be more forceful next time."

Clive leans back in his chair, studying me, then looks contrite. "I'm sorry, Dawn. I know Valentine is not easy to deal with. I can never figure out what games he's playing. The Valentines were one of the most vicious families during the war. That's why they have so much power now. It's the reason they were given Denver as their territory."

I know that Denver is strategically located and an incredibly valuable city. Only twenty walled cities remain in the United States, and ours connects the five in the West with the other fourteen to the east. If we're ever taken over by vampires, then the country would be split in half. The two closest cities, Salt Lake City and Wichita, aren't within a daylight's ride of each other. No way to send reinforcements during a fight or flee to safety elsewhere. If we fall, the rest will follow.

"You know what they called Lord Murdoch Valentine during the war, right?" Clive asks.

"The Bloody Valentine," I say.

"And for good reason. Just be careful out there. I don't want to lose you, too."

Clive was the second person to see the burned carriage that held my parents on the road. He left his footprints in their blood and he can't wash it off.

"Overall you did a good job for your first time solo. Your parents were wonderful people. They would be proud of you."

"Would they?" I ask, and Rachel's eyes go wide.

Clive hesitates, but knows I'm speaking out of frustration. "That'll be all."

Rachel and I step into the elevator. I'm staring at the numbers, watching them go down. Still, I can feel her gaze boring into me.

"Your parents *would* be proud of you," she finally says.

"I don't want to talk about them."

The rest of the ride down is silent. I didn't mean to snap at her, but I have some unresolved issues with my parents. Ones that will never be addressed because all I have left of them is a tiny box filled with their ashes, and there aren't any answers to be found there.

Chapter 9

By the time I get to school, the hallways are silent and empty, except for the occasional student heading to the principal's office. In a way, I'm glad no one is around as I open my locker. Since I became a delegate, it's been a little weird at school. With my new position came certain perks. I don't get in trouble for being late to class. I can turn in homework whenever, if at all. The students resent my privileges, and I can't blame them. But their bitterness adds to the challenges facing me these days, so I wish they wouldn't take it out on me.

After getting to the gym and changing into my sweats, I am more than ready for a strenuous workout. Vampire Defense is more popularly known as Kick Vamp Ass.

As soon as I walk in, I spot Michael. He's talking to some other boys, but seems to sense my arrival and turns around. Tearing away from his group, he comes over to me. God, he's hot. And the way he looks at me makes me glad to be here.

"Hey, you," he says, hugging me tightly.

"How was your training session last night?" I ask.

"Who cares," he says, laughing a little. "How was your first night flying solo?"

Okay, until I found out what Victor really is.

"Fine," I say.

He waits for me to elaborate. When I don't, he echoes me, "Fine?"

"Yeah. Fine. Boring, really."

"You're in front of *the* head of the Valentine family, by yourself, in the middle of nowhere, negotiating for the lives of everyone in this city, where a single mistake can get you killed—and it's boring?"

"Well, when you say it like that . . ."

He hugs me again, taking all the humor out of the situation. "If you don't want to talk about it, it's all right. I'm just glad you're okay," he says.

"Michael . . ."

"I didn't sleep at all last night. All I wanted was to see you again. Nothing else mattered."

I sink into him, want to tell him all that's happened, but I can't burden him. "Everything's fine," I say. "I won't see him again for two weeks. Until then, it's just paperwork." I'll discuss things with Rachel and she'll keep me updated of where things stand with the Agency, but at this point, I'm more of a figurehead—except for my encounters with Valentine.

"Promise?" Michael asks.

"Promise."

He pulls back and smiles. Maybe we should skip school. Take some time for us. After what I went through last night, I deserve a little spoiling.

"Well, isn't this cozy."

I glance over to see Lila Hursch walking toward us. Her red hair is pulled back into a ponytail that swings with her movements. Three words can sum her up: *bitch*, *bitch*, and *bitch*. I'm surprised she wasn't standing beside her father while he was ranting at the blood site. She's Daddy's little darling. Whenever she gets in trouble, his money and influence bail her out. She hates me because I barter with vampires. Even though I'm doing it to protect her neck, she doesn't care. Besides, she's been after Michael for some time now. It's no big secret.

"There's no kissing allowed at school," she says, stopping in front of us, hands on her hips.

"Dawn was just telling me about her visit to Valentine," Michael says, trying to keep things cordial.

"Yeah, so how'd that go?" she asks.

"Top secret. You'll have to wait until my report is released to the press," I tell her.

"Daddy can get it. He should be the delegate, not you."

"Your father believes we should stop giving blood to the vampires."

"Don't have a problem with that," she says smugly.

"You don't get it. It would provoke them into attacking

us to get what they need," I tell her.

"We'd destroy them during the day, when they're sleeping."

Frustration causes me to grit my teeth. "You really need to pay more attention in history class. We tried that, remember? It cost us thirty years and a few billion people. If we couldn't do it then, we sure as hell can't do it now."

"Coward," she spits out.

"Hey," Michael interjects sternly. "Dawn's the bravest person I know."

I don't think I've ever been so touched by Michael's words. I wrap my hand around his and squeeze. He squeezes back.

"Maybe we should take a field trip beyond the wall sometime; let her prove it," Lila says.

"That's not going to happen," I tell her. Lila knows the rules as well as I do—the government thinks anyone underage is too immature, too willing to get turned by vampires, to allow them outside at night. But that doesn't stop teens from wall-walking. The wall surrounding Denver is so large that while there are patrols, not every area can be scrutinized. Kids sneak out there and scour the wall, looking for ways out of the city. Not many people find one, because the wall is sealed pretty tight. Which is good, because a spot to get through works both ways—if kids can get out, vamps can get in.

But I wouldn't put it past Lila to wall-walk, to have the mistaken impression that it would make her appear tough instead of reckless. Even now fury burns in her eyes. She can't stand the fact that I'm the exception to the under-twenty-one rule.

"You're not the boss of us," she says.

"Real mature. You're definitely ready to go out of the city on your own."

"I can handle myself better than you."

And before I know what's happening, she takes me down. My head and hips slam against the wooden floor, the air in my lungs rushing out all at once. Straddling me, she pulls a fist back.

I let her throw the punch, knowing it's going to be weak. I grab her wrist with both my hands before it connects, and in the blink of an eye, I roll her over. I take a deep breath to get my air back and watch her struggle against my grip.

I smack the side of her face. The crack is followed by *ooh*s from our gathering audience.

"Give up?" I ask, half question, half demand.

"Not as long as you breathe."

I'm about to hit her again, but she looks so pathetic squirming on the floor that I hesitate. Big mistake. She wiggles out from beneath me, kicking me in the gut along the way.

When we stand up, the students surrounding us chant our names. I can't tell who they're rooting for the loudest.

Lila comes after me with the same blind rage her father blasts when he's preaching his antivampire propaganda, even screaming a little as she charges. I use her fury against her, easily throwing her onto her back with a simple move that Jeff taught me. She lands with a satisfying thud.

Suddenly a strong hand clamps onto my arm and I'm yanked away. Mr. Timmons, the head defense coach, is holding me. His assistant, Ms. Richards, is stopping Lila from lunging at me. I take pride knowing the bigger teacher immediately moved to restrain me, not Lila.

"Save it for the vamps," he says in a commanding voice.

"She started it," Lila whines.

I just roll my eyes. Unbelievable.

Mr. Timmons shoves me toward the dummies. "Stake practice!" he yells.

I wrench free of his hold and head toward the torsos that line the wall. Kids are shuffling out of my way, and I know my movements and expression are telegraphing, *Don't mess with me.* The only one who dares to follow is Michael.

"Why didn't you tell Timmons that Lila attacked you first?"

"I have more important things to do than worry about her." I walk past the dummy and grab a stake from the wall where they are neatly stored. I pick a nice, heavy metal one. I plunge it into the dummy. A direct hit to the heart. I know because red gel begins to ooze around the stake.

A vampire's heart bleeds out so fast that nothing can stop it. As long as the stake is held in place, the wound can't heal. Within four to five beats, the vampire dies. Bullets can't do the trick. Too small. The heart will heal, pushing any bullet out or sealing up after it if it passes through. That's why stakes work. The first hit stuns them, weakens them just enough for the human to hold them down while they bleed out.

"You ever think about doing that to Valentine?" Michaels asks quietly.

To Valentine and now Victor. I've never been on a first-name basis with vampires. I don't like it. "All the time." As a delegate, I'm supposed to be neutral, the perfect arbitrator between vampires and humans. An image I'm expected to project at all times. But after my fight with Lila, I'm in no mood to play diplomat.

I slam the stake into the dummy again, overdoing it and lodging it deep within its plastic torso. Gripping it, I try to pull it out, but it's in too far. I'm about to put my foot just below it for extra leverage when Michael takes hold of it.

"Easy," he says with a smile. "You're really worked up, huh?"

I take my first real breath since the scuffle with Lila. God, she just gets under every inch of my skin.

Michael twists the stake and slowly pulls it out, then flips it and hands it to me. "Still up for watching the Night Train roll in this evening?"

The Night Train is the *only* train that runs across the country; it moves practically non-stop, twenty-four hours a day. Literally, one train, one track. It was written into VampHu as the only alternative for long-distance travel, now that airplanes are outlawed. It's slower, bumpier, and less reliable, but it gets the job done. It mainly redistributes blood and other goods among all the cities, taking passengers on and carrying mail. I know, it sounds boring. And during the day, it would be. But at night . . . rolling across those empty plains, just an inch of steel separating the passengers from thousands of hungry vampires—the thought makes me shudder.

Each city is an island. That is the core plan of the VampHu. Getting supplies from one to the other is hard enough, but passing information is almost impossible. The vampires didn't want humans to compare notes anymore. We might get an agent once a year who's making the rounds on the Night Train, updating all the cities on the comings and goings. But besides that, it's quiet. All news is local news. All radio and television shows are made within the city, for the citizens. Sometimes, it feels like the world outside these walls could simply disappear one day, and it would take us years to notice. The vampires destroyed all means of communicating with others beyond our wall. There's a tradition whenever people visit other cities: they bring back as many newspapers as they can. Even if they're irrelevant to us, the news outdated by the time we even read them, it still helps us feel like we belong to a larger world. It makes us feel part of the human community.

The Night Train serves as a symbol that while we may be isolated, we are not alone in our struggles. We are tenuously connected.

Michael and I have a little ritual that began when we were kids: We watch it coming into town together. I'm not exactly sure when it started, but it's always felt as natural as a heartbeat since.

I smile at him. "I wouldn't miss it." I touch his arm. "Or being with you."

I can tell that he wants to kiss me, but this is the one class where he strives really hard to make a good impression and follow the rules, because without a good evaluation from Mr. Timmons he won't get to stay in the elite program.

"Me too," he says. "I have practice after school. Wanna meet at Daylight Grill when I'm finished?"

"Yeah, okay, that'd be great. I have to stay after school to work on a project anyway. Shouldn't take me too long."

"Be sure you get there before dark."

I smile. "Right." His protectiveness makes me feel warm all over. I know Michael would do anything to keep me safe.

And then, as if to prove his skill to me, he turns and stakes three dummies in a row, each one drawing red ooze. His motions are calculated and efficient.

I have a feeling that if Michael ever went beyond the wall he'd survive . . . for a while, anyway.

Chapter 10

After defense class, I head to Vampire Methodology, one of my few classes with Tegan. She's specializing in vampire psychology, the inner workings of their ancient minds. Which means she raises her hand for every question the teacher asks, and when our latest tests are handed back she, of course, blew the curve for all of us. So, all in all, nothing new. When the bell rings, Tegan and I head to the cafeteria.

"It's all over school that you and Lila got into it this morning in kick-ass class," Tegan says.

"Who do they say won?" I ask.

"Depends where they stand on the delegate issue. Most are giving the win to Lila, but my money's on you."

I grin. "I was still standing when they pulled us apart, so I'd say you'd get paid."

She laughs, a bubbly sound that always makes me smile, even on my worst days. "She's such a bitch."

In the cafeteria, we get our trays and slog through the line. The entrée server places a plump piece of chicken on my plate. "Need to keep up your strength," she says with a wink.

The veggie lady gives me half a portion of rice and beans—along with a snarl.

Such is my new life as a delegate. I've become a love-her-or-hate-her kind of girl.

Tegan takes her tray and follows me to an empty table by the window. Michael usually joins us for lunch, but he's back in the gym getting in some extra practice, since we have plans for this evening.

As soon as we're settled, Tegan wastes no time asking the big question, now that we have some privacy. "How was it last night—being alone with Valentine for the first time?"

"Kinda scary, if you want to know the truth."

"I always want the truth. Especially when it comes to Old Family vamps. Everything they do is so . . . calculated."

I think of Victor and know the same applies to him. What was he really after when he came to my bedroom? And why give me advice regarding his father?

"Maybe I could go with you next time," Tegan says. "Just to see him in person would be so awesome."

"No way you're coming."

"Come on. I could help you. I could even help the Agency. I'll pick up on things you can't. I mean, you're good, Dawn. But you don't have the understanding of vampire psyches like I do."

"No, Tegan," I respond harshly, to shut her up. "You don't know what he's like. He's not a lab rat for you to study. Trust me."

She's disappointed, and plays with her chicken, a small pout on her face that won't get her anywhere with me.

"So I take it you didn't tell Michael about the hot Night Watchman," she says after a while.

I stare at her blankly for a moment, then realize she's talking about Victor. Yeah, right, I haven't told her yet that he isn't a Night Watchman. I should tell her. She could do her little psych eval thing and help me figure him out. Then again, she'd tell everyone that an Old Family vamp was in the city; I might as well give her a megaphone to do it. No, I need to control that information and release it when I want and to whom I want. So instead, I hear myself saying, "About that. I sorta promised him that we'd keep our encounter with him a secret."

"Oh, absolutely." She leans forward. "But here's the thing. I've been giving it a lot of thought, and I have a little black hole of time. From the time we left the party until I woke up in the car—even allowing for the vamp attack you told me about—it just seems like . . . I don't know. Too many unaccounted-for minutes. So what were we doing?"

"Just driving around." Guilt gnaws at me. Why am I being loyal to Victor and lying to Tegan?

"So you don't know how we get in touch with him? Seriously?"

"No."

"Wish we could have him come talk to us—for career day or something."

Like that's going to happen.

"Wonder if we'll ever see him again," she muses.

"Probably not," I lie.

A girl can hope, can't she?

After school, as I scour the few research books our school has, I'm glad I have something to occupy my thoughts. This project should have been turned in last week—but I was spending extra time with Rachel preparing for my first solo encounter with Valentine. Today my history teacher, Mr. Chen, simply handed me the classroom keys and told me to lock up when I was finished.

My report details the major battles during the war. I pay particular attention to the Battle of Lonely Hill. It was the last battle my brother fought in before he returned home and got a job at the Works. My writing isn't polished, and not all my sources are properly cited. I'll get a C, maybe a B. But I'll pass in the end.

I check my watch. I've been working on this stupid thing longer than I thought. Sunset should be creeping in. Michael is probably already waiting for me at the Daylight Grill.

I grab my messenger bag, place the paper on Mr. Chen's desk, and head to the door. As I lock up the room and slip the key into my pocket, I realize the school has become very creepy. I hear footsteps echo every once in a while, maybe another student staying late, wandering the corridors. Somewhere a door slams shut; another creaks open. It's like being surrounded by ghosts. I can hear and feel them, but can't see anyone.

A shiver runs up my spine, and I feel ridiculous for letting this place spook me. I deal with Valentine, for crying out loud. But I can't shake that feeling of being watched. The hairs on the back of my neck stand up.

I amble down a hall with most of the lights off, an attempt to save electricity now that school is out. Just before I get to the doors leading outside, I see that they're padlocked.

"Unbelievable," I say aloud as I rattle them.

I'll have to try to find another way out.

That's when I feel it: movement, right behind me. I turn around and see someone staring at me from the end of the hall I just came from. He's wearing a hoodie pulled up, completely covering his face. It's dirty, covered in black soot. He just stands there, watching me.

I listen for the sound of anyone else, someone who might help me in case this guy is more than just a voyeur. Nothing. Silence fills the hallways.

I quicken my pace and go down another corridor, unsure where it will lead, because I've never been down here before. This place can turn into a labyrinth fast, and the deeper you crawl in, the harder it is to get out. I glance behind me and Hoodie isn't following. That's a relief, but I quicken my strides until I turn the next corner and . . .

There he is. Staring at me from down the hall. I would've

heard him. Even if he knew a shortcut, I would've heard him. This guy is either out to spook me or worse.

He isn't too big, so I might be able to fight him. But I like my chances at running a lot better. I make a break for it. I pick random corridors and run down them, hoping they don't lead to dead ends.

I'm running full blast now when I slam into a wall. At least, it felt that way. I land on my butt and look up to see Hoodie right in front of me.

I hit him with all my weight and he didn't budge. He moved so fast I can't outrun him. He's completely silent. I know exactly what he is.

A vampire.

Too many shadows cover his face for me to get a good look at him or see the fangs, but I know they're there. I quickly yank my stake from my boot and scramble to my feet. I balance myself on the balls of my feet for quick movements and grip my stake.

"If you want my blood, you're going to have to fight for it," I tell him.

He tilts his head, as if confused or even disappointed. Then he turns around and begins to walk away. The back of his hoodie has a design on it, or it did at one point. It's eaten away now, faded nearly to the point of oblivion. I can't tell what the original image was, but the remains look like a giant snake.

Funny how you notice those things even when your heart is pounding a million beats a minute.

I don't dare follow him. With the right combination of

speed and stealth, I might be able to land a fatal blow in his back. But what's the point? One false move and I'm dead. Maybe when he got up close he decided I wasn't his type. Some vampires are like that. It has to be A-positive, or B-negative, or O. I might've lucked out and gotten a picky one. Or maybe he's just tormenting me, getting the blood warmed up for later.

I keep my eyes on him until he disappears down the hall. A crack of thunder rolls through the building, a dry storm starting outside.

Making my way through the school, I realize how really flustered I am. It takes several minutes of walking the hallways before I find a janitor to let me out.

"You know a guy who wears a hoodie with a snake on the back?" I ask, hoping it was just some maintenance guy with a demented sense of humor.

"Nope. I just mop the floors." He unlocks the door, pushes me through onto the steps. The door shuts with a clang that seems to reverberate through me.

Dark clouds are blocking the sun. I start running for Daylight.

Chapter 11

Day has shifted into night by the time I arrive at the Daylight Grill. I'm disappointed to discover that Michael's not here yet. I order a hot chocolate and sit at an empty table near one of the windows. I can't seem to control my trembling. I wish I hadn't missed the sunset. It's strange, but I love watching it, even though it's a signal for the monsters to come out to play. It calms me.

On Day Street, it's a very different experience. As the shadows lengthen and creep between the buildings, huge street lamps come on. Before long, it's daylight again. Eventually all of Denver will be like this: daylight all the time so people feel safe. Unfortunately, an artificial sun isn't much of a deterrent to vamp—

"Is this seat taken?"

Case in point. I jerk my gaze around to find Victor

staring right at me, cup of coffee in hand. It's a shame a face that gorgeous has to belong to a vampire.

And he is absolutely the very last person I want to see at this precise moment.

"Yes, as a matter of fact, it is, so get the hell away from me."

Completely ignoring my protest, he plunks himself down across from me, wrapping both hands around his mug as he sets it on the table. His gaze is so intense, like he can see straight into my soul. "What's wrong?" he asks.

"I'm expecting someone," I emphasize, not bothering to hide my irritation.

"No, you're shaking. I can feel the vibrations over here."

Vampires have incredibly keen senses.

"I want you gone."

"Something happened, Dawn. Tell me." He places a hand over mine. It's so warm it makes me realize how cold mine is. I jerk my hand out from beneath his. I don't want him comforting me. That's Michael's job. Where the hell is he?

"It's none of your damn business," I say to Victor. But then my anger overtakes my fear and I lean forward, whispering harshly. "There're getting to be too many vampires in this city."

Victor eyes me curiously. "I keep a pretty good head count. It's not that high."

"Well, then, you do a bad job of keeping them in line. And the next time one of them comes near me, I will shove my stake—"

"Another vampire attacked you? Where?"

Is that anger I hear in his voice? Not directed at me, but at my unseen foe? It rattles me, makes me rethink what may have happened. "No, not attacked. Just followed. At school. I don't know what he was trying to do." I cross my arms over my chest and rub my hands up and down them. "Scare me, maybe. Maybe it wasn't even a vampire; the sun was still out, even if it was cloudy. I didn't get a good look at him. He was wearing a hoodie pulled forward. It doesn't matter."

"If the sun was out, it couldn't have been a vampire."

Logically, I know that. It's just that this guy was so . . . weird. But more, I don't like appearing to be irrational in front of Victor. "He could have a nest somewhere in the school."

"That's possible. My father . . ." He hesitates.

"What?" I insist.

"He may have ordered someone to follow you. I know he had someone following your parents."

"You're kidding me."

"You don't really think he relies on the delegate to bring him all the information, do you?"

"Son of a bitch." I glance out the window. Where's the real sun when I need it? Then I glare at Victor. "Is that why you're in the city? To spy for him?"

"I'm not here doing his bidding."

"Then why are you?"

"Maybe if we were friends—but, well, you said that won't happen—so I'll keep my reasons to myself. But I promise you that my presence puts no humans in danger."

"Yeah, right. You'd have to say that, wouldn't you?" I rub my brow. "I should tell the Agency you're here."

"You didn't tell them?"

I hadn't meant to confess that. "There wasn't a good opportunity to bring up the subject. I was crunched for time. Had to get to school, so discussing the negotiations with your father took precedence."

"Thank you," he says, his low, seductive voice sending pleasure spiraling through me.

What's wrong with me? Why do I care if he's happy?

"Can you please go?" I ask.

"I won't stay long."

"Don't you get it? I'd rather you not stay at all."

He studies me for a minute as though he's trying to judge the veracity of my words. Other than threatening him with a stake, I don't know how to get my point across.

"Fine. I came here to give you this. I meant to give it to you this morning . . . but, well, I was a little distracted." He reaches into his jeans pocket, then sets my cell phone on the table between us.

I snatch it up. I hadn't yet worked up the courage to tell Rachel that I'd lost it. And I sure could have used it when Hoodie was following me through the school. "Oh my God, you went back for it?"

He shrugs like it's no big deal. But there could have been other vampires around. Or Night Watchmen investigating a trolley that was no longer running. One with dead vamps in it. I don't want to be grateful to him, but I am, dammit.

I open it. There are the texts from Michael. The missed calls. "I don't know what to say."

"Thank you?"

I look up at him, totally unable to understand his motivation. What does he want from me? Vamps never do anything without expecting some sort of payback. "Yeah. Thank you."

"You're welcome," Victor says, like we're back at Valentine Manor, having to be all formal and polite.

Since it's obvious he's not leaving, I decide a little interrogation might be in order, and if it makes him uncomfortable, all the better. I'm not in the manor now, and I'm not under his father's scrutiny, which means I've more freedom to ask what I want. "So did you fight in the war?"

He hesitates, then says quietly, "Yes."

"How long?"

"From the beginning."

Thirty years. I stare at him, not sure what to say. Brady fought for only two, and the change in him after he returned was so extreme that even at my young age, I noticed it. Once happy and optimistic, he became severely depressed. I remember sometimes he just stared off at nothing, and there'd be no way to get him back. No telling what horrors played through his mind every night. After only two years. I wonder what toll it took on Victor to have fought for thirty. I'd never considered that vampires, with their immortality and their ability to heal quickly from almost all wounds, would never get a break from the fighting.

Uneasy with my silence, Victor says, "I should probably
go."

"Yeah, definitely."

"I'll see if I can find out anything about this guy who
was bothering you at school."

"Don't." I don't want him doing me any more favors. I
don't want him having an excuse to come talk to me. "My
boyfriend will take care of it. Michael is really capable. As
a matter of fact, you *really* don't want to be here when he
gets—"

"Victor, oh my God! I was afraid I'd never see you
again," Tegan gushes as she drops into the seat beside
him as though we'd invited her. I'm not surprised to see
her here. Daylight is hangout central for everyone at my
school. Still, her timing seems like a curse from the gods. I
was finally getting rid of him.

"You look like you're feeling better," Victor says, smiling at her. The control he has to keep those fangs from
emerging when he's surrounded by humans is amazing.

"Totally. I'm so embarrassed that you saw me at my
worst." Tegan looks at me, at Victor, back at me. "So what
are you guys doing here?"

"I'm waiting for Michael to finish up practice. Victor
just happened along."

"Amazing. That our paths would cross again so soon.
Right? Must be destiny."

"Probably not," Victor says. "I have to go."

Tegan leans against him and whispers, "To protect the
citizens. I know. But your secret is safe with us."

Victor slides his gaze over to me. "I'm counting on that."

I get this really weird sensation—like we've connected on some level that never existed before. *He's the enemy*, I remind myself, then realize that it's not a good sign that I *have* to remind myself.

Tegan doesn't take her eyes off him as he walks out the door. To be honest, neither do I. His strides are long, confident, relaxed. Powerful. He could probably destroy everyone in the building in the time it would take me to pull my stake out of my boot.

"Wow! I can't believe we ran into him again." Tegan twists back around to face me. "The way he was looking at you . . . I think he *likes* you. You know. Really likes you."

"What? No. Absolutely not. He just . . . he returned my cell phone." I take it out, show it to her, like I need proof to back my words. "He found it."

"That was pretty lucky."

"He knew the area where I'd lost it. It's no big deal."

"Why are you flustered?"

"I'm not. And I'm not a vamp, so don't psychoanalyze me."

An awkward silence swallows us, and I know her perceptive mind is picking me apart. Yeah, she loves her vampire psychology class, but it's surprising how easily that knowledge translates to humans. So I'm grateful when Michael arrives.

"Hey, you," he says, and slides into the chair beside me, wraps his hand around my neck, and leans in to give me a lingering kiss. I feel so safe with Michael, and the last vestiges of both strange encounters—the guy at school and Victor—drain away.

"Geez, why don't you two get a room somewhere," Tegan mutters.

Michael is grinning when he draws back and drops his arm around me, holding me near. "Wasn't expecting to see you here," he says to Tegan.

"So you didn't see me? Aren't Night Watchmen in training supposed to be observant?"

"We are. Which is why I know something's wrong." He looks back at me. "You were . . . distracted a second ago."

Tegan mouths, *Uh-oh*, and I know she thinks it's because of Victor, and maybe part of it was. But Hoodie is also still on my mind.

"Just a random thought," I assure him.

"Come on, Dawn, what's going on?"

I know he won't let up. It's the hunter in him. "When I was leaving school . . . a vamp was chasing me through the hallways."

"Hell's horses, you didn't tell me that," Tegan says.

"I didn't get a chance. Not that you could do anything about it." But Michael . . . I can see him shifting into hunter mode. I wonder if telling him was a bad idea. He's good, but he's never actually faced a vampire.

"Are you sure?" he asks.

I nod, then shake my head. "I don't know. I didn't see any fangs, but he was fast, faster than he should have been. When I threatened him with my stake, he just walked away."

"Was the sun still out?" Michael asks.

"Yes, but it was cloudy; maybe he made a dash for the school. Or maybe he came in last night and was waiting for me."

"Or maybe it wasn't a vampire," he says.

"Yeah, fine. Maybe I'm just crazy." I hate that my word isn't enough.

But Michael takes my hands. "No, that's not what I mean. I heard a rumor a few days ago that some kids wanted to mess with you. Antidelegate kind of stuff, probably Lila's idea."

"You didn't tell me?"

"There are lots of rumors out there, and I didn't want to bother you with it, not with your big solo outing just around the corner."

That makes sense—a lot more than some crazy rogue vampire walking away from me when I was an easy target. Lila has a lot of influence over her underlings, and maybe she was trying to impress Daddy by scaring the delegate: a little revenge for this morning's Vampire Defense class.

"I'll look into it," Michael says. "I'll find out where the rumor started, don't worry. From now on, though, no more late days at school, okay? I'll try to be around you whenever I can."

He squeezes me tight and I feel better. Michael's probably right: Some idiot kid in a hoodie wanted to rattle my nerves.

My phone rings. I dig it out of my jeans pocket and look at the display. *Rachel*, I mouth before answering. "Hey."

"Where are you?" she asks.

"Daylight Grill with Michael and Tegan."

I hear a little sigh and I know she's torn between protecting me and letting me stretch my wings. She doesn't have any experience at being a parent, but she's learning the ropes quickly. "Michael and I are going to watch the Night Train roll in. I won't stay out late," I promise, figuring that's her dilemma. "And Michael will walk me home."

"I'm not sure that's such a good idea," she begins.

"People will be out. We'll be fine. We always do this. You know that."

"Just be careful. And come straight home afterward."

"Okay." I hang up and shrug. "Rachel doing her parenting thing. I can't stay out late."

Michael's brow is furrowed, but I don't think it has anything to do with the fact that I've been given a curfew. "Thought you lost your phone."

My gut tightens. I hate lying to him, but I don't want him ferreting out the truth. "Oh, yeah, well, turns out it was just in the bottom of my messenger bag. Dead battery. I couldn't find it with all the junk in there. I probably should clean that out tonight. The bag. Not the phone."

I'm rambling, I know, trying to cover up my lie. I'm lying to everyone lately, and I hate it.

"Happens to me *all* the time," Tegan says, covering nicely.

"So are you going to watch the Night Train with us?" I ask, deflecting Michael's attention to Tegan.

"No. I'm just going to hang around here. Who knows?

Maybe someone interesting will show up."

She wiggles her eyebrows and I know she's hoping Victor will come back.

"We should probably go," Michael says.

"Have fun, kiddies," Tegan says, waving her fingers. "Don't let the vampires bite."

I wonder how she'd feel to know that not less than ten minutes ago, she was flirting with one.

Chapter 12

As we head for the one and only train station, Michael wraps his hand around mine. When we were kids, we held hands so we wouldn't lose each other in the crowd. Now we do it because we like the sense of belonging to each other that comes from the contact.

"If you see this creep who was bothering you at school, point him out to me," Michael says. "We'll have a little heart-to-heart."

"I probably overreacted." All of a sudden, it's like I'm seeing vampires everywhere.

"You don't overreact. Not even when you were a kid."

"How about that time on the playground when I shoved you off the swing because you hadn't gotten me a present?"

He grins. "I didn't know it was your birthday."

I was eight. I thought he was supposed to give me a gift

because we were friends. After school he did.

"I still have it, you know. The rock you gave me," I tell him.

"That's fair, since I still have the scar on my elbow that I got when I hit the ground."

I smile. Michael always knows how to put things in perspective. He's been in my life for so long, for all the big and small moments. I can't imagine him not being there.

The sidewalk begins to get congested with people. I imagine that before the war, the streets were often like this, filled with people doing things at night. Now it happens only when the Night Train comes through. More police, guards, and Night Watchmen are out. People feel safe. Or maybe they just need this one night when they can pretend they're not afraid of the dark.

It's a party atmosphere, with people laughing, talking, shouting. Some are even singing. Giddiness is in the air.

We see the milling crowd gathering around the station. The Night Train is a big deal, not so much for the goods it delivers, but because of Ian Hightower. The single greatest vampire hunter to ever live. The only human to kill an Old Family vampire single-handedly, to drive a stake right through its evil heart. He's the king celebrity now. And he's in charge of protecting the Night Train and its cargo.

"All right, Dawn," Michael says when we reach the mass of people, "work your magic."

When we were younger, we would have to dodge between people's legs and often got yelled at for cutting through to the front. That is no longer an issue.

Standing at the thinnest part of the crowd, I hold up my badge. "Agency, let me through. Agency, step aside." People turn around and look pissed until they see Michael holding on to me. Using his hands like oars, he rows us through the sea of people. A few cops try to stop us, until I hold the shining piece of metal up to their faces. Then they wave us through.

We get to the police barricades. "Admit it, Michael. You became my boyfriend for the front-of-the-crowd pass that I can provide."

He grins broadly. "That and your kisses."

To prove his point, he plants one on me. He draws back, and we find ourselves pressed against the barricade. On the other side, several cameramen and news reporters from the local station stand by, earpieces in and mics held high. Even though it arrives several times a year, the Night Train is still newsworthy. Or at least, Ian is.

A few minutes later a black plume of smoke rises in the distance, and excitement thrums through everyone. The massive crowd surges against us, pushing us painfully into the barrier. I get scared for a moment, certain I'm going to be crushed. But Michael gets behind me, puts his hands on the metal bars, and pushes back. His arms surround me protectively. I feel his weight press into me, providing a shield. "You know, this is my favorite part of coming here," he says. "It gives me an excuse to be really close to you."

I laugh. "Like you need an excuse."

"Think we'll ever grow tired of doing this?" he asks.

"Can't see that happening."

The behemoth train rolls in, its whistle going off to the cheers of thousands of people watching. The entire thing is encased in thick, black metal, making it seem like the night itself is on the tracks, moving from city to city. Dents and scratches mar it, evidence of the failed attempts by vampires to get on board and feast on the humans and blood bags it carries.

The reporters next to us begin blabbering.

"The Night Train has just come in. We'll see if we can catch a glimpse of Ian. Maybe he'll grace us with his presence. Help lift everyone's spirits."

A few passengers step onto the platform and are greeted by family members with great big hugs and kisses. I see a kid folded into the arms of loving parents, and push out the memories of a burned carriage, and Clive's sad face when he delivered the awful news that Mom and Dad weren't coming home. Rachel was there to comfort me, but Clive took on the responsibility of crushing my heart.

Next, the conductor comes out and begins signing clipboards, initialing here and there, before telling the station agents where the cargo is to off-load.

A tall man hops off the first railway car and the camera lights explode with flashes. The crowd behind us yells and screams, reaching out, frantically trying to brush up against a celebrity. Ian squints from the onslaught, and waves at everyone. His short-sleeved shirt shows the patchwork of tattoos on his arms, each one spotty and jagged, like it was done in the very trenches of the war in which he fought so bravely. A leather belt crosses his torso, a dozen metal stakes threaded through it for easy access. His short black hair moves with the strong winds.

"I want to be him someday," Michael says.

"You'll be a greater vampire hunter than Ian," I reassure him.

I can tell that my words please him. It's not a false compliment. I have absolute faith in his hunting and defense capabilities. But I also know the danger it'll put him in, and hope that when that time comes, he'll move about the city incognito, so Valentine doesn't center his attention on him. Ian, on the other hand, is far too recognizable now.

The great hunter strides over to the barricade and begins jotting his name on whatever scraps of paper people dig out of their pockets or purses. A few people manage to capture the moment on film, leaning across the metal barrier and putting an arm around his shoulders while their friends snap a picture. I can tell he doesn't enjoy it, that he sees it more as a duty to keep morale up, a job just as worthy as protecting the train.

When Ian gets to Michael and me, it's so deafening from people yelling to get his attention that I can't even hear myself think. I'm always amazed by Ian's appearance. His face is fighting to be young—he's only in his thirties— but the scars that run along his jaw and neck age him. He's tall and strong, and his massive hands swallow the tiny pen. I stare at those hands, thinking of them wrapped around a stake, plunging it into a vamp's chest, just like I've always wanted to do. There's something so powerful in him. Something so . . . intoxicating.

And then he's gone. Moving on to the next person. The reporters try to get him to answer a few questions, but he skips them. I see him grab a baby, look into a camera, and hand the infant back to its mother before he disappears among the outstretched arms of rabid fans.

Then I catch a glimpse of one of those fans. Only he's not rabid. He's as still as death.

It's Victor.

What the hell is he doing here? Victor's gaze shifts, locks onto me. I can't move. I can barely breathe. Because I know what I should do. I should shout, *Vampire!* Ian would go into hunter mode. Michael would join him. So why don't I? Why don't I alert everyone that there is a vampire in our midst?

Someone bumps into me and I lose sight of Victor. When I turn back, he's gone, vanished into the crowd. I'm left wondering if I really saw him at all.

"I can't believe what a rush it is to be here, even after all these years. Ian is so *cool*!" Michael says, his arms tightening around me. "Hey, you're shaking."

"I'm just a little cold." He pulls me even closer to his side. His warmth penetrates me.

"Let's get you home," he says.

We cross the street and, with fewer people around, begin moving easily. I can't help wondering if some of them are vampires.

"Here," Michael says, shrugging out of his duster. "I can't believe how much you're shivering. You didn't see that creep from school, did you?"

"No."

But seeing Victor seems to have shut down my body temperature controls. I'm freezing. So I slip into his duster. It smells like him, and it's carrying the heat from his body. I snuggle into it. The hem drags on the pavement. "It's going to get dirty."

"Who cares?" He slips his hand around mine. "The warmth can travel from you to me."

I laugh. "Smooth move."

"I love your laugh," he says. "It's always amazed me that you can still laugh after everything that's happened."

The streets are crowded again as everyone rushes home.

"I can almost forget that everything isn't perfect when I'm with you." I groan. "That was corny. Can't believe I said it."

"I like it. Hey, I've got an idea." He grabs my hand and starts pulling me down an alley.

"Michael, what are you doing? Rachel said no lingering."

"So just tell her we got slowed down by the crowd."

We're back on a street, heading in a direction opposite to the one we should be going.

"Where are we going?" I ask.

"Trust me."

"I do. You know that."

He retrieves a flashlight from one of the pockets of his cargo pants. The bright light illuminates our path better than the occasional street lamp. More out of habit than worry, I glance around, taking in our surroundings. I'm familiar with the area, but the street is deserted. No glow coming from any of the windows we pass.

We reach a large brick building with a chain fence around it. Dawson Elementary. Like all the schools, it was named to honor a war hero.

"Here, hold this," Michael says, and hands me the flashlight. Focusing the beam on him, I watch as he removes a small object from a pocket, opens it, and takes out two metal instruments. He sticks them in the padlock.

"Are you picking a lock?" I ask, stunned. "Where did you learn to do that?"

"Advanced vampire defense training isn't only about fighting moves."

"You're kidding."

"Nope. We have to be able to get to the vamps." He grins as the lock opens.

"Can you teach me to do that?" I ask.

He pushes open the gate. "Sure."

He takes the flashlight from me, then folds his hand around mine and leads me into the schoolyard.

"Never thought we'd be breaking into a school," I whisper, not certain why I suddenly feel like we need to be quiet.

"Not the school. The playground."

We walk around to the back and my gaze falls on one of the swings.

"Remember—" he begins, but I don't wait for him to finish.

I run to the swing and jump onto the bench, standing

with my hands wrapped around the metal links. Once a
traveling trapeze troupe arrived on the Night Train. They
set up in the street and gave an amazing performance. It
was shortly after Brady had died. Although I thought I was
too old for swings, afterward Michael and I snuck off here
one afternoon. We had the best time.

"Daring Dawn returns!" he announces, setting the
flashlight so the spotlight is on me.

"And what about Amazing Michael?"

"I'm here, too," he says.

He places his hands above mine and puts one foot on
the wooden bench before shoving off with the other. We're
bigger than we were before, and the swing protests with a
loud squeak and moan.

"Is this going to hold us?" I ask.

"Guess we'll find out."

We start moving in tandem, a rocking motion that takes
us higher and higher. Our bodies brush over and over with
our movements. It's different now from when we were
kids. There's an electricity here, an awareness. Michael is
so much taller than me, and I have to bend my head back
to see his familiar features, to meet his gaze.

He's always been there for me. I know he always will be.

"I don't remember us going this high before," I say as
we swoosh forward, then back. It's a little frightening.

"We weren't as strong. Didn't have as much weight."

"We thought it would be so exciting to run away with
that troupe," I remind him. "I wonder why they never
came back."

"Maybe they found a place they liked and decided to stay."

"Maybe." I like his explanation better than the one that was traipsing through my head: that vampires got them.

Michael releases his hold on one of the chains and cups my face with his palm. Our weight is no longer balanced, and we swing wildly. I scream and Michael covers my mouth with his, swallowing the sound. Then the crazy careening shifts to my heart as we deepen the kiss. Our motion slows as we're concentrating on each other rather than the swing. His other arm comes around me, pressing us close. When we're barely moving, he draws back and touches his forehead to mine.

"That is certainly a trick we never performed before," I say.

"I liked it."

"Me too." I touch his bristled jaw. "I needed this. The past few days, weeks . . . it seems so hard sometimes."

"Yeah, I know."

For a moment I look past him, to remember this hallowed ground of memories even better. And that's when I see the two black orbs in the bushes, reflecting the moonlight. My pulse kicks up. "Michael, we're not alone."

He leaps off the swing and is gripping his stake in a fighting stance before I even realize what he is going to do.

"Where?" he asks.

I jump to the ground and take my place beside him. "It was over there, near the side of the building, in the bushes. It looked like two black eyes. I don't see them now."

"Maybe it was a cat or something."

"Maybe. But it was an awfully tall cat."

Slowly he crouches, snatches up the flashlight, and sweeps it around the playground. Nothing.

Suddenly a bloodcurdling scream rips through the night. It seems to be coming from near the school, near where I saw the eyes. Then a heavy silence descends that's almost as frightening as the scream.

"Stay here," Michael orders.

I grab his arm. "No, Michael. We go together." My mouth is dry, but my palms are damp.

"Yeah, okay, but stay behind me. Watch my six," he says, meaning I should keep an eye out and make sure no one is sneaking up in back of us.

Cautiously, we move toward the school, around the side of the building. The entire way Michael is sweeping the flashlight over the area. We step around the hedges, and in front of us lies a prone figure. Michael's light falls onto the still body.

In the distance, I hear the echo of pounding footsteps as someone speeds away.

"Don't go after him," I say, knowing that's what Michael wants to do, but already the sound is absorbed by the night. He'd never find him.

Michael sends the beam around us, illuminating the area. Except for the fact that someone died here, it looks undisturbed. The light returns to rest on the victim, spotlighting him more clearly. His mouth is wide open. Fangs protruding. Half his throat is gone, like someone—something—tried to devour him.

"A vampire," Michael says in a low voice. "What the hell happened?"

My mind jumps to Victor. Did he save me again from a vampire?

"Why is his throat like that?" I ask.

"No idea," Michael says. "The bite marks, the savagery . . . it looks like vampire work."

"A vamp killing another vamp?"

"I don't know. Maybe he mistook him for a human and tried to feed. Realizing his mistake, he went for the heart."

He shines his light on the wooden stake jammed into the vamp's chest.

"I need to call Rachel," I tell him.

"Sure, go ahead."

I can tell he's in ultra-alert mode, once again using the flashlight to scour the area around us.

I remove my cell phone from my pocket, so grateful to have it again. I dial her number, wondering how I'm going to explain what Michael and I have discovered: We have a new kind of monster in the city.

Chapter 13

"What the hell part of 'come straight home' did you not understand?" Rachel's voice is quaking with anger, or fear, or both.

Lights are sweeping all over the area. She and Jeff arrived shortly ahead of the Agency's disposal unit, which deals with dead vamps. She, Jeff, Michael, and I are standing off to the side, while the unit works.

"We just . . . we just wanted to mess around for a while," I say, knowing it's an inadequate answer.

"You don't get to *mess around*, Dawn." Yeah, that's definitely anger. "You're a delegate now—"

"It was my idea," Michael says.

Rachel glares at him. She's shorter than I am, but at that moment I think she might terrify even Valentine. "What? Did you tie her up, sling her over your shoulder, and drag her here, kicking and screaming?"

"Uh, no."

"Then she had a choice, and she should have done what I—"

"Rachel," Jeff cuts in quietly.

Now she turns her evil eye on him.

"It's done. She's safe. It's not like you were never a teenager. Sometimes she's gotta rebel a little."

"Are you not looking at what I'm seeing here?"

Jeff rubs his jaw. "I'm not saying she should make a habit of this, but it's always safest when the Night Train comes through the city."

"*Safest* does not mean there are no dangers." She glares pointedly toward the vampire.

"I know, but she was with Michael. I've seen him in training. He's good."

I meet Michael's gaze, give him a secretive smile. To have Jeff's endorsement means a lot.

"Don't do it again," Rachel demands.

"Yes, ma'am."

We hear footsteps and glance up as the coroner approaches. Everyone refers to him as Reap—an homage to the Grim Reaper. Sometimes I think it's not so much because of what he does, but how he looks. He's tall and wiry, with slightly hunched shoulders, as though dealing constantly with death drags him down.

"Well?" Rachel asks.

"I've never seen anything like it. Bite marks on his throat are sloppy, done in haste, like a lot of vampire attacks. But the victim *is* a vampire; their blood is useless to one another; it provides no nourishment."

"Then why?"

He just shrugs. "No idea." Reap checks his watch and makes a note for approximate time of death. "We'll take him back to the morgue, do an autopsy before we place him in the sun for disposal, but I don't think we're going to find any answers."

"Okay," Rachel says. "Tell your team this incident is confidential, need-to-know only. I don't want the public getting wind of this until we figure out what the hell happened."

"Right."

After he walks away, Rachel turns to us. "You're not to tell anyone about any of this."

"What about Valentine?" I ask.

She shakes her head. "No. Not yet, at least."

"Maybe it was a mad dog or something," Michael suggests.

"Whatever it was, it obviously doesn't like vampires," Jeff says.

"So maybe we have a new ally," Michael muses.

Only I'm not sure it's an ally we want.

The only advantage to what happened tonight is that at least now Michael and I are traveling in an Agency car, holding hands in the backseat. Jeff and Rachel are in the front. None of us seem to have much to say.

"Hope you don't get in trouble with your mom," I

whisper. She's superanxious and prone to worry, but that's no wonder. He never knew his dad. He died during the war, shortly after Michael was born.

"No problem. I'll just tell her I had late practice. If she's even home." His mom works two jobs, and he's pretty much been taking care of himself since he was twelve. A lot of kids have stories like that.

We draw to a stop outside Michael's apartment building. Since the war, the rebuilding efforts have concentrated on erecting apartments instead of houses. People like living in communities, where they can feel safe.

Michael gives my hand a squeeze. "See you at school tomorrow."

"Yeah." I lean in and give him a quick kiss—even though I know he's not comfortable with it in front of Jeff. "You were amazing tonight."

He grins. "Thanks. You, too."

He slips out and I settle back as Jeff drives away.

When we get home, Jeff comes upstairs with us. It's after midnight now. And I'm exhausted. "I'm going to bed." I walk over to Rachel and hug her. "Thanks, Rachel. Thanks for coming to our rescue."

"Don't make a habit of this," she says.

"Trust me. I don't need any more adventures."

As I'm walking to my room, I call over my shoulder, "And you two had better behave as well."

Rachel gasps; Jeff laughs. Definitely something going on between them. And I'm glad. Rachel needs a guy in her life.

Everything seems to catch up to me once I close the
door to my bedroom. I feel like I'm moving through molas-
ses as I get ready for bed: showering, putting on flannel
pants and a tank, crawling into bed. I'm trying really hard
not to think about what happened earlier.

But as I'm lying there, it keeps flashing in my mind.
After a while, I hear a soft rapping and figure Rachel can't
sleep either. I sit up and am about to call out to her when
the knock sounds again. It's coming from my balcony
doors. I consider lying back down and ignoring it. Maybe
it's a bird pecking at the glass. Yeah, right. It comes again,
and I know he's not going away.

I turn on the lamp, clamber out of bed, grab the stake
from my nightstand, and pad over to the balcony. Drawing
back the curtains, I see Victor's tall silhouette. I open the
door. "At least you knocked this time. Still, just go away."

"I need to talk to you."

"Victor—"

"I heard a vampire died tonight."

"Vampires die every night. They keep the Night
Watchmen busy."

"Not this one, Dawn. I need to know exactly how he
died."

There is a chance that he isn't talking about the one
Michael and I found, but if he is, I have to do some damage control. As much as I hate breathing the same air that
he is, I sigh, step out onto the balcony, and cross my arms
over my chest. "*What* exactly did you hear? And how did
you hear it?"

"Someone saw a commotion near Dawson Elementary. He went to investigate, but couldn't get close enough to see much with all the Agency people hovering around. Still, he could sense everyone's . . . fear."

"There's always fear when we have confirmation that vamps are within the wall."

"He overheard someone say the vamp was bitten on the neck, possibly fed on." His voice is thrumming with impatience. I guess I can't blame him for wanting information.

"Okay, look, I'll tell you what I know, but you have to promise not to tell your dad about this."

"Trust me, Dawn. I'm very good at keeping things from my father."

"Okay, then. Yes, the vamp had bite marks on his neck. Really savage ones. Michael and I—" I stop as something else occurs to me. "I saw you at the Night Train."

"I know you did. I saw you, too. That guy you were with—"

"My boyfriend. Michael."

"He seems . . . capable."

"Very capable." I let my voice reflect my pride in Michael's skills. "So why were you there?"

"Getting to know my enemy."

"Ian Hightower doesn't hunt vampires anymore unless they're messing with the train."

"Not Ian. You."

I feel like he just punched me in the chest. I've always considered vamps as the enemy, hated them beyond belief for what they did to my brother. But I never reversed it, never considered it from their side. Never saw myself as *their* enemy.

"I thought you were the one who wanted to be allies— friends. Besides, how can you say I'm the enemy when I work as a delegate to ensure there is enough blood for the vampires?"

"How can you view me as the enemy when I've not attacked a human or taken blood directly from one since the war ended?"

I narrow my eyes at him. "Clever wording, Victor. Did you think I'd miss it? You *have* in the past. Probably by force, against their will."

"During the war, yes. I did what I had to do to survive. Like all soldiers."

Black and white. I've always viewed the human-vampire relationship in black and white. They take. We give. But he's mixing things up, showing me shades of gray, complicating matters that should be simple. I don't like it. Then another thought occurs to me. "You didn't follow me and Michael, did you? After we left the station."

"At first, until I realized you might want some time alone."

I slam my fist against his shoulder. He barely moves. "You creep!"

I reach for the door—

He grabs my arm, but I wrench free.

"Dawn, after your encounter at school, I just wanted to make sure you were safe."

"I don't want you following me."

"You're right. I'm an evil creature to try to protect you."

He makes me feel petty and small, but I don't want him in my life. Still . . . "Did you see any vamps in the area?"

He hesitates. "Some, but they were harmless."

"There are no harmless vampires."

"You think that only because you haven't taken the time to get to know any. Yes, a lot of Lessers tend to lose their humanity when they're turned, but it's not due to the process. It's because they become enamored of their new selves: their strength, their invincibility. They become deranged. But others adapt well. They're no different from you."

"Do not compare me to a vampire."

He sighs. "I just meant that they aren't like the vamps on the trolley. Those were the equivalent of human juvenile delinquents. But if you could see some of these others, you might appreciate your role as a delegate more."

"I appreciate my role just fine. And it wasn't a vamp at school. It couldn't have been. It was just some kid. I don't need you to protect me."

I can feel him studying me. I don't want to be out here standing with him; I don't want to wonder if maybe he's right that not all vampires are the same.

Victor backs up a step, as though he realizes that I need distance between us.

"You're right about it being some kid at the school. Before I came here, I checked it out. I couldn't find any sign of a vampire nesting there."

"You would say that, though, wouldn't you? I'll just have Michael check it out, if you don't mind." Even though I no longer believe it was a vampire. I'm just being stubborn. Victor does that to me.

"So even when we agree, you're going to argue with me?" he asks.

"Pretty much, yeah. I don't trust you. I don't like you. I don't want you in my life. How can you not get that?"

He releases a sigh of frustration. "Okay, then, let me get the info I need and I'll go. Is there anything else you can tell me about the vamp that was killed tonight?" he asks, his voice solemn, almost sad, as though he's finally accepted how very much I dislike him.

For some reason, that bothers me, as though I've hurt him. I have to remind myself that he's a vampire. He doesn't have feelings. I swallow hard. "His throat was nearly ripped out. A stake through the heart. That's all we know right now."

He moves to the edge of the balcony, away from the pale light coming from my room. Still, I can see him gripping the rail and bowing his head. He whispers something that sounds like *thirst*, but I'm not sure.

I ease toward him slightly. "What?"

He shakes his head. "Nothing. I need to see him. Where did they take him?"

"The disposal morgue, but you won't be able to get in."

"Let me worry about that. Where is it exactly?"

I give him the address.

"Thanks," Victor says.

I'm unsettled by his gratitude, by this entire visit, actually. "Why is all this important?"

"Hopefully I'm wrong and you'll never have to find out."

"What does that mean?"

"I can't tell you."

Before I can object, he throws a leg over the railing, disappears over the edge. I rush up and look over, but I can't see him. Vampires are like cats. The drop, even from this high up, won't hurt him.

As I turn to go back into my room, my gaze falls on a long white box with a red ribbon resting on the balcony chair. I hesitate, then pick it up and carry it into my room. I lock the door behind me.

Studying the box, I notice the corner of a card sticking out beneath the ribbon. I remove it gingerly, as though I'm expecting it to explode.

For when you next face the night.

Setting the stake I picked up earlier back on the nightstand, I fold my legs beneath me on the bed and tentatively begin unwrapping the box. I can't remember the last time someone gave me a present. My parents, maybe. On my seventeenth birthday. Inside the box is a belted holster made of the finest supple leather. I slide out what it holds: a shiny stainless-steel stake. Its balance is perfect, and the light glints off its surface as I turn it.

I can't believe that a vampire would give me such a nice weapon, one that I could use to kill him.

Moving to the mirror, I wrap the belt low around my hips, secure the buckle. Perfect fit. I fasten the holster to my thigh with the leather strips. I yank out the stake. It slides free with an ease that thrills me. But why did he do this? Why am I touched? He's a vampire. My enemy. I take it off, shove it into a bottom drawer of my dresser, and cover it with T-shirts. I back up until my legs hit the bed, and then I plop down.

If the gift were from Michael, I'd be ecstatic, because not even a diamond necklace would have pleased me more.

I know I should tell Rachel, but I'm determined to face Victor on my own terms, and going to Rachel feels like . . . defeat. I refuse to be defeated.

Still, it's scary how well Victor Valentine knows me.

That night Victor invades my dreams. I roll over and Michael replaces him. We kiss, but when he pulls away, it's Victor again. I see his fangs just a moment before they plunge into me. And then I wake up. Sweaty, breathing hard, trembling.

I scramble out of bed, walk onto the balcony, and stare at the fading moon. The sky turns gray, then blue. The sun finally begins to rise. Chasing away the darkness and monsters.

And yet I can't help but feel that both are still lurking nearby.

Chapter 14

I'm still unsettled when I head to school, and little things begin to irritate the hell out of me. The fact that the sun is hiding behind thick, dark clouds. The fact that I'm running late. The fact that the zipper on my hoodie broke. The fact that I can't shake the feeling that I'm being watched.

The sidewalk is crowded with people going to school, to work, to shop. To do all the things they can while the sun is up. I spin around—

Catch sight of a dark hoodie pulled up. Another guy shoulder-checks me, knocks me back a little, and I lose sight of the guy in the hoodie. I spot an alley he could have ducked down.

I rush over to it. But it's empty except for the garbage littering the ground. I turn around, search faces, see other hooded sweatshirts, but not in the dark shade I'm looking for. And I don't see any with snakes on the back. A girl gives me an impatient glare as she walks around me.

I take off in the direction of school. Picking up my pace, I'm determined to get there before the morning bell. I make it in time, and as I stream in with other kids I find myself paying close attention to what everyone is wearing, searching for that stupid snake.

When I get to my locker I'm not happy to see what's waiting for me. My photo was taken for the *Denver Times* when I was named the new delegate. Now that article is taped to my locker door with a bubble coming from my mouth with the words, *Ooooh! I loooove vamps!* scribbled inside it.

I hear snickers, glance over, and see Lila standing with a couple of her clones.

I rip the picture down, wad it up, and throw it to the back of my locker.

"It's hard to handle the truth," Lila says as she sidles up to me. "One day Michael will realize where your loyalty lies. Then you won't be able to hold on to him."

After my stupid dream, her comment hits a little too close to home.

"It's going to take more than a cheap photo and one of your boy toys stalking me to hurt my feelings." I know she sent Hoodie after me. Michael hasn't found the rumor's source yet, but I'm looking at it. I can feel it.

"Whatever, Dawn. I don't have to do anything except watch. Your downfall is inevitable. Then my father will become the delegate, and my family will be more famous than yours."

Dumbfounded, I stare at her. "You don't get it. This isn't a popularity contest, Lila."

"I know that."

Only I'm not sure she does.

Tegan suddenly appears next to me. "Don't worry about her," she says half to me and half to Lila. "You'll just feed into her craziness no matter what you say."

She's right. Lila has some kind of warped agenda. The best thing I can do is ignore her. I turn to my best friend, grateful to have her support.

"Besides, *we've* got things to discuss," Tegan says.

"Like what?"

Out of the corner of my eye, I see Lila stomp off. Score one for Tegan and me.

"The new guy," Tegan says.

"Who?"

"You haven't heard?" she asks, as though it's incredible I made it this far in life without hearing of the *new guy*.

"No."

"You're gonna love this," she says as we start walking down the hall. "He arrived on the Night Train. From Los Angeles. Can you believe it? I've never met anyone who actually traveled on the Night Train. I have, like, a million questions for him."

When we get to our classroom, I immediately understand what all the buzz is about. The new student stands at the front of the room next to Mr. Chen. He's good-looking, easy competition for Michael in the hottest-guy-in-school category. His hair is longish, falling just below his eyes, which are dark, as if they've spent an eternity in shadow and like it there. He's wearing nice clothes, which means he has money. Wealth and looks—with those two things, he immediately has the attention of the girls in the class. Tegan included.

"Hello, future boyfriend," she whispers. She smiles at him on the way to her desk.

"You're nuts," I say as I sit down beside her. "You don't know anything about the guy."

"He's hot. What else do I need to know?"

Before I can answer, the bell rings and Mr. Chen calls the class to order, then says, "Everyone, this is Sinclair."

"Sin," the new guy corrects him. "Everyone just calls me Sin."

"He looks like he was made to sin," Tegan murmurs in a low voice beside me.

I roll my eyes at her, but secretly have to admit that she's right. He looks like he could be trouble. The good kind, though. The fun kind.

Sin's eyeing the room. I feel his gaze pause on me, ana-lyzing the delegate, before moving on to the next student. He just stepped into the lion's den of high school, and it's like he's already in control.

Mr. Chen points to an empty chair that just happens to be beside Tegan. I'm afraid she's going to pass out from exultation. Sin takes his seat. Mr. Chen tries to lecture, but it's a lost cause. Everyone only cares about the new kid.

Even I'm not immune, stealing glances whenever I can. It isn't long before he's whispering to Tegan, and she laughs or nods and smiles. He seems as infatuated with her as she is with him. Not that I can blame him. He'd be nuts not to be interested in her. So many guys are. What intrigues me, though, is to see that Tegan isn't in flirt mode. She seems to be truly fascinated by him.

When class is over, Tegan and Sin walk out together before parting in the halls. She hops over to me and takes my arm to balance herself.

"Oh. My. God. Is he hot or what?"

"Definitely hot."

We start heading to our next class.

"I think he's going to ask me out," she says.

"All guys ask you out," I remind her.

"But he's different. Or I want him to be different. I want what you have with Michael."

She's never told me that before, but then I remember how she was glad that Michael couldn't join us at the party, how she didn't want me to call him. Maybe my developing relationship with Michael has been hard for her. I never really thought about it, because she is such a guy magnet. I thought she liked it that way. Still, I feel a need to point out, "But I've known Michael forever. You just met Sin."

"We could still have that connection." I hear the stubbornness in her voice. "We *do* have that connection," she insists. "You like him, right?"

She's put me on the spot. "I don't really know him. I wasn't the one talking to him."

"You'll like him," she assures me. "He's perfect for me."

I take her word for it. I've got my own romantic connections to worry about. Namely, why the hell am I dreaming about Victor?

I'm grateful when Tegan veers off and Michael takes her place, wrapping his arm around me to draw me in against his side. Strong. Solid. There's comfort here, familiarity.

He leans down and whispers, "Anything more on what happened last night?"

"No." Reap called Rachel this morning. Autopsy revealed nothing new. I wonder if Victor got in to see the body before it was placed in the sun for disposal. "Reap asked if we wanted the fangs."

Some people collect them as trophies. I'm not sure why I'm suddenly bothered by the practice.

Michael appears appalled. "Why would I?"

His reaction reassures me, makes me want to hug him. "Collecting them seems kinda barbaric, doesn't it?" I ask.

"Yeah, I've never understood people who do that." He shakes his head, then shifts to a new topic. "So, have you heard about this new guy?"

"Yeah. Sinclair: goes by Sin, came in on the Night Train from Los Angeles."

"Whoa!" He looks taken aback. "Do delegates keep details on everyone?"

I laugh. "No. He's in my first class."

"What did you think of him?"

"I wasn't nearly as impressed as Tegan. I think she's going to pick out her wedding gown after school."

He smiles. He has the best smile, nice and fangless.

At the gym, we split off to go into our respective dressing rooms. With no friendly faces among the girls of this class, I quickly change into my workout sweats and head into the gym.

Lo and behold if Sin isn't in there with us. His sweatpants and a tight-fitting shirt reveal more about his physique. He's slender, but every muscle is so defined he could be studied for anatomy labs.

The teacher barely acknowledges him, simply marking him off on the updated roster. But I can see Michael checking Sin out, trying to measure his worth. Since he's been accepted into the elite training program, he looks at everyone a little differently, assessing strengths and weaknesses automatically. His competitive side also seems to have doubled, becoming a beast all its own. I suppose he always feels he has something to prove now; he has to show that he deserves to be in the Night Watchmen more than anyone else.

"Okay, ladies, you're with me," Ms. Richards says, and takes us to one side of the gym.

We begin the routine: running and then quick-drawing our stakes; running and then striking the dummies with our bare hands; running and then staking them through the heart. I imagine that each one is Victor, but I find myself missing the blows. Strange. So I switch to picturing one of the vamps I encountered on the trolley—the ones Victor saved me from. Dead center through the heart every time. If I ask Tegan about it, she'll probably say that subconsciously I don't want to kill Victor. She'd be wrong.

Suddenly I notice that I'm the only one still doing drills. All the other girls are simply standing there, staring across the room. I ease around one of them to see what's going on.

The guys have paired up and are wrestling one another, practicing complex throws and moves on the mat. I don't think it's a coincidence that Michael has paired up against Sin.

Without realizing it, we start moving toward the action, and it isn't long before the other guys stop what they're doing and surround the dueling pair. Michael and Sin are locked in battle. It's only training, of course, and they aren't trying to kill each other, but they are definitely trying to prove something. I think Michael was looking for an easy fight; he wanted to quickly dominate Sin so that the new kid would know who the top dog in this school is. But it's obvious Sin is going to make Michael earn that title. They're both skilled fighters.

Michael grabs Sin's arm and tries to throw him over his shoulder, but Sin's too fast, his wiry body finding a weak point and exploiting it. Somehow, it's Sin who manages to ground his opponent. Michael's body hits the mat with a resounding thud. It's the first time I've seen someone standing over Michael, victorious. But it's only for a second. Michael kicks Sin's legs out from under him, and he lands hard on his back.

"This is good," Lila says, her attention so caught up in the two guys that I doubt she knows I'm next to her.

The audience surrounding the spectacle isn't cheering for either side, but I'm rooting for Michael, of course. And not just because he's my boyfriend. It wouldn't be fitting for the new guy to win. I mean, he's the *new* guy! I know how hard Michael works and trains.

But as the pair continues, I grow nervous. They seem equal, as if each were fighting a mirror opponent. The only difference is that Sin seems to be smiling more, enjoying himself, and maybe breathing just a little easier.

Then he gets too cocky and charges in. I gasp as Michael uses Sin's momentum against him and, in one final move, lifts Sin off the mat and slams him down. I cringe at the sound of what has to be bone breaking. The room is still as everyone waits, wondering if the fight will continue. Michael stands tall right now, but he isn't prepared to keep going. He wants this over.

It's almost as if Sin picks up on that, too. He reaches his hand up, and Michael takes it, lifting Sin back to his feet. Some kind of man language passes between them. Nothing is said, but everything is understood. Michael will remain at the top, but Sin is close behind. There is scattered applause from the class, and the guys wave us off. Mr. Timmons blows his whistle and begins herding everyone back to their assignments.

I dash across the gym and place my hand on Michael's shoulder. I can feel him trembling from the adrenaline rush. He turns to look at me, and I can see the warrior in his eyes. For him, this wasn't just some exercise. He was in combat mode.

"You were awesome," I tell him.

"The guy's good."

"He just got lucky."

"Maybe."

I hug him hard. I don't care who's watching. "I always feel safe when I'm with you."

"Hey, what's this?" He puts me at arm's length and studies me.

I don't know if it's the stupid dream, or watching Michael fight so hard for his place as the best soldier in the school, or the craziness of the past couple of days, but I say, "I just want you to know that you're important to me."

Michael grins with triumph and pleasure at my words. "I do know."

"Colt!" Mr. Timmons yells.

"Later," Michael says, giving me a quick kiss before darting across the gym to where the guys are working out.

I go back to the girls' side and we finish our drills. I've never seen anyone come close to besting Michael, and Sin's smile, even in defeat, makes me wonder what secrets he brought with him from Los Angeles.

Chapter 15

"Pleeease tell me you're free after school," Tegan says, as we settle into our seats for the last class of the day.

"As far as I know," I say.

"Good, because I want you and Michael to hang out at Daylight Grill with me and Sin."

"Whoa, that was fast."

"What can I say? When I see something I want, I take it."

"And you want Sin?"

"Absolutely. What's not to want? He's hot. He's traveled. I mean, he's been on the Night Train. And did I mention that he's hot?"

Only every time that our paths crossed throughout the day.

I start scribbling in my notebook. "Yesterday you were interested in Victor."

I'm not even sure why I said that, why I brought him up, why I'm drawing two Vs, one on top of the other. I scratch them out.

"That was yesterday," Tegan says. "Besides, it's not like I made the best impression on him. With Sin, I have none of the I'm-going-to-be-sick garbage hanging over my head. And everyone's talking about how he kicked Michael's butt—"

"Actually, he didn't," I hear myself saying, sticking up for my boyfriend automatically. "He might have come close, but Michael won."

"Still, Sin's practically a god. And since I'm already a goddess—"

The bell rings, cutting her off. I've never seen her react this way to any guy. She always has guys hanging around her, is never without a date on the weekend. But this is different. I can't tell if it's a good or a bad thing. I just know I don't want her to get hurt.

Hanging out with her and Sin will give me a chance to see if he's good enough for her. After all, she's my best friend. I want only the best for her.

After school two arms encircle me at my locker. "Guess who?" Michael's voice is cheery.

I turn into his embrace. He is all smiles as I tell him Tegan's plan. Apparently he had another class with Sin and they formed a bond of mutual respect.

"The guy can fight," he says as we wait outside. "He'll make a good bodyguard if he wants."

"Not as good as you," I say loyally.

Tegan and Sin aren't holding hands as they approach, but they're so close everyone can see they're an item already. How does she work so fast? It must be her psychology background; she picks up on signals that fly under my radar and knows how to volley them back.

The attraction between them is obvious. I have to admit that they make a cute couple.

It's just small talk as we head to the Daylight Grill: boring classes, terrible weather, and the rolling blackouts that have been plaguing the city lately.

"I hope you don't like your lights too much," Michael tells his new friend. "They seem to have a mind of their own."

Once we get inside, it's an average Tuesday for the place, half the tables taken, kids from school shooting pool, others drinking the famous lemonade. We take a booth in the back and order.

Outside, the sun drops below the horizon, and a hushed calm descends as everyone pretends not to watch. My parents wanted a world where sunsets could be beautiful, instead of feared. I have to remind myself that I want that, too. That's what I'm fighting for.

"I always hate watching the sun disappear," Tegan says.

"Don't tell me you're afraid of the dark," Sin jokes, eyeing her like she could hold back the night.

"I'm fearless," she parries.

"I like that in a girl," he assures her.

Michael reaches beneath the table and squeezes my

knee. When I glance over, he gives a little eye roll and I
wonder if he thinks Sin is trying too hard. Michael and
I have always been comfortable together. Our first kiss
knocked off our socks, made us really aware of each other
in a more-than-friends way, but we never went through a
getting-to-know-each-other phase. Or maybe we did, but
it was so long ago, and we were kids. We've just never had
to impress each other.

We eat our burgers; at least, that's what they look like.
Our city now has a gigantic, multistory greenhouse that
produces crops year-round. Harvested vegetables are diced
up and mixed with artificial flavors to give it the look,
taste, and texture of meat. I think it's delicious, but I've
never had the real thing, so what do I know?

"So what's it like to ride on the Night Train?" Michael
asks as he takes a fry and dips it in ketchup.

"Pretty awesome," Sin says. "Especially at night. Lot of
vampires out there."

"Did they attack the train?" Tegan asks.

"Only a couple of times. I think it's young vamps just
being wild. They know it's impenetrable."

"I don't understand why they attack it at all," I say.
"VampHu allows for the train to deliver goods across the
country from city to city. If we can't get the goods we need
from other cities . . . how can we survive? And if we don't,
how will the vamps?"

"I know," Sin says. "It's totally crazy, this whole setup. No
one obeys VampHu's laws, not even the vampires who created them. If you ask me, things won't stay this way forever."

I feel Michael go into alert mode. "What are you talking about?"

Sin glances around as though afraid of being overheard. "The Night Watchmen are great. We have them in Los Angeles, too, but . . . there are some underground movements. . . . I probably shouldn't discuss it."

"Is that where you got your training?" Michael asks. "From some underground group?"

Sin grins. "I have a very simple philosophy: If you want something, you have to be willing to do whatever it takes to get it."

Tegan beams at the strength in Sin's voice and inches closer to him in the booth.

It gets kind of quiet while we finish eating. I think Michael and I are trying to decipher exactly what Sin is talking about. When the waitress takes our plates away, Michael challenges Sin to a game of pool.

"Is Sin awesome or what?" Tegan asks me as we trail them to the pool tables.

"Yeah," I say. "He's pretty cool. But his whole 'simple philosophy' is a little worrying. I assume he's talking about vigilante groups."

"Yeah, so?"

Okay. I can tell by her tone that she doesn't like me questioning Sin. "I have to do everything within the confines of VampHu, so if you're going to get involved in something . . . *underground* . . . don't tell me, all right?"

"He just got here. He's not talking rebellion—although I'm not sure that would be such a bad thing."

Before I can respond, Michael is holding a cue out to me. "So, do we want to play partners or do you ladies just want to watch?"

"Partners," I say, taking the cue.

"We're going to kick their butts," he whispers in my ear, and a familiar thrill shoots through me. We're a team. Michael and me.

Tegan breaks. She gets a ball in the pocket, misses the next one. I go next, get two good shots before I miss and rejoin Michael against the wall. It's Sin's turn, and he's making the most of it. I watch Tegan's smile broaden with each ball that Sin sinks.

"He's good at everything," Michael says, studying his opponent's game.

"Kinda like you."

Appreciation lights his eyes, and he lowers his head to kiss me. I rise up on my toes to meet him and curl an arm around his neck. He moves his mouth over mine with purpose.

"Ahem."

Michael jerks his head up, and Sin looks at him apologetically. "Sorry, I scratched. It's your turn."

"I'm halfway tempted to forfeit."

"I don't blame you," Sin says, and winks at me.

I feel my cheeks warm. I can't deny he's charming, but he doesn't appeal to me in the same manner that Michael does. I watch as Michael strides over to the table, his long legs eating up the distance. There's a beauty to his movements—whether he's handling a cue or a stake—that comes from confidence and constant practice.

A few quick strikes and it's all over. We win. Michael starts racking up the balls for a rematch while Sin goes to the bar and returns with some lemonades. I take a sip, wrinkle my nose. There's something different about it.

Tegan must have thought so, too, and said something to Sin, because I hear him say, "I had him add a special ingredient."

Tegan's eyes widen. "Booze? How did you talk him into that? We're underage."

He just grins and says, "I know how to get what I want."

"You're all about sin, aren't you?" she says with a giggle.

He puts his arm around her, draws her in, and kisses her. Based on the dazed look on her face when he pulls back, I think she found the kiss more intoxicating than the drink.

Time gets away from us as we play one game after another—and Tegan drinks one lemonade after another. When waiting for her turn, she leans against Sin like she can't stand up without his support. I see horrible flashbacks of the party where everything went wrong.

When Sin goes to take his shot, I scoot over to Tegan and whisper in her ear, "Don't forget what happened the other night."

"You worry too much."

"How are you getting home?"

"Sin, of course. Loosen up. Have some fun."

The last time I did that, we nearly lost our lives. If Victor hadn't shown up—

And then, as if I conjured him with my thoughts, I see him in the corner of the café.

He's watching me, and as soon as our eyes meet, he starts to walk toward us.

"Oh, no," I mutter.

"What?" Tegan glances in the direction I'm looking. Her eyes brighten and she smiles as he arrives. "Hi, Victor."

"Hello, Tegan." He looks at me. "Dawn."

I want to ask him if he's crazy. How can he just show up here again like he's . . . not a vampire? Michael is suddenly at my side, and I can feel the tension radiating off him. If he could, I think he'd mark me as his territory. Maybe he can, because his arm comes around me, clamping me to his side. The message is clear: *She's with me.* Sin looks up from the shot he was about to take, and I can see speculation in his eyes as he saunters over to join our awkward little group.

"Who are you?" Michael demands.

"Oh, this is Victor," I say, and make introductions.

"Dawn, I need to talk to you for a minute," Victor says.

"So talk," Michael says.

"Privately," Victor replies, clipping the word sharply and reminding me of his father and how he expects to be obeyed.

"I don't think so," Michael says, clearly shifting into protective mode. Maybe even a little jealous.

"Michael—" I begin, not certain how to reassure him, and hating that Victor has put me in this position. But before I can say more, Tegan speaks up.

"It's okay. It's probably Agency business. He's a Night Watchman." Her eyes go wide and she slaps her hand over her mouth. "Oops! I wasn't supposed to say that. I'm sorry, Victor, one special lemonade too many, I guess."

I can tell that Michael is conflicted. He doesn't like Victor, but if he's a Night Watchman—how can he not admire him?

"Uh, yeah, Tegan's right. Agency business. I'll just be a minute." I grab Victor's arm and herd him toward the hallway that leads to the restrooms. When we get to the dimly lit, empty hallway, I whisper harshly, "What were you thinking? Why are you here?"

"I need your help. I was waiting outside your apartment, got impatient, and came looking for you."

"Victor—"

"I need blood."

Anger explodes through me. I was so stupid, beginning to wonder if he was different: saving Tegan and me, caring about my encounter with Hoodie, giving me a stupid gift. Like all vampires, he was really after only one thing. "And you think I'm going to become your fang diva? I don't think so." There's a black market for blood donors. People who let vamps—for a fee—take blood directly from the source. Vampires claim that nothing compares to blood taken straight from the neck; as it passes through the still-beating heart it has a warmth and taste unparalleled to anything else. Many vampires protested the blood bank terms of VampHu for that very reason and try to find humans desperate for cash.

But those who serve as blood divas are ostracized. Arrested if caught. All blood donations are supposed to go through the Agency, where control is kept tight.

"Not from you. From the blood bank. About a dozen bags. I figure as a delegate you have access."

I do.

"Blood will be delivered to your father on Friday. Get it from him then."

"That'll be too late."

I don't see how it could be. Victor is vibrant, energetic. Hardly the image of a starving vampire. "You're just like him. Greedy, just wanting to drink all you can."

Disgusted, I turn to go and he grabs my arm. "Dawn—"

"Get your hand off her," Michael barks. I didn't see him arrive, but the fact that his stake is still holstered reassures me that he didn't hear the crux of the conversation.

The testosterone level is so high that I feel like it's battering me.

"Victor, please," I say, my voice low, because I know that if it comes down to a fight, he'll take Michael out.

"You force me to do what I don't want to," he says, his voice equally low. He releases me, spins on his heel, and strides down the hallway to the back exit. The door shudders with the force of him opening and closing it.

I want to rush after him, stop him. Is he going to attack someone, take blood by force? Have I condemned an innocent citizen? I should tell Michael and Sin. They could go after him, but I know by now that he's disappeared. They'd never find him. Besides, I don't want to put them in danger.

Michael wraps his arm around me. "You okay? You're trembling."

"I'm fine," I say, snuggling against him, finding reassurance in his strength.

"What the hell did he want?"

"Agency business. I can't talk about it." And even if I did, what would I say? *There's a rogue vampire out there?* I could tell the Agency about the theater, but I doubt Victor will be there tonight. All I can do is hope that the Night Watchmen are ever vigilant and Victor keeps to his no-blood-direct-from-a-human policy.

"Anything to do with last night?"

"No."

He furrows his brow. "Lot of secret stuff goes on at the Agency."

"Not really. Just seems that way."

"I'm not judging. I guess I just never realized how much of a burden it is to be a delegate. Maybe we *should* have run off with that trapeze troupe."

I laugh as Michael leads me back to the pool table, where Tegan and Sin are waiting.

"Let's really kick their butts," he says.

"You got it." And I'm grateful for anything to take my mind off Victor.

Chapter 16

I have a restless night, tossing and turning, waking up to every little sound. Expecting to see Victor hovering over me, coming for my blood. But my balcony doors stay closed.

The next morning I'm dragging as I get ready for school. When I go into the kitchen, Rachel is pacing the floor, phone to her ear.

"How could it have happened? You're sure they'll be okay? All right, yes, we'll just have to deliver what's left." She snaps her phone closed, spins on her heel, and comes up short at the sight of me.

"Trouble?" I ask.

"Someone broke into blood site five and stole a dozen bags of blood. Had to be a vampire. The guards saw a blur just before being knocked out. They have a headache this morning, but that's it. I guess the good news is that this vamp—whoever the hell he is—took legally obtained blood and didn't drain the guards. Of course, the bad news is that you'll have to explain to Valentine why we're short." In the long run, a difference of a dozen bags doesn't mean much, but Valentine will make sure I hear about it—and demand reparations.

Rachel sits down and starts stirring her oatmeal like she expects to find some answers there.

I ease onto the stool in front of the bowl she set out for me. While she eats hers plain, I absently pour sugar over mine. It had to be Victor. I'd feared he would attack someone—and he had, but not in the way I'd thought. A thousand questions are running through my mind.

It's hard to believe after everything that's happened lately, but today is only Wednesday. "We have a little bit of time. Maybe we can get some additional donations by Friday," I suggest.

"Yeah, maybe." Her brow is so deeply furrowed that it has to be painful. "Makes no sense. If he was going to sell it on the black market, why take only a dozen? If he was that desperate for blood, why risk breaking into a guarded facility at all? And then why not take it from the guards themselves?"

The same questions occurred to me, only I know where to get the answers. And then I'll make sure he understands I won't tolerate his stealing blood.

Before I leave for school, I go back to my room and open the jewelry box on my dresser. It was a gift from my dad. When it's opened, a tiny ballerina pops up and spins with the music. But what makes the box so special is that it has a little hidden compartment. My dad used to hide things in it for me to find. I never knew when he would or what it might be. Little things, silly things. A shiny penny. A stick of gum. A note that said, *I love you*.

Now it holds the key that Victor gave me to the theater the night he rescued Tegan and me. Then, with a deep breath, I pull open the drawer where I stashed the present he left me. For some reason, the stake looks much more lethal than the one I carry in my boot. I grab it and stuff it in my messenger bag. If he didn't want me using it, he shouldn't have given it to me.

I know it's dangerous to even consider confronting him, but I'm tired of his games, of his constantly making me think that he's something he isn't. I know the smart thing is to alert the Agency about him and the theater, but Victor has made this personal. I want to be the one to bring him down, with no help from anyone.

All through my classes, the key burns a hole in my jeans pocket as I review my strategy. Tegan and Michael are still so enamored with Sin, peppering him with questions about his life in Los Angeles between classes and during lunch, that they don't notice how distracted I am. Michael has practice after school and invites Sin to go with him. Tegan wants to hang out with me, but I tell her that I have Agency business. Which is true.

I have a vague idea of where the theater is, and I hop on a trolley that runs through that neighborhood. I have a stake hidden in my boot and Victor's gift in my bag, but the sun is still out, a much more effective weapon. I get off the trolley and start walking through the maze of abandoned buildings in this part of town. Hearing a sudden clang, I spin around. Rats scurry away from a Dumpster as a cat stalks them from its edge.

I don't know why I'm so jumpy. I continue on. A few minutes later, to my immense relief, I spot the theater.

It looks different during the day. It's lost its romance, its majesty. Instead of an ancient relic fighting against the sands of time, it seems more like a hollowed shell supported by broken frames and broken dreams. I imagine the owner, fifty years ago, smiling at the giant lettering and the glass cases that hold posters of movies long erased from memory. He had no idea what it would become.

Yet the theater is just like me. Something different at night. It transforms with the setting sun, just as I transform into a delegate, into someone who has to put the citizens' needs above my own wants. Glancing around, I don't see anyone. I take the key from my pocket, slip it into the padlock, and—

To my immense surprise it opens and the chains roll out. I was worried that Victor would have changed the lock by now. I shove open the door and walk through into the quiet. My heart is thundering. I should have a cadre of Agency guards with me—but my encounters with Victor flash through my mind. Maybe I want to give him one more chance to prove he is different from the others.

I pull out my flashlight, click it on, and pluck the stake from my messenger bag. The weight of what I'm doing settles on me like a heavy stone as I strap on the holster. I'm not even sure why I put it on. All I care about is the stake, and right now I've got a death grip on that. I walk through the lobby and turn down the hallway. He could be anywhere, but I suspect the room where he placed Tegan on a bed is his nest, the place where he sleeps during the day.

I creep up the stairs and stop outside the door; just beyond it is the room where we waited out the vampires when I thought he was a Night Watchman. When I thought he was human. When I . . . liked him.

Slowly I open the door. Victor is right where I expected him to be—stretched out on the cot. The slumber of vampires is so deep, it's one of their only weaknesses. Even with my flashlight shining right into his eyes, they don't open. His chest doesn't move. He's like the dead.

Do vampires dream?

Why do I care? I move over to the small refrigerator that had housed the canned drink he gave me. I open it. It's stuffed with blood bags.

The disappointment that ricochets through me is astounding. Until that moment, I didn't realize how desperately I wanted to be wrong about him. In my heart, I didn't want him to be like other vampires. But here's the proof. Greedy, selfish, caring only for himself and his never-ending quest for blood.

I walk back over to the cot. He's so gorgeous, but it's just a facade to hide the monster that lives within. I want him out of my city—him and all vampires. And if he doesn't leave—

The sun must have set, triggering Victor's internal clock,

because his eyes spring open. No, it isn't the sun, it's too early for that. It's something much more inescapable: the blood running through my veins. Even in his deep slumber, he could scent it.

The Old Family vampire stares at me now, the beautiful blue of his eyes capturing me. He doesn't seem surprised to see me; in fact, he gives no reaction at all. Just studies me.

"I see you got my gift," he finally says.

My anger spikes and I can't keep it out of my voice. "I don't understand you, Victor. You seem . . . almost nice, but then . . . you stole blood from the blood site."

He rolls into a sitting position. "You left me no choice."

"I didn't tell the Agency yet, because I owe you for saving Tegan's life and mine, but I'm taking the blood—"

"No, you're not." He brushes past me to the fridge as though I'm simply a fly that's irritating, no real threat.

Livid, I glare at him, unsure why I haven't plunged the stake through his heart. He snatches up a backpack, opens the fridge, and starts stuffing the blood bags into his pack. "I have to get these delivered tonight. It was too risky last night."

"I can't let you take them."

He stands up, shrugs the pack onto his shoulders. "You can't stop me, Dawn."

"Vict—"

"So come with me and see why I had to take them."

I'm not sure what I was thinking when I accepted his invitation. Maybe that I would learn more about this illegal operation and could provide the Agency with names and vamp hidey-holes. We waited in silence for nightfall before leaving the theater. Now we're maneuvering our way through the darkness over debris, slipping through alleys. I stumble.

Victor grabs my arm, stops me from landing with a splat.

"Sorry we can't use the flashlight," he says. "It'd reveal our location to any watching eyes. Just stick close and I'll guide you."

He takes my hand, threads our fingers together. Vampires can see in the dark. I realize now that the first night he brought Tegan and me to the theater, he used a flashlight for our benefit. And as just another layer to disguise what he truly is.

We don't talk. Another method to keep our movements undetected. What amazes me is how quiet Victor is. Wearing black, he's lost in the night's shadows. If his hand didn't grip mine, I might think he wasn't even beside me anymore. He makes no sounds at all, steps cautiously to avoid landing on anything that would give away his position. My father once explained to me that not all vampires exhibit this kind of stealth. It's limited to Old Families, the ones who are born into a vamp's body, and are comfortable with all its capabilities. Those who are turned very seldom completely assimilate into the vampire form. At their core, they're human—they've just acquired an invincibility, an agelessness, and a craving for blood.

I'm not even sure where my father got all of his

information. But as a scholar, he was always scouring through ancient texts and documents.

It seems like we've been walking forever. I can see why we didn't drive here. It's so run-down, so littered in these narrow streets. My imagination is running wild, and I can envision all sorts of illegal deals going on here. Blood for money, blood for drugs, blood for food. The precious crimson that runs through my veins has become the currency of the new world.

Eventually, he stops at a building and opens a door I hadn't even noticed. We slip inside.

"Stairs," Victor whispers.

Reaching out with my free hand, I grab a banister. It makes going up easier. I count the steps, count the flights, just to keep my mind occupied and away from the fact that I'm in the middle of nowhere with a vampire.

At the fourth floor we start walking straight. I hold my hand out and feel it brushing against a wall. We're in a hallway, one that hasn't seen the light of day in quite some time. Bumps and bruises cover the wood, water damage from years of rain seeping down, rotting the building from the inside.

Victor stops and I hear a quiet knock. A door creaks.

"Victor," a soft feminine voice says. "Thank goodness."

Victor brings me inside. When the door closes, a light comes on. I see the flashlight in Victor's hand. He releases his hold on me and sets it upright on the table. It fills the room with a weird glow. I see a woman who must be the one who opened the door. She's slender. Her eyes are hollow.

"Martha, this is my . . . friend Dawn. How is Justin?" Victor asks.

"He hasn't moved all day. If it were possible for him to die, I think he would have by now."

Shrugging off his backpack, Victor walks through an open doorway, the broken hinges the only evidence that a door ever hung there. I glance around and decide to follow.

The light from the flashlight creeps into this space and casts an eerie glow on a young boy of about nine lying beneath the blankets on a bed.

"Hey, Justin," Victor says, opening the backpack. "I brought you something."

He takes out a bag of blood and presses it to the boy's mouth. Without hesitation, Justin's fangs emerge and pierce the bag. The coppery scent of blood wafts up as he greedily devours the contents. I watch his throat working to swallow the lifesaving fluid, knowing I should be repelled. But instead I'm fascinated. With just a few ounces of blood, Justin already looks worlds better. Never before have I understood the full extent of the miracle of our blood. Now I understand that they need it to live—in some weird way, maybe even more than we do.

"His father turned him, turned us both," Martha tells me, her voice quiet, as if she might disturb them. "He returned from the war a vampire and couldn't stand the thought of facing eternity without us." She sighs, looks at me. "You're the delegate."

I nod, not sure why I'm uncomfortable with her scrutiny or feel as though I've let her down.

"I know we're not supposed to be in the city, but I don't like it beyond the wall. This has always been our home."

I'm at a loss for words. The apartment, the vampires, it's all very surreal. Like something I would've seen on television and then had a dream about.

Given where I am and what surrounds me, I should be afraid. But I'm not. These are the kinds of vampires Victor was telling me about the other night: the ones not much different from me.

"Before I was turned, I saw all vampires as monsters," Martha says quietly. "Funny, now I think it's the humans. I laugh and cry and feel just the same as they do. I'd never hurt a soul, but if I walked these streets openly, I'd be staked. If the Night Watchmen ever find us, they'll kill us. And the next day, in the papers, there would be a small column written in praise of the slayings. My son and I would just become numbers, notches on their belt."

"How did your son get so weak?"

She rubs her hands up and down her arms. "My husband, Robert, works for Valentine, beyond the wall. Valentine doesn't give rations to those of us who live in the city. To do that would be to acknowledge that there are vampires in the city." I hear the loathing in her voice. "And that would be against VampHu. He's supposed to be our lord, but he doesn't care about us. Robert brings us what he can, but it's never enough, and it's difficult for him to get into the city. It's been three weeks since I saw him."

I can tell that she's worried about him. He could have run into a patrol, Night Watchmen, or a vigilant citizen.

He could have even run into that creature from the other night.

"All the while, Justin has been wasting away," she says. "Slowly at first, but now his cries echo through the night, and I can't do anything except hold him close and tell him it'll be better tomorrow. In another week, he'd just be an empty shell, alive inside, but unable to move until he feeds. My fear is that before then, he would have left the apartment out of desperation and killed somebody. I've tried to teach him that all life is precious and that he can't take blood from people's necks, but I know the pain he's feeling, and how quickly those lessons are forgotten."

"What's it like?" I ask. "To be without blood?"

"Horrible. You spend so much time trying to keep the monster under control, but when you are starving for blood, everything just goes. It's like a temporary insanity. Nothing else matters until you feed. It's absolutely terrible. And now my son is suffering it."

But not for long. Within an hour, Justin is running around the apartment. His mother takes her share of the blood Victor brought.

When Victor and I are back outside, I ask, "Why didn't you tell me what you needed the blood for?"

"You didn't give me a chance. And you weren't exactly receptive to believing me anyway."

"Can you blame me? From the moment we met, you've lied—"

"I've never lied to you, Dawn. I may not have told you everything—"

"You deceived me. You made me think you were hu—"

Without warning, he pushes me into a crevice, backing me up against a brick wall, his body pressed against mine.

"What—" I begin.

"Shh. Watchmen." Victor's voice is soft in my ear, his cheek touching mine.

I hear them then. The scuff of boots. The low murmurs.

One of my palms is flattened against Victor's chest, and I can feel the hard thudding of his heart. It matches mine.

"Stupid," he says, his voice so low that if his lips weren't brushing over my ear, I wouldn't catch his words at all. "To bring you with me, to put you in danger. I just wanted you to understand that not all vampires are monsters."

We hear a crash, someone turning something over. Victor goes so very still, as still as death.

"Because I'm the delegate, right? So I'll be more sympathetic to the vampires?"

"That's not the only reason." He pauses; a silence stretches between us as I wait for him to explain. "I've known humans," he finally says, "but I've never known anyone like you, Dawn Montgomery. You're so passionate in your beliefs. We live forever and have started to take so much for granted. You appreciate everything."

I don't know why he's telling me these things. Maybe he's trying to distract me from how very close we are to each other.

"I'm going to try to draw them away," he whispers. "If I don't come back for you, stay here until the sun comes up."

"No." I realize I'm clutching his T-shirt. Silly of me to

think that I have the strength to hold him here. "Just wait."

And he stays. He doesn't say anything else. Our hearts slow. The long, interminable minutes pass. The night air seems to be growing cooler, but Victor's body radiates warmth. I know the Watchmen wouldn't kill me—if they recognized me. But they wouldn't expect me to be in this part of town, at this time of night. And if they find the bags of blood Victor still has, too many questions would be raised.

Everything grows quiet. No more footsteps. No distant voices. Then I hear the sounds of tiny creatures starting to stir once again.

"They've moved on," Victor says. "Thank you for not calling out to them."

He eases back then, and I'm hit with the realization that he never covered my mouth. That I could have yelled to the Watchmen, could have turned Victor over to them. And not once did it cross my mind to do so. I tell myself that it's only because I was taken by surprise. That I didn't shove him away or draw attention to us because if the Night Watchmen found us, I'd have a lot of explaining to do to the Agency. I was just protecting myself. That makes much more sense than me worrying about Victor getting killed.

Taking my hand, he guides me out of the crevice. Carefully we make our way over the debris and hurry on. We make two more stops, but we don't go inside either place. He just slips the blood through the narrow crack when the door opens to his knock.

As we're walking away from the last one, I say, "You've never stolen from the blood sites before, have you?"

"No. I usually steal from my father's stash, but these vampires couldn't wait. They don't die, Dawn. They just suffer, withering away until all they can do is sit in a corner, unable to move, waiting to be staked by a wandering Watchman or for the sun to pierce them through a window. A vampire can spend an eternity like that, alone with his thoughts."

I shiver. Tonight I was given an uncomfortable view of vampires as a . . . family. And seeing Victor as some sort of Robin Hood, stealing game from the king's forest in order to deliver food to the poor. Only in his case, it's taking from the blood bank to give to the vampires in the city, those neglected by Lord Murdoch Valentine.

It's also strange to realize that he's holding my hand again. Yes, we're in the dark; yes, he's guiding me. Yet somehow I can't help but believe that it's more than that. Something changed between us while we were in that stupid crevice, and I feel guilty when I remember Michael.

"How many are in the city?" I ask, trying to regain my original intent of using this as an intelligence-gathering mission.

"What does it matter, Dawn? If they're not hurting anyone, why can't they live here in peace?"

It doesn't escape me that he avoided answering my question. "But they know to come to you if they need anything?"

"I do what I can."

"Does your father know about all this? Know what you do?"

"Does Rachel know everything you do?" he asks.

"I hate when someone answers a question with a question."

"Then stop asking questions."

I know that he's holding back secrets. In spite of everything that happened tonight, he doesn't trust me any more than I trust him. The realization saddens me.

Still, I can't help wanting to know more, to test whether he has any trust in me at all. "So why does your father insist that I dress in Victorian garb? It's like he's obsessed with that era."

"We were at our height during that time. We understood the world. And then all the technology came, and suddenly humans knew more than we did. We're not creative. We can't envision possibilities like you can. We have very little imagination."

"I never knew that."

"Painting, writing stories, poems, or plays . . . it all eludes us. But what I *can* imagine is a world in which humans and vampires coexist. Where humans willingly donate blood so we're not forced to suffer. Where we serve as the protectors against evil, instead of being viewed as monsters."

I try to picture this world he's describing. I want to, but it seems impossible, and I wonder when I became such a pessimist.

"Speaking of evil . . . did you discover anything when you saw the vampire at the morgue?" I ask him.

"I didn't know him. All I know is that he was attacked by something rabid."

As soon as we get to a section of the city with some light, I work my hand free of Victor's. I'm not sure exactly where we are, but eventually we reach trolley tracks.

"I can get home fine from here," I say, not looking at him.

"I'm not letting you travel through the city alone. It's almost ten."

I release a little groan. "Rachel is going to kill me." I pull out my phone. Sure enough, missed calls and text messages. I'd muted it when I was going into the theater because I didn't want it to go off and wake Victor before I was in place.

"She'll forgive you once you're home safe," he says.

"I doubt that." Part of me wants him to take my hand again, wants to feel his touch. So instead, I cross my arms over my chest, just to make sure that my hand isn't within easy reach of his. "Doesn't it bother your father? You living here? I mean, an Old Family vampire, subjecting himself to a human city. It isn't exactly . . . proper."

Victor smiles. "You know him pretty well. That's exactly what he said. But I don't care."

"I thought it was a son's duty to obey his father."

"You're quoting stuff straight out of Old Family textbooks." I see the frustration in his face.

"I'm sorry," I say automatically.

He waves it away casually. "No, it's a testament to how much you learned from your father, how much you've studied us. There aren't many people in this city who know as much about vampires. I mean, it's one thing to read textbooks; it's another to see vampires in the flesh. Only a handful of humans have ever talked to my father and lived. It's given you a unique perspective, experiences few people have."

"My parents had them," I say. I'm not sure why. But I think I want Victor to talk about them. He must've known them. Their death opens up a chasm inside me, like a wound that's suddenly bleeding uncontrollably.

A long, drawn-out silence follows. Our eyes catch from time to time, neither of us wanting to speak.

"Did you know them?" I ask finally.

He shakes his head. "I'm sorry, Dawn. I was in the city during their tenure. On the few trips I ever made to the manor, I never saw them."

I nod, accepting it. For some reason, I thought Victor could heal that wound better than anyone else. It's strange to think that this vampire, the embodiment of all my hatred, could act like a suture.

Thank goodness, the trolley finally arrives. Only a couple of people are on it. We climb aboard and sit down on the back bench. Victor's thigh touches mine. I think of a time when I would have been repulsed. Now I draw comfort from his nearness. Or at least a feeling of safety—the prince of the night is escorting me home.

We don't talk during the ride. Or when we disembark. Or when we walk toward my apartment building. Only when we stop across the street does our silence end.

"I should give you back your key," I say, reaching into my pocket.

"Keep it. You never know when you might want to stop by and watch a movie."

"You really have movies?"

"It would be kind of pointless to have a movie theater with no movies."

"Yeah, I guess. Where do you get them?"

"I have a friend in Los Angeles who sends them to me whenever he runs across one."

I never really thought of vampires as having friends, as doing small, special favors for one another. Victor's becoming more and more human all the time.

"A Carrollton?" I ask. They're the Old Family that rules the vamps in that part of the country.

"That's right. I guess you know all the Old Families by name—and their territories. His name's Richard. You'd like him, I think."

"Not if he's a vampire."

"You don't say that with as much conviction anymore."

It's true; I don't. Since meeting Victor, everything that I've ever thought about vampires is being turned inside out. I feel like I should thank him, but I'm not sure for what. "Okay, then. I'd better go."

I start to cross the street, stop, turn back. "You're not what I thought."

He smiles. A devastatingly beautiful smile.

I race across the street to my apartment building, to home and safety. Because that smile scares me for reasons I can't explain. I only know that it makes me want to see him smile again.

Chapter 17

Rachel's glare when I walk into the apartment is almost as fierce as Valentine's was when I told him there was no additional blood.

"I know, I know," I cut her off before she can say anything. "I've been sitting in the stairwell thinking."

Both her eyebrows shoot up at my lie. "Why? Did something happen?"

I plop onto the couch and draw my legs beneath me. "I don't feel like I'm making any contribution as a delegate."

"You spoke with Valentine. His vamps aren't storming the walls."

"But being a delegate is more than that. My parents used to do blood drives." All these thoughts bombarded me as I rode the elevator. "They had that five-K blood run—"

"Which garnered zero pints, as I recall."

"What was the reward? A T-shirt? No one's going to come for that."

She joins me on the couch, tucking her legs up against her chest and wrapping her arms around them. It makes her look young. It's easy to forget that she's not even ten years older than me. We all have to grow up fast these days. "So, you want to start paying for blood?"

"No, but . . . we take blood from anyone who is at least seventeen. But I don't know anyone at school who gives blood. So teens are an untapped resource. How do we get them to donate blood?"

She presses a well-manicured finger against her chin. I can see that she's seriously considering what I'm saying.

"I mean, most of the posters around the city are focused on parents giving blood to protect their children," I point out.

"Because that's who we've always thought was most likely to give. But you're right. If we can get the teens into the habit of donating, they'll carry it into adulthood. So do you have some ideas for how we do that?"

"A dance?" I suggest. "Donate blood and get a free ticket?"

She puckers her brow. "I think it needs to be more than a dance. I think it needs to be a kick-ass party."

I grin. "I like the way you think."

"Write up some plans, some justification for the expense. We'll run it by Clive on your way to school in the morning."

"Thanks." I pop off the couch, stop, and study her.

"Rachel, have you ever known a vampire? Other than Valentine, I mean?"

"By 'known' I assume you mean for longer than it takes to put a stake through their hearts?"

I nod. "Yeah."

A sadness touches her fudge brown eyes. "A lot of what I know about vamps I learned from one I considered a . . . friend. I was younger than you; the war was still raging. He would come into the city at night. It was easier then—we didn't have the wall. We would talk. Then one night . . . he needed blood. He wanted mine. And when I said no, he tried to take it. I screamed. People rushed out of their homes and . . . they killed him. I felt guilty for a long time. Because he was just asking for help."

"If he were really your friend, he wouldn't have tried to force you."

"No. He wouldn't have. But if I were really his, wouldn't I have given him what he needed? Relationships with vampires are complex, Dawn. Remember that. Valentine will never be your friend."

She's right, he won't be. But I'm not thinking of Valentine. I'm thinking of Victor. Could we be friends?

"So here's what we're gonna do. After school, we'll all go to blood site five and donate blood. Rachel is going to arrange for a news crew to be there so we get coverage. We're going to start a special blood drive—the Teen Initiative—and every teen who donates a pint of blood between now and next Saturday will get a ticket to a party at the Daylight

Grill. Free food. Free drinks."

I'm sitting at a table in the lunchroom with Tegan, Michael, and Sin. I can see the wheels in their heads turning as they try to decide whether or not to embrace this incredibly cheesy idea. The Agency kept the blood bank theft under wraps, so no one knows about it. No need to scare the already frightened citizens.

Rachel and I met with Clive before school this morning. My delegate training paid off, because it took me fewer than five minutes to convince Clive to let us give the Teen Initiative a shot.

After my trip with Victor last night, I'm determined to see the blood donations increase. It's part of my duties as a delegate, something I've been slacking off on. I have to admit that Victor's outing helped me see the value of our blood.

"You sound like you've gone a little pro-vampire," Michael says after a couple of minutes.

"What? No. It's just that they need our blood. And I'm supposed to ensure that we get enough of it to Valentine"— although if some went to Victor, who was going to know?—"to keep the peace, and I thought this would be a fun way of doing all that."

"Unfortunately I gave blood just before I left Los Angeles," Sin says. "So it's a little too soon for me. But I'll definitely spread the word, maybe even help set up the party."

"I hate needles." Tegan gives a visible shudder, then grins at Sin. "But if you'll hold my hand, I'll do it."

"I'd hold your hand without your giving blood, but of course."

I glance over at Michael. "Michael?"

"Yeah. Okay."

I wish he'd seen what I did last night. I know he'd be more enthusiastic then. I'm trying really hard not to compare his reluctance to Victor's willingness to risk so much to procure blood for vampires on the verge of starvation. It's an unfair comparison, because Michael would do anything for humans. Although Victor didn't hesitate to save Tegan and me that night on the trolley.

"Think you could convince some of the guys around school to come with us? They're not listening to me much lately," I say.

"I'll talk to the guys in the training program."

"Thanks." Reaching out, I thread my fingers through his and am unsettled to realize that the fit doesn't feel quite as perfect as it did with Victor last night. That's crazy. Michael means everything to me. And Victor . . . I don't know what to think about him anymore.

A news crew is waiting at blood site five when I arrive with my small entourage: Tegan, Michael, Sin, and four of Michael's buddies. Half a dozen other people are in various stages of donating. Even I'm surprised by the positive turnout.

I smile, stretch out on the recliner, and roll up my sleeve as though I'm about to have the most exciting time of my life. Michael takes the recliner next to me, and Tegan's on the other side of me. She's pale. Sin takes her hand.

Several Agency guards are strategically placed at doors and elevators. This place is practically the Fort Knox of blood now. Only donors ever get to see this floor, but beneath it are several levels of frozen and chilled blood, all waiting to be delivered. During the day, of course. Placed outside the manor in insulated containers every Friday.

"So, Dawn," the reporter with the mic begins as the nurse rubs the inside of my elbow with a cold, alcohol-drenched cotton ball, "if you weren't our delegate, would you be donating?"

"I would, Chip," I say, recognizing him from other news stories he's done. "Vampires can't survive without our blood. Giving my blood . . . I see it as charitable."

"Some people consider vamps parasites."

"It's true that they need our blood in order to survive. But recently, I had the opportunity to visit with a vampire family." Standing behind him, Rachel widens her eyes, and I know I'm going to have to do some explaining after this. "They feed only on legally drawn blood. I guess . . . I think we have an obligation to do what we can to preserve all life. We can either give our blood to the vampires or have it taken from us. By giving it, we control how it's taken and how much is taken. Meanwhile, negotiation is the best path to reclaiming our place alongside vampires rather than beneath them."

Rachel gives a subtle nod of approval. When I asked for this publicity op last night, she gave me a list of talking points to memorize.

"Do you honestly think Valentine will ever consider us equal?"

Not him, but maybe his son. But Chip doesn't specify whether he's referring to Lord Murdoch Valentine or Victor, so I simply say, "With time, yes."

I grimace as the needle slides into my vein.

"With all due respect, Dawn, you're a kid who Valentine can't possibly take seriously—"

"I don't hear much respect there, Chip. I'm young, yes, but I learned a lot from my parents. And I don't carry the hatred that those who fought in the war do." Sometimes delegates lie. "I truly believe I can make a difference for the citizens of Denver. I wouldn't have accepted the position otherwise."

"Well, here's one reporter who hopes you and the Agency know what you're doing."

"The Agency knows exactly what it's doing, and has full confidence in Dawn," Rachel says, stepping forward. "As you can see, several teens came in with Dawn. Under her guidance, we're starting a new program that we're calling the Teen Initiative. To help get it off the ground, we're throwing a party a week from Saturday at the Daylight Grill. There will be a live band, and free food and drinks for any teen who donates blood during the next week."

As she fields the tougher questions, I relax, pressing my head against the pillow. Cameras are clicking. Michael reaches over and wraps his hand around mine.

"Not exactly the most exciting date we've ever had," he says.

I laugh softly. "Maybe we can do something about that afterward. Thanks for coming."

"All finished," the nurse says, as she removes the needle. She has me press a cotton ball to the tiny wound and raise my arm until the bleeding stops. Then she slaps on a bandage.

"Okay, kiddo," Rachel says. "Good deed done for the day. Let's go celebrate."

She and Jeff take our little group to a Chinese buffet. Michael peppers Jeff with questions. It's no secret that he was a Night Watchman before he became a bodyguard for the Agency.

After dinner, Jeff gives everyone a ride home. I'm thinking I'll get a chance to see where Sin lives, but he gets out of the car with Michael. Apparently they're going to practice some defense moves together.

As we drive away, Rachel says, "What do you know about Sin?"

"Not much. Why?"

"Just like to keep up with who you're hanging out with."

"Afraid he's going to get me in trouble?"

"He does give off that vibe."

I look out the window. Yeah, he does.

From the front seat, Rachel turns around completely to face me.

"So . . . speaking of who you're hanging out with . . . care to explain how you came to spend time with a vamp family?"

Busted!

"They were at Valentine Manor," I tell her, and wonder how many lies I'm going to have to spout. It seems like I've turned into a serial fabricator since Victor entered my life. "I thought mentioning them might be the best way to humanize vampires."

"Only they're not human."

"But we need the citizens to see them as not exactly monsters. Or at least, not all of them as monsters."

She studies me for a moment. "I'm impressed by how quickly you're coming to understand your role as delegate, but why didn't you mention meeting them when we were discussing everything that happened at Valentine Manor?"

"I was a little more freaked out by Victor Valentine's presence."

"You didn't seem freaked."

"Geez, Rachel, I'm not the enemy here."

"I just don't like it when I don't know everything that's going on. Yes, you've had two months of delegate training, but it takes years to become truly proficient at dealing with vampires—especially someone like Valentine. Don't kid yourself, Dawn. You're still a novice. I need to know everything, so I can advise you and keep you safe. And keep the citizens safe. So what else haven't you told me?"

A lot. I should tell her about Victor.

"Nothing."

Through the window I can see the lights of the Works. We're nearing home. I'm tempted to ask Jeff to drive a little faster.

Chapter 18

When we get to the apartment, Jeff comes in with us. I sink onto the couch and turn on the TV. We're immediately greeted with the image of Roland Hursch outside the blood site we were just at.

"The Agency is making slaves of us all!" he shouts from a makeshift podium that I swear he carries around with him. A small crowd has gathered beside the raging warmonger. News cameras capture his rant, and flash photography bounces off his sweating, angry face. "Now they're targeting teenagers, our own children. They are asking them to trade their souls for a party. A party! The Agency isn't satisfied draining adults. No, they've moved on to our kids. This is a tragedy!"

"Wow," I say, "can you believe it?"

No answer.

I look behind me. Rachel and Jeff are in the kitchen, definitely standing closer than they need to be. I hear them talking quietly and feel like an intruder, or worse yet, some kind of roadblock for this blossoming romance. Muting the TV, I call out, "I'm going to my room. I've got some homework to do."

"Okay," Rachel says back.

Closing my bedroom door, I'm just as relieved at having a moment of privacy as they are. I tuck my legs beneath me on my bed and start writing a report that I can give to our public relations department about the Teen Initiative. If they can spread the word throughout the city, maybe it'll generate some excitement at the other schools. It should be a nice counter to that idiot Hursch.

It's nearly midnight when I have outlined some suggestions for how to promote this event. Satisfied that my work is done, I flop back on my bed and stare at the ceiling. I wonder what Michael and Sin are doing. Since Sin's arrival, Michael and I have had even less time for each other. Or maybe the fault is mine. Lately, so much of my energy is focused on figuring Victor out.

I roll off my bed, cross the room, open the French doors, and step out onto the balcony. The night is clear, the moon is bright, and the electricity from the Works is strong. The entire city looks like a collection of fireflies.

I sit down in a cushion-covered wrought-iron chair. Closing my eyes, I take a deep breath. A familiar scent is in the air, one I spent way too much time inhaling last night.

I open my eyes, unsurprised that Victor is standing

at the edge of the balcony. His tall figure leans carelessly against the railing; he's unafraid of the perilous fall waiting for him if he tips over.

"What are you doing here?" I ask.

"I wanted to thank you. I saw the news tonight. Your . . . Teen Initiative."

I shrug. "Just doing my job."

"Were you?"

I don't want to examine my motives, and I especially don't want him examining them, so I say, "You probably shouldn't be here. Jeff is inside." I think. I didn't hear him leave.

"I know. I can elude him easily enough if necessary." He looks out over the city. "I wish I could see this place when the sun is out."

I look across at the streets covered by the choking smog coughed up by the Works. "I wish I'd seen it before the bombs destroyed so much."

"I used to enjoy walking around here before the War. Everything was much brighter back then, and overflowing with life. Right over there"—he points to an intersection through which cars seldom travel—"I saved a child from being hit by a truck. He was human then. Now he's a Lesser."

"Justin?"

He turns his attention back to me. "Yes. He was maybe three or four when he ran into the street. But early in the war, his father was turned. He came back here to preserve his family in the only way he knew how. The thing about

Lessers . . . they never age, never change from how they were when they were turned. Justin will remain a child forever. Never mature enough to outgrow his toys, fall in love, or dream of changing the world. I despise when vampires turn children—even when it's their own."

I don't know what to say. So much about Victor can leave me speechless.

"People are either reviled by vampires—or they want to become one," he says. "But forever isn't what anyone expects it to be."

"It's never appealed to me. And then there's the whole new diet. Blech."

He grins, looks back out over the city.

I find myself more curious about him than I should be. Four hundred years. I can't imagine. Seventeen years have been hard enough for me. I wonder if the years mean less to him than they do to me.

"What happened to your mom? I never hear anyone talk about Lady Valentine."

"There is no Lady Valentine." Unlike his father, Victor holds my gaze. "I'd been around for a century when my father got rid of her."

"What? You mean, like, divorced her?"

"Banished her. That's how it works with us. Vampires don't do the whole until-death-do-us-part thing."

"Yeah, I guess I can see that. For you, it really would be marriage for eternity." I tuck my feet beneath me. "So your dad just got tired of her?"

"He wanted more children."

It's strange to think of Valentine as a loving dad. I think of him as a lord and master, as a monster, as my enemy.

"A female of the Old Family can give birth only once. Then she becomes sterile." Victor shrugs. "And you have to be born a vampire to conceive a vampire. Those who are turned can't reproduce. I guess it's nature's method of birth control for an immortal species."

"My father once told me that a vampire can't have children with a human."

"True. Your father knew his stuff."

I can hear the respect he had for my father in his voice— even though he never met him.

"So *did* Valentine have other kids?" I ask.

"Yes, a daughter. Faith."

"I never knew that. Does the Agency know?"

"I don't know. It's not their business."

"I guess not." I look out at the Works and think about Brady, wondering if Victor appreciates having a sibling. "Brady, my brother, had a job there. At the Works. After he returned from the war."

"You miss him."

"All the time."

"Share a good memory of him with me."

I jerk my attention back to Victor. What he's asking seems a simple request, but Brady is personal, so personal. He was my big brother. Sometimes when I close my eyes, I can still hear him laughing. He had the best laugh. But the most horrific scream.

I can't talk to Victor about his death. Even though I was

only nine at the time, and Brady was twenty, the memory is still fresh, raw. He died because of me. We were living in an older part of town then. My parents were working late at the university when the vampires came, and Brady shoved me in a closet. To keep me safe. To protect me. I was scared. I didn't want him to leave me. To calm me, to reassure me, he said, "Don't be afraid of the dark." They were the last words he ever said to me. Then he shut the door. After that all I heard was the fighting. And the awful screaming. I curled up into a tight ball, wanting to get so small that the vampires wouldn't see me if they opened the door. It was hours before the door opened, and when it did, my mother pulled me onto her lap. Brady was gone.

I can't find the words to tell Victor the anguish that still consumes me after all these years. Brady died protecting me. His death influenced me, shaped my hatred of vampires. Every vampire I see is the faceless one who killed him. I live with his screams; it's like he's always in the next room, and I'm still trapped in that closet, listening with my hands over my ears, praying for an ounce of sunlight to come in through the windows. But it never did. I know it's not rational. I was only nine, a kid. I just wish I could have saved him.

I want Victor to leave me alone. Brady is too personal, too private, too painful. I shake my head. "I can't talk about him." My voice is scratchy, as though I've been crying, but where Brady is concerned I have no more tears left.

Victor crouches in front of me. "I share with you pieces of my world. Tell me something about Brady. Help me to understand . . . your heart."

Victor can be persuasive. Suddenly I want him to know about this place inside me that still bleeds. He's shown me another side of vampires; maybe this will enlighten him about humans a bit more.

With my finger, I trace a circle over the back of my left hand. "Somehow, when he was working, coal dust got embedded in an open cut on his hand, and when the wound healed, the dust got trapped. It looked like a small flower blossoming, no bigger than a thumbnail. Sometimes he'd color with me in my coloring book. I'd watch his hand move as he carefully filled in between the lines, and the little petals would move back and forth like they were being brushed with a gentle breeze. They fascinated me."

At least, I remember it looking that way.

They never found my brother's body. After I became a delegate, I was able to get my hands on the Agency report of the incident. It said they'd found so much blood, they suspected he died in the apartment and the vampire dragged him away, maybe to the sewers or a vampire lair. I hate that image the most: a horde of vampires slowly feasting on the remains of the boy with the flower tattoo on his hand. Not knowing what became of him leaves me to imagine the worst.

"I've been wondering something," I say quietly.

He doesn't say anything. Just waits. I guess when you live for eternity, patience comes naturally.

"You seem to know the vampires who live in the city. I don't suppose you ever heard who took him. Whether he died quickly or slowly."

"I'm sorry. No. I never heard anything."

I sigh. "Just thought I'd ask."

"I can understand how his death shaped your opinions about us. But please know that we're not all monsters."

"Yeah, so I'm starting to realize." I look back toward the Works. I can't look at him, because I'm afraid that if I do, something inside me will crumble, that this protective shield will melt away. And I'll care about vampires. Worse, I'll care about Victor.

Chapter 19

Friday afternoon, Michael and I head to the Daylight Grill after school. I need this time with him. Last night with Victor was too intense, encompassing a riot of emotions. It made me feel like a traitor to Michael. I know he wouldn't approve of my spending time with a vampire. And I care about Michael so much. I love everything about him, and I drink in the details as we walk. The way his muscles bunch when he moves. The way he smiles when he looks at me.

At the Daylight Grill, we sit across from each other and hold hands. I just can't seem to touch him enough.

He furrows his brow. "Is everything okay?"

"Yeah. Sure."

"That guy in the snake hoodie isn't bothering you again, is he?"

"I don't think so."

"You don't *think*?"

I shake my head. How to explain without sounding like I'm losing my mind? "Sometimes I feel like I'm being watched. And I thought I saw him the other morning on my way to school, but when I went after him—"

"You went after him?"

"It was fine. The streets were crowded. I don't even know if it was him. I lost him."

"Okay, starting Monday morning I'm walking you to school. I'm not going to let anything happen to you."

He sounds so confident, so sure. But then, so did Brady.

Tegan and Sin come in and join us. We talk for a while, but the conversation seems to drag. Finally I suggest we play some pool.

"Don't you guys ever get bored with this place?" Sin asks.

"Yeah," Tegan says quickly, which is news to me.

"What do you say we do something different, then?" Sin asks.

"Like what?"

I don't like where this is going.

"How about we go wall-walking?" he asks, a gleam in his eye.

I knew he would bring trouble.

"Forget it," I say. "We can't make it to the wall before sunset."

He has to be crazy to suggest it. During the day is one thing, but at night . . . we'd just be asking to become a late-night snack. I've heard of people setting up stakeouts to wait for the vamps so they can ambush them. Personally, I'll leave that job to the Night Watchmen and wall guards.

"Come on," Michael says. "It's fun."

I stare at him. "You've done it?"

"Sure. Well. Kind of. I mean, I went there once during the day, walked along the wall for, like, three hours. Found some really weird stuff, you know. But couldn't find a hole to the outside."

"Trust me. It's too dangerous. Maybe tomorrow afternoon, but not at night."

"That's when it's more fun," Sin urges. "Michael and I will protect you. No one's going to bother us."

"I'm not worried about people. I'm worried about vampires."

"Don't be," Michael says. I can tell he loves the thought of protecting me against any fanged enemies.

"I'll only go if Dawn goes," Tegan says, turning to me.

Great. That's her way of saying, *If you don't go, I'll be mad at you because you blew my chances with Sin and now everything is ruined and blah blah blah. . . .*

"How about this," Michael says. "We start out, and if you want to turn back, just tell me, and we'll go. No questions asked. No complaints. We'll do a one-eighty and head home."

Tegan widens her eyes and mouths, *Do it!*

It's a bad idea, but then, I seem to have a track record lately of embracing bad ideas.

"Fine."

* * *

We catch the trolley, but as I feared, the sun has set by the time we get to the end of the line. This is the farthest I've ever been from the city's center and still within the wall. Normally, when I leave for Valentine Manor, Winston takes the carriage along the main road that goes straight from the heart of the city to the large main gate. But we're far from that well-traveled path. Or from any of the other streets that lead to the south and west entrances, and plenty of little ones in between. Some say that's why the city isn't secure: too many ways in.

"This way," Sin says. "I've got a good feeling about it."

I have a feeling, too. That I'm going to regret this.

We head down a row of abandoned town houses, all lined up and identical except for which windows are smashed. They look prewar, and I can see what Michael meant when he said he's found weird stuff out here. There's no telling what's in those houses. Relics from the past, family photos of people no longer alive . . . or vampires. The Night Watchmen like to do raids in this area, hoping to find small groups of vamps hiding in an old basement. I wonder if Michael is hoping to catch them in action and join in.

"It's like a ghost town," Tegan murmurs, her voice hushed.

"Are you scared?" Sin asks.

"Maybe just a little."

He pulls her to him. She squeals and laughs. I exchange a look with Michael. He shrugs.

Sin opens up his backpack and pulls out four flashlights, handing them to us.

"You knew we were going to do this, didn't you?" Michael asks.

"I had a hunch."

They're high-quality flashlights, all metal, bright bulbs.

"You can keep them," Sin says. "A gift for helping me relieve my boredom."

The farther we move down the street, the more destroyed it looks. It's like the entire neighborhood was submerged underwater for a hundred years and then drained. The wood isn't just shattered; it's rotting. The lampposts aren't just bent; they're rusted, and the street signs haven't been legible in years.

"There it is," Michael says once we round a corner.

The wall is a stone's throw away. I imagine the city architects deciding on its placement, the engineers building it. Maybe they put it here in hopes of renovating these homes, making them livable again. At the time, it might've seemed like the right idea. But now it just looks like it's keeping the hideous town homes from escaping into the night. Maybe the wall is holding back the ghosts that walk these streets from haunting the rest of the world.

The wall seems bigger at night, looming over us like a slumbering animal as we approach. Here, it isn't as nice as in other areas. It's thick steel, with vertical girders bracketing it to the ground every few yards. The paint wore off a long time ago, and it's warped over time, as if they miscalculated its weight and it's now collapsing upon itself. Looking to the left and right, seeing it stretch into the distance, I can see the curvature that nature and time have forced upon it. What was once uniform has taken on a demented life of its own. Normally, at the top of the wall, there is a walkway for guards to patrol. But not here. Maybe everyone just wants to forget about this part of the city.

We each touch the wall and then begin walking along it, letting our hands glide over it.

"This is too thick," I say. "We'll never find a weak spot or a hole that leads to the other side."

I'm not sure whether that's true, but I want to go home. We've seen the wall. Isn't that really the point?

"I think I might know a spot," Sin says.

Of course he does. He's been in town for only a few days, but he already seems to know everything.

We walk down another block. The wall is to our right, and long streets and corridors dart away to our left. As I look down them, the light from our flashlights disappears almost instantly, barely penetrating the inky night. We're swallowed up by darkness, and much as I'd like it to be, I can't help admitting to myself that Michael's presence is not as comforting to me as Victor's was.

"Maybe we should leave," I say to Michael, who's behind me.

"But we're so close."

"You don't know that."

"If Sin says he knows a spot, then—"

"You promised me that if I wanted to go we would. This is stupid."

It's cold and dark, and my feet hurt, and dammit, I deal with enough crap every day; I don't need to go on dangerous field trips just because the boys want to. But looking at Tegan, I don't think even she'd be on my side; she's more infatuated with Sin than anyone.

"A little farther," I relent. "But then we're—"

"Got it!" Sin exclaims.

We run over to meet him. His light is shining on a pile of debris that he's pulling away from the bottom of the wall. Behind it, there's a hole just big enough for a person to crawl through.

"From the outside in," Sin says. "Vamps must've done this."

He holds his light to the twisted metal, all of it pointing toward the city, as if someone had been pushing from the other side.

"Then let's not go," I say. "If vampires know about this hole . . ."

"Come on," Michael says, irritation in his voice. "We're right here."

"They could be waiting on the other side."

Sin ducks and shines his light through the hole. "Nothing moving," he says.

"See?" Michael says. "It'll be fine."

"You said—"

"I know what I said! But we're not going to get another chance like this. We don't get to go beyond the wall like you do, Dawn. I've never even seen the outside. Neither has Tegan. We've been stuck in this city for our entire lives! You don't understand what that's like, okay? I'm not going to leave you here alone, but this is important to me. I want to go, and that means you need to come with me."

I'm angry that he's doing this. Beyond angry, actually. But I swallow it, not wanting to make a bigger scene in front of Sin and Tegan. Besides, the longer we're out here, the more likely something bad can happen. I just need to get this over with and deal with my anger at Michael later.

"Fine," I say tersely. "Let's go."

"We'll stay right at the wall," Sin says. "That way we're just a few feet from the city."

As if that can keep us safe.

Sin goes first, his slender body easily passing through to the other side. He waves to Tegan and I follow her. Michael joins us last.

We stand next to the wall and peer out into the night. I've seen the outside, not much, but more times than I'd care to. Sin, having traveled on the Night Train, is no stranger to it either. But Tegan and Michael gaze around eagerly.

"I've seen it before through binoculars," Michael says. "But to be here . . ."

"I've never seen it," Tegan says. "I always thought that it would be . . . I don't know . . . beautiful. But it's just . . . it's nothing."

It's flat. It's desolate. You can hear the wind trying to move things, but there's nothing to move. The grass is barely alive, struggling to find nutrients in the ground. The plains just stretch out for an eternity; they might as well be an ocean. The mountains in the very, very far distance are no more attainable than the stars.

"It always reminds me how small the cities are," Sin says. "Imagine, people used to walk right here, right where we're standing, without any fear. It's all gone now. Taken."

In a war we started, but now isn't the time to remind them.

"Where are the vampires?" Tegan asks.

"Out there." I gesture to the plain. "Most of them have found hills to carve homes into. Little more than hollowed-out coffins, just big enough to avoid the sun. If you go far enough off the main roads, you can find vampires living in what were once towns. They're just shells now, after years of bombing during the war. Or so the Agency says. I've never seen them."

"And the city," Michael says. "Sometimes I think there're more vamps in there than out here. Like it's all a big conspiracy to keep us scared from moving outside the walls."

"They're out here," I say. "And we should head back."

"There's plenty of time," Michael replies.

If none of us objects, he'll stay until the sun rises, assuming we survive the night. I'm just realizing that the flashlights we used to get to the wall might've attracted some unwanted attention. Now I'm not only worried about vamps catching us on the outside, but waiting for us on the inside. Michael has no idea how right he is—there are plenty of monsters within the city as well.

"Michael. It's time to go," I say in my sternest delegate

voice, the one that leaves no room for negotiation.

"Dawn, this is important."

"I know. You already used that excuse. We've seen it. Let's go."

Michael looks at the others, but they quickly turn away, not wanting to get involved.

"Fine," he says curtly. And I know he's not happy, but then neither am I.

Our little group separates into couples after we disembark from the trolley near the center of the city. While Tegan and Sin talked the entire way back, Michael and I didn't. I think we both have been playing the next conversation in our heads.

At my building, Michael and I walk past the guard and take the elevator to my floor. When we reach my apartment door, I put the key in. It's been a game of chicken to see who will speak first. I break.

"Good night."

"Why did we have to leave?" he asks.

I turn and face him. "Because it wasn't safe and you know it. I can't believe I went that far."

"Well, I wish you hadn't."

"What does that mean?"

"If it'd just been me tonight, I would've stayed out there even longer. You can't understand what it's like being trapped in this city, in these walls."

"You're right. You should've just ditched me, your girl-friend, at the Daylight and gone off with your new best friend who you've known for only a few days to sneak out beyond the protection of the walls just to see a flat, empty plain."

"It may be stupid, okay? But being beyond the wall—it's important to me. Besides, it doesn't hurt anybody."

"Don't you get it? Tonight we were lucky. People set up ambushes on our side of the wall, hoping to have a chance to attack vampires. You don't think vamps do the same thing on the other side, hoping to capture idiotic humans?" God, why is he listening to Sin and not me? Why do I even have to explain this? "If you want to be a Night Watchman, then you need to realize what's stupid can get you killed."

He's stung by that.

"Don't you think I can take care of myself?" Michael asks.

"Of course I do. But no one can fight off a whole pack of vampires. So why take the risk?"

"Because I'm tired of being told how to live, what we can and can't do. You're the delegate. Do something about it."

His words hit me like a physical blow.

"Sin's not afraid of anything, Dawn. Last night we went hunting—"

"What? You mean for vampires? Just the two of you?"

"Yeah, an area called Fang Alley. He said a lot of vamps live there."

My tension ratchets up a couple of notches. Was that him and Sin that Victor and I heard last night? If they'd found us, Victor would have attacked them. They wouldn't have backed off. He could have killed them. Now my fear for Michael has swirled into my anger, creating a tornado of emotions.

"How could you be so reckless? Do you not comprehend the unnecessary risks you were taking?"

"He told me not to tell you. I should have listened. You just don't get it. You're all about negotiation. I'm about action. I'm tired of waiting."

"Michael, it's too dangerous, what you and Sin are doing."

"At least we're doing something."

He storms away. I want to go after him, but I think he just needs to cool down so we can talk. Sin is filling his head with crazy ideas. I hope Michael will think about what I said, that he'll realize I'm right and he's risking his life needlessly.

When I walk into the apartment, there's no sign of Rachel. I'm glad, because I don't want to have to explain where I've been, and I'm getting tired of lying.

I plop down onto the couch, put my hands to my face, and moan. I'm beyond frustrated. I wish time would just stop for a few years while I sort out everything. But the gears just keep turning, and I have to keep up somehow.

Chapter 20

"Too bad Michael couldn't join us," Tegan says.

We're walking down the dusty streets, the sun high, but in a way it seems just minutes from setting.

"I know it isn't any of my business," Sin says. "But is something going on between you two? I was sparring with him earlier today and he was . . . off. Like he couldn't focus and was easily frustrated. That's not like him."

Even on Saturday, Michael practices his defensive maneuvers, and Sin has obviously become his favorite partner. The best two in the class, steel sharpening steel.

"We're just disagreeing on some things lately," I say, simply to get them off my back. I had called Michael to see if he wanted to go with us, but he spit out an excuse in a frosty voice that chilled me.

"I hope the little wall-walking trip didn't make things worse," Sin says.

Yeah, it did, in a lot of ways. But it'll just annoy Tegan if I find fault with Sin. Besides, Michael is the one who is being difficult.

"We'll be fine," I assure him. "We're both just super-busy."

We turn a corner and then zigzag through an alleyway. In this city, sometimes it's difficult to tell what's a street and what's a shortcut through two buildings. If I'm not familiar with the area, I can get lost easily. Even though Tegan's leading the way, Sin's completely comfortable, and I'm impressed with how quickly he's mastered his new location.

Eventually we reach our destination.

"Ted is the best junker in town," Tegan says. "If it's broken, he can fix it."

The broken item in question is Tegan's cell phone. She dropped it two days ago and it shattered, completely busted. She was almost in tears when Sin offered to pay to have it fixed. Not exactly a cheap thing to do.

We walk into Ted's shop. It's huge, but he has so much worthless junk piled from floor to ceiling, you have the feeling of being caught in a garbage tornado.

Scavengers bring this stuff in from all over the city. Maybe they found an old building with a prewar basement: The broken TV is worthless, but bring it to Ted and he'll buy it from you, then strip it for parts. Same for that half-destroyed microwave and melted laptop. Useless by themselves, but once a good junker gets his hands on them, he can pull the usable bits out and throw the rest away. Like Tegan's cell phone. The body from an old pre-war phone, but the electronics inside are from three or four different devices. Wires from a VCR, circuitry from a heart-rate monitor, antenna from an old remote-control car. It's amazing what Ted can do with a little patience and know-how. And a lot of money from his customers.

"Hey, Ted!" Tegan says, approaching the old man. The guy seems to be caked in a permanent layer of dust. He's wearing a headband fitted with multiple magnifying pieces. I know they're to help with his delicate work, but it looks as if he's always prepared for an optometrist's exam. His clothes, like the things he creates, are a hodgepodge of different fabrics, styles, and maybe even centuries.

"You remember me, don't you?" she asks.

"No."

I doubt he remembers anyone. He lives in a world of machines, not people.

Tegan tries to sweet-talk him, butter him up, but stops halfway through the attempt and just hands him her phone.

"Kids these days!" Ted says. "Don't take care of nothin'! I break my back finding the right keypad for this thing, and you go and bust it!" Machines, Ted remembers. People, not so much.

"It wasn't on purpose."

"Ahhh, humbug!"

He takes her phone and cracks it open. After muttering

to himself for a minute, he turns to a mammoth-sized cabinet behind him with dozens of drawers of different sizes.
He goes through them, opening one and then another,
closing them with renewed frustration every time.

"Can't find anything in this place!" he shouts.

"Maybe if you kept it a little cleaner," Sin suggests.

"Ahhh, what do you know, young'un?"

Sin laughs.

Eventually, the junker finds what he's looking for and
begins outfitting Tegan's phone.

"How much is this going to cost?" she asks.

"How do I know? It ain't fixed yet!"

Ted's the best in the city. He's also the crankiest. And
priciest.

I wander through the makeshift aisles of the shop.
Here is the closest I can get to the past. I run my hands
across the mountains of old things: TVs and computers
and phones and car engines. All the stuff that made the
world turn. Now they're only good for parts, used to create
Frankenstein monsters of technology. A gold pocket watch
catches my attention. As I pick it up, I think it would make
a nice gift for Victor. I immediately drop it.

"Careful over there!" Ted shouts.

I wave him off. What's wrong with me? Why does
Victor keep popping into my thoughts?

By the time I return to the counter, Tegan's phone is
repaired and she jumps for joy. Until Ted names his price.
Tegan almost has a heart attack, but Sin just puts his
hand on her shoulder. He pulls out a thick wad of money.

Both Tegan's and my jaws drop. I've never seen someone with that much cash. Even cynical Ted isn't beyond being impressed as he licks his lips at the imminent payday.

"Here's a tip for your trouble," Sin says, giving him extra.

"Yes, sir. Anytime, sir. You, too, little lady."

As we walk out, Tegan looks up at Sin as though he's a god.

I don't know why I'm so bothered by that wad of cash. The rarity of it is unsettling.

"What does your dad do?" I ask.

"He's involved with the Night Watchmen. I can't say anything beyond that." He winks at me. "You know how it is."

"Yeah, I—" I stop, the words backing up painfully in my throat. The sun has almost finished its descent, and there, in the distant shadows, is a guy in a hoodie. It could be anyone, really, and I tell myself to relax.

But then that blackened hood turns my way and I can feel his gaze. All I can see is the pale flesh of his chin and his lips, which curl into a smile.

"What is it?" Tegan asks.

"That's him. The guy I saw at school, the one who followed me down the halls."

"Sin, he was hassling Dawn," Tegan says. "Do something."

"No—" I begin.

"I'm on it," Sin says, and I hear in his voice that he's going into protection mode. "Hey, you!" he shouts, and starts walking toward Hoodie.

Hoodie waits for just a heartbeat, and I can feel his gaze still focused on me. But when Sin gets too close, he turns and runs.

"No, Sin, let him go!" I yell, but it's too late. He's already taken off after him and rounded the corner.

Okay, if my stalker was just some kid sent by Lila as a prank, then why would he be here? That's taking it a bit too far. So maybe he isn't some kid. Maybe my first instinct was right: He's a vampire.

Tegan, as if reading my thoughts, pulls her stake from her backpack and grips it tightly. I realize I'm holding mine as well. I don't even remember taking it from my boot.

"That guy's creepy," Tegan says. "I couldn't see him clearly, but he was giving off weird vibes."

"I wish Sin hadn't gone after him."

"He'll be fine. He's really tough. I can't tell you how safe I feel with him."

"So you really like him, huh?"

She shrugs. "Yeah, I do. It's a little strange just being with one guy, but since I met him, I'm not looking for anyone else. What about you?"

"What about me what?"

"What's going on with you and Michael? Seriously. When I met up with Sin and asked Michael if he was coming, his expression was so cold when I mentioned you that it was giving *me* chills."

"He thinks I don't have faith in him. And I was annoyed at him for dragging me out beyond the wall. But maybe it's more than that." I give her an earnest look. "You have to promise not to tell anyone."

"Cross my heart. Now spill."

"I've sorta been spending some time with Victor."

"The Night Watchman? Whoa! That's kinda major. So, Michael found out?"

"No, I just . . . I'm confused. I think I'm starting to like Victor."

"What's not to like?"

Why did I start this conversation? I can't tell her everything.

"I don't know. Victor and I . . . we're not right for each other"—vamp and human—when has that ever worked out?—"but he just always seems to be there when I need someone. And Michael often . . . isn't. But I know Michael's better for me." Human, human. No species conflict. No lifestyle conflict. No diet conflict.

"Victor is sexy, so I can't blame you for having an interest in him. But then, so is Michael. Tough call. On the other hand, in some ways, Victor reminds me of Sin. They both project this don't-mess-with-me attitude, which is an additional hotness factor."

"Michael does, too," I say, feeling a need to defend him.

"Yeah, but it's not as . . . intense. Sin is just . . . God, okay, I admit it. I'm nuts about him. And it's not just because he's gorgeous and rich and tough. He listens to me. He makes my heart speed up just by looking at me. And he's an amazing kisser. Complete package."

And the package is walking back toward us, brushing

his hair out of his eyes, only to have it fall back into place.

"The dude was fast. I couldn't catch up with him."

"Were you able to get a good look at him?" I ask.

"No. Sorry. But now I know to keep an eye out for him."

"Thanks."

"Not a problem." He slips his arm around Tegan and she melts against his side. "Let's head to the Daylight Grill."

"I'm not in the mood to be a third wheel," I tell them. "I'm going home."

"We'll go with you that far," Tegan says.

As we start to walk away, I glance over my shoulder. Hoodie's long gone, but I have to wonder why he was following me at all.

Chapter 21

I didn't hear from Michael all weekend. As I'm rushing down the hallway at school Monday morning, I'm anxious to see him, to make things right between us, to regain some balance in my life.

I come to a staggering stop at the sight of Michael with his forearm pressed to his locker door. He's smiling down at Lila, who is backed up against his locker. Her hand is flattened against his chest as if she needs to count his heartbeats. She's got this insipid grin on her face like he just hung the moon for her. Or handed her a pair of vamp fangs.

"What the hell?" Tegan says as she comes up beside me and nudges my shoulder, like I'm not already seeing what she's seeing.

"Were you at Daylight this weekend? Did you see them

together there?" My throat is suddenly so dry that I can barely get the words out.

"I was. And I didn't. You need to get over there and shove her butt down three lockers to her own, where it belongs."

"Yeah." I should. But instead I'm rooted to the spot.

Lila releases an irritating giggle, pats Michael's chest, and walks away. Still wearing a broad grin, he watches her retreating back. Passing me, she gives me a satisfied smirk that sets my blood to boiling. Then Michael notices me. His smile disappears. He turns to his locker and opens the door.

"Uh-oh," Tegan says.

"I'll see you in class," I say, before wending my way around the students in the hallway until I arrive at Michael's side. "What was that about?"

"What?" His voice echoes from inside his locker. Apparently he's suddenly fascinated by the arrangement of his books.

"You know what. You and Lila."

He slams his locker closed with such force that I jump. He meets and holds my gaze, his unforgiving. "We were just talking. She and I have a lot in common."

"Like what?"

"Wall-walking, for starters. She's never done it at night, but she thinks it would be cool to go with me."

My heart drops to the floor. "Michael, don't do this. You don't have to prove anything."

"I know that."

I'm not sure he does. But I want to change the subject. I want everything to go back to the way it was.

"Michael." I press my hand to his chest, realizing too late that I've placed it in the same spot where Lila was resting hers earlier. "I have absolutely no Agency business to take care of tonight. And Rachel is working late. I thought maybe you and I could have an intimate picnic on the balcony, maybe even sneak a bottle of wine out of Rachel's cabinet, the one she doesn't think I know about."

"I can't. I have something else to do."

His words are like a slap in my face.

"I gotta get to class," he adds.

He's walking away from me before I can protest, and I refuse to chase after him. Suddenly Tegan is at my side.

"If body language is any indication," she muses, "I'd say that didn't go well."

"You have a gift for understatement."

When school is finally over, I go outside to discover the clouds have grown dark and heavy with rain. They reflect my mood. Michael totally ignored me in kick-ass class. He sat with Lila at lunch. She was so smug about it that it set my teeth on edge.

I stare at the gathering storm clouds and feel like they're inhabiting me. I've had this feeling before. I know what I have to do.

At home, I quickly gather my things and put them in my backpack.

I look out the window one more time. The clouds have thickened, blocking out the sun. Vampires could come

out now if they wanted. The cloud cover offers enough
protection from the harmful rays of the sun. But I'll take
the chance. Lightning flashes across the sky, stuck in the
clouds, turning them from deep grays to light blues for just
a moment. Ten seconds later, thunder echoes. My dad told
me once that if I counted the time between the lightning
and thunder, I'd be able to figure out if the storm was close.
This one is. It's just what I need. What I want.

By the time I get outside, the rain has started. I pull the
hood on my raincoat over my head as I move through the
streets. With my eyes on the ground, I watch the puddles
grow around my shoes, every step making a bigger splash
than the one before it as the rain picks up. I'm enjoying
the pitter-patter of water droplets against the plastic hood;
it echoes until it drowns out the world and it's just me and
the sidewalk.

It's a long walk, past the areas of Denver that have been
rebuilt. When I get to my destination, I take a moment to
just look at it. The building used to be called Greene Tower,
then Tower Eight, then Abandoned Building Thirty-six,
before ending up as Demolition Site B. A massive fire
ripped through the building several years ago. It was so
fierce that, in spite of the efforts of the fire department,
what remained after the flames were doused wasn't livable. So it was simply abandoned, like so much of the city.
Abandoned, like I'm feeling today.

It's thirty stories high. My parents and I lived halfway
up. Before they were hired by the Agency, they were profes-
sors at the local college, and this was all they could afford.

It used to be somewhat nice, but now it's an empty shell with pieces of walls and windows missing, entire floors collapsed, stairs with so many crumbling steps they're unusable. No lights. No water. Just shadows and memories.

I step inside and the rain stops beating against me. Some transients might be left, trying to live in the few rooms that haven't been infested with rats and roaches, but I've never seen anyone inside, not since it was condemned. Even though the storm has intensified, enough light comes through the clouds to illuminate the building through holes and cracks and windows. It's gray and weak, but it's enough. I know where I'm going.

I cautiously make my way deep into the building before coming to the right set of stairs. My goal is the eighteenth floor, but I'll have to navigate a maze of steps and hallways to get there. It used to be as simple as entering the stairwell and going up. But not anymore. Too much rot and decay. I have to zigzag between flights of stairs to get there, and even then, if I don't watch my step, I'll fall down a new hole that wasn't there last time.

When was the last time? Two months ago, I think. At this rate, I'll never finish.

No artwork remains in the building, so the place looks like nothing more than a series of walls and beams thrown up to create an intricate, towering box. I often got lost in them as a kid, running around and banging on strangers' doors until they pointed me in the right direction.

When I was seven years old we had a neighbor named Mickey. He was my first real crush. Just an innocent kind

of thing. I wanted to, I don't know, kiss him on the cheek
and then run away, or give him a giant bouquet of flowers,
because I thought maybe boys liked dandelions. I knocked
on his door one day so I could invite him to my birthday
party. I'd already arranged the seating chart so he'd be right
next to me. I was so proud of my cunning ways. But when
the door opened it was a different family. My parents said
Mickey had "gone to a new school" and his parents had to
move. A few months ago I looked through the Agency files
on Mickey, hit with a sudden curiosity. He was killed in his
sleep by vampires. His entire family was drained.

It's difficult to believe that I was ever that innocent—or
young. Sometimes I feel as though I've been acting like an
adult forever. I don't know why my parents didn't move.
The war was in its last days. Maybe they thought things
would get better when the peace negotiations were final-
ized. Maybe they truly believed that VampHu would keep
vampires on the other side of the wall. I hate knowing that
my brother, after surviving the war, returned to us here
and was the one to dispel that myth.

After the last flight of stairs, I finally arrive at the eighteenth floor. I walk down the hall, bits of light coming in
through the doorways, since most of the doors have been
stripped off their hinges. I step around one of the holes in
the floor and almost trip on a bit of torn-up carpet. Rats
must've chewed through it, because I don't remember that
from last time.

When I get to my old apartment, the place where we
lived until Brady died, it's the brightest one on the floor.

But that's only because the entire outside wall is missing. I'm ten steps from plummeting to the ground. We weren't the last tenants, of course. There was always someone more desperate ready to fill an apartment back then, even one vampires had attacked. So the sparse furniture crumbling in the corner isn't ours; nor is the small crib in the next room.

I sit cross-legged near the ledge. It provides a good panoramic view of the city. I couldn't really appreciate it as a kid. It doesn't face the Works or the downtown district. No huge buildings are in the way. Just the streets below and the row houses and the wall and the mountains beyond that. The wind lashes, and raindrops splash on the already soaked hardwood floor. It was carpeted once, I think. Hard to remember now. Details like that fade.

I unzip my backpack and pull out a photo of my parents and me. Back when we were happy, or as happy as humans were allowed to be. Just the three of us smiling in front of the water fountain in the North District, a fountain that stopped working long ago. My father's holding the camera at arm's length to capture all of us.

I'm thirteen in the photo, my hair pulled back in a French braid I thought was so mature. We'd moved into the apartment that I now share with Rachel, courtesy of Dad's new prestige within the Agency. He was initially hired as a consultant on vampire affairs. The Agency provides housing for all its employees. Mom looks happy; maybe she finally found the security she always longed for. The thought of making a better future for their only surviving child must've been powerful. It must've brought smiles to their faces every night as they tucked me into bed.

And then they died. Together. On the road to Valentine Manor. Because Mom couldn't stand the thought of Dad facing Valentine alone. Like I now have to.

I put down the photo and pull out a box of matches from my jeans pocket. I light the corner of the Polaroid. It curls inward, carrying the yellow flame with it. The fire erases my dad's face, turning it black and charred, then consumes my family until we are just ash.

I come here to let everything out. This way it doesn't affect my work; it doesn't affect my studies. I purge all my emotions here, in this abandoned building. I don't know if it's big enough to house all my anger and sorrow. Maybe that's the reason it's falling apart. The weight of my emptying heart tears it down piece by piece.

This is why I don't talk about my parents to other people. I don't want to be reminded of the pain. This is where I do my remembering. I burn photos of them, slowly, one at a time. Maybe one day they'll all be gone, and so will the despair I feel. And the nightmares.

I cry a little less every time. It's just a trickle now, so little I can't tell the difference between the tears and the rain already on my cheeks. I'm afraid my relationship with Michael is like this building, deteriorating until it's beyond repair. I don't know how to make anything last. How to hold on to Michael. Or if I even should.

The photo's almost finished burning. I wish my emotions drained that fast. The wind carries the ash outside, where the rain beats it down to the ground.

"You shouldn't be here."

I turn around. Victor's standing in the doorway, his back against the frame, arms crossed. His heavy coat is soaked through. He didn't bother to wear a hat, just let the storm have its way with his hair.

"I have to be here," I say. "It's the only way I can survive the days."

"And what about the nights? Vampires are going to be out soon. They'll come here, looking for the homeless."

"I'll take the risk."

"One day you might not come back."

"What's there to come back to?" I shake my head. "Sorry. This place just brings that out in me." The encounter with Michael at school didn't help. I may have lost him. Ironic when all I want is to protect him.

"Then why come here?" Victor asks.

"To mourn. To forget. I can be sad here, and no one will see that maybe I'm not as strong as everyone thinks."

He walks past me and lowers himself onto the ledge, his legs dangling over the side.

"I'm sorry you lost your parents, Dawn."

"How can you be sorry? You didn't even know them."

"But I know you. And I'm sorry because I can tell there are pieces of you missing. I wish I could fill them somehow. But I also know that those scars you feel inside are the things that make you strong. They make you who you are. Your parents' lives define you as much as their deaths."

"Sometimes I'll go a whole day without thinking about

them. I feel guilty about that."

"You shouldn't. I've lived long enough to know that all things fade in time. All things turn to dust. Buildings. Monuments. People. Even memories. The pain you feel, that anger, that hopelessness . . . they'll disappear in time. One day you'll understand their sacrifice, and then you'll feel that spark of hope again."

My parents were so sure the world would turn out to be a safe place for me, a better place when they were finished with it. But then they died, and I couldn't tell a single difference they'd made. I'm only seventeen; how can I even begin to do a better job than they did? At times it feels impossible. But then I realize their legacy for me wasn't a better world; it was raising me to be strong and confident and smart, and then I decide I have to try because I can't let them down.

"It's really coming down now," Victor says, as a crack of thunder rolls through the sky.

Scooting nearer, I join him at the very edge. My own feet hang over. Eighteen stories up.

"You'll catch me if I fall, right?" I ask.

Victor smiles. "I'll catch you before you even slip."

I believe him. A few inches from certain death, in a bad storm, and I feel completely, totally secure.

"Why are you so different, Victor? Any other vampire would've taken my blood by now. Probably would have killed me. Why not you?"

He's quiet for a moment, and so still. I wonder what he's thinking. Is the question so hard, or does he not trust me completely, the way I've begun to trust him?

"I like you, Dawn. I've seen a lot of humans, from far away and up close. I've never met one like you. I think you're the closest thing to a sunrise I'll ever see."

My heart squeezes in my chest. The feelings I've been walling off come crashing in. But maybe here, in this building, I can let down my guard a bit. It's a dangerous thing to do, especially with a powerful vampire involved. But I'm already at the edge; what's another risk?

"I like you, too," I admit. Even though I know I shouldn't. I should want Michael here, but it feels right that it's Victor.

"I'm glad you can't resist my charms," Victor says with a smile. Then he turns serious. "I know I've complicated your life, Dawn. But you've complicated mine, too."

"How's that?"

"I'm always fighting my baser instincts. We can dress well, conform to proper manners. But at heart we're monsters—just like you accuse us of being."

"You're not," I rush to assure him. "You rescue people—Tegan and me. You help vampires. Granted, by breaking the law and stealing blood, but your intentions are good." I can't believe I'm striving to convince him that he's not evil. "You're not a monster, Victor."

"I wish that were true. But when I'm around you, all I can think about is . . . the temptation of you."

My chest tightens, and I work hard not to let fear sneak into my voice. "My blood?"

"I'm a vampire. Blood is the first thing we scent, the

first thing that draws us to humans. I fight it. But I can't deny it's part of who I am. I would never take your blood, though. No matter how strongly it calls to me. You have to believe that."

"I do." My voice lacks conviction. We've never discussed the differences in us except in anger. To admit to them now, in this place, is scary. Makes the differences more powerful, because I wish they didn't exist.

"It's not just your blood that tempts me," he admits. "In four hundred years, I've never dreamed. Vampires don't. But after I saved you on the trolley that night, you invaded my sleep. In my dreams, we're the same. We can touch, kiss, love. And every dream ends with us . . . being together forever."

"I'm mortal. I don't get forever. Not unless I'm turned, and I'd never . . . I'd never willingly—"

"I know. It's just a dream."

But I can see in his eyes how he wishes it weren't. There's something developing between us that I don't understand, that I never wanted. His nearness makes my heart pound, my skin grow warm. Maybe it's just this building, but here I consider that impossible things could actually become possible.

"Is it scary? Being turned?" I ask. "Hypothetically speaking."

"I wasn't turned, so I can't speak from experience, but from what I understand it isn't. I'd take your blood, give you mine. And then you'd die. It wouldn't have to hurt. You'd just . . . wake up and be everlasting."

Victor and I are so close together that if I shift my weight even a little, I could touch him. It would be easy to nestle my face against his shoulder. To draw comfort from him.

"I should probably take you home," he says.

I look out and realize that night has fallen.

Victor starts to get up. A loud crack of thunder makes me jump, and I slip. But as he promised, Victor grabs my arm before I can even inhale to scream, and he pulls me up and away from the ledge. So quickly that I bang into his chest. He's staring down at me, his arms circling me, clutching me to him. He's so warm and solid. Part of me longs to stand here forever, locked in his embrace.

"Thank you," I whisper.

His gaze drops to my mouth. I'm barely breathing. Just waiting. Not even sure what I'm waiting for. I can't deny the attraction I feel, even though I know it's dangerous. But sometimes I can almost forget he's a vampire.

Then, as quickly as he snatched me from death's door, he releases me, steps back, and shoves his hands into his jeans pockets. I'm disappointed; an emptiness worse than anything I've ever felt washes through me. First Michael rejected me, and now Victor is. For some reason, the second one hurts more.

"Have you ever seen a movie in a theater?" he finally asks.

"No." Entertainment isn't a high priority on the rebuilding efforts.

"Would you like to?"

"I've seen movies on TV." I'm trying to pretend nothing

just happened. And I have to resist the temptation to spend more time with him. But why should I? Michael is probably with Lila.

"It's not the same as seeing one in a theater," he insists. "We're not that far away. . . ."

No, we're not. And the trolleys are still running. The truth is, I'm not ready to say good night to Victor, either.

"Yes. I'd like to see a movie."

Victor's hand holds mine gently as he leads me through the darkened theater, up a different set of stairs than I used before. I try not to think about how much I like the feel of his touch.

"How does hot buttered popcorn sound?" he asks.

"Unhealthy."

"Which is what makes it so good."

We round a corner and go into an alcove that smells heavenly. I hear a click, realize he hit a light switch. It's still not very bright, but I can see Victor move around behind the stainless-steel counter. He's opening doors, flicking other switches. "I used to love to come here before the war. The first time I ever saw the world in sunlight was when I watched a movie," he explains.

I jump when the popcorn starts popping. He turns to it, scoops some into a bag, and adds butter. Lots of butter.

"How do you get this stuff?" I ask, as I take the bag from him.

"I have ways." He retrieves two sodas from a small refrigerator.

He starts switching things off, leaving the lights for last. We plunge into shadows. "Let's get comfortable."

I follow him into a theater and realize we're up in a balcony section. The lights are low, and he leads me to a row of chairs that actually look fairly decent. When I sit, the chair rocks a little.

"I'll be right back," he says.

I twist around and watch him move along the top row to where a projector protrudes through a hole in the wall. He reaches in and suddenly there's flickering light and a steady clicking sound.

When I turn back, colorful images are dancing on the screen. Victor returns and sits beside me.

"*Singin' in the Rain*. One of my favorites," he says.

I reach for the popcorn at the same time he does. Our fingers brush. Still. I wonder briefly if coming here was a bad idea, but then again, doing anything with Victor is a bad idea.

"You eat food?" I ask to break the tension.

"Just for the sensual experience. I derive no nutrition from it."

He moves his hand aside, and I grab some popcorn. I can't remember the last time I had any. Still, I barely notice its flavor. I know being here is the latest in a series of bad decisions I've made lately. But I'm still glad that I'm here.

I shift my attention back to the movie, try to concentrate on it. There's so much vivacity on the screen. People are dancing and singing. They're just . . . happy.

I glance over at Victor. The lights and images from the

screen are playing over his handsome face.

I can't believe it—he's mouthing the words that the guy on-screen is singing. Victor must feel my gaze on him, because he slowly turns his head to look at me.

"Was it really like that back then?" I whisper. "Were people so happy?"

"People were sad, too. The movie is all illusion. How people wish things were." Slowly he reaches out and pushes a few strands of my hair behind my ear.

"Are you working your powers on me, Victor?"

"You mean am I controlling your thoughts and desires? It's a myth that vampires have that capability."

"It can't be. Too many people—"

"Fall to the lure of the vampire? It's easier to blame us for humans' lack of control than to admit their weakness."

"I'm not weak."

"No, you're not. That's what I like about you. You're strong, bold . . . reckless."

"I prefer the word *adventurous*."

He gives me a small smile. "That, too."

"Why are we here, Victor? Why are you suddenly in my life? What do you want with me?"

"Things I shouldn't want."

He cups his hand behind my head, then leans toward me. I know I should move beyond his reach. But I don't. His lips touch mine. A whisper at first. Soft, gentle. Between one heartbeat and the next everything changes. Passion rises up, and there's a hunger between us that I don't understand. That I've never felt, not even with Michael. I feel the point of his fangs, know I should be frightened or repelled by the reminder of what he is, but I'm not. I'm lost in the pleasure of a kiss that is anything but simple.

Michael and I have kissed. A lot. Yet I've never felt anything like this—a kiss that seems to encompass and inflame all of me. Is it because Victor is a vampire? Does he have a special power, despite what he claims? Or is there something between us, something primal that I don't want to acknowledge?

When he finally draws back, we're both breathing heavily. One of his palms is resting lightly against my throat, and I know he can feel the rapid pounding of my pulse, the rushing of my blood.

"I know I should resist. Vampires and humans . . . they never work out." Victor's words are only halfhearted, and he leans in to kiss me again. But this time it's bittersweet.

"I should take you home now," he says, "before I do something I'll regret."

I don't want to leave. But he's right. If I don't go, *I* might do something *I'll* regret. Because I'm not a hundred percent sure where Michael and I stand. We've never fought before. I don't know if our relationship is over.

Victor doesn't even bother to stop the movie. It just continues to play as we step out into the hallway.

"There!" someone yells.

And suddenly, Night Watchmen are rushing toward us.

Chapter 22

Four Watchmen are on a collision course with us, their black dusters flowing behind them as they run at remarkable speeds. Their faces are covered in dark cloth that hides everything but their eyes.

I've never seen them in a group, but I understand instantly why vampires fear them. It seems like they've become the new rulers of the night.

I don't have much time to admire them, though, as Victor rushes forward to meet the elite guards who've come here to slay him.

The Watchmen fight him with the respect he deserves, whether they know he's Old Family or not. Stakes drawn, they dance around him, trying to disorient the vampire. One goes in, and Victor easily takes his stake before throwing him across the floor. But the timing of the squad is perfect, like a clock whose gears have kept pace for centuries, and the next Watchman darts forward. His stake fails to find its mark, but comes so close that I scream.

Victor throws him against the wall, and the guy lands in a heap. The third Watchman moves up, but Victor punches him hard and I hear his nose shatter. As the fourth and final hunter comes in, Victor wastes no time, shows no mercy. With amazing speed and force, Victor drives his stake through the attacker's thigh. He cries out in agony.

Victor whirls to me. "More are coming."

His vampire ears, so sensitive, pick up the approaching footsteps before my own can. He takes my hand and we run down the hall, heading toward a part of the theater where I've never been before. The darkness here is all-consuming, but I trust Victor's sense of direction. I trust him.

The Watchmen are right behind us.

Victor kicks open a door, and the faint light from distant street lamps barely illuminates an abandoned alleyway. He lets go of my hand and runs over to something that looks like a pile of junk covered by dark cloth. I'm unsure why he's wasting his time on it, until he tears the cover off in one sweeping motion, like a magician revealing his assistant to a mystified audience.

"You ever been on a motorcycle?" he asks, as I stare at the two-wheeled beast.

"No," I say.

"Well, no better time to learn."

He hops on, revs the throttle, and I quickly slip on

behind him. The romance of being this close, the tension of our bodies touching, is lost as the door to the theater bursts open, three Watchmen tumbling out.

Victor blasts past them, and though they give chase, they quickly give up. Minutes pass; street signs fly by.

"Where are we going?" I ask, shouting into the wind of our movement.

"A friend's."

We're barreling through the city at breakneck speed. I'm clinging to Victor as though my very life depends on him. I feel like I'm following Victor down the rabbit hole. I don't know what his plan is, but I trust him.

Victor is driving so fast that everything is a blur, but I realize we're heading into the Far West District, known for its sparse population, vast empty spaces, and abandoned buildings. Agency posters and street signs fly by. As usual, few people are out, but those who are stop and stare. Motorcycles are rare. Especially one like this shiny restored model. Riding it makes us stand out, but then, not riding it would have meant Victor's death and quite possibly mine. I have no way of knowing if the Night Watchmen would have recognized who I was before they'd rammed a stake through my heart. Or maybe they would have decided it was enough to find me guilty by association.

Once we reach the Far West District, the alleyways get very narrow. Without slowing down, he cuts through them, and we find ourselves on streets that could barely be called that. A car could never make it through the sharp turns and tight passageways.

The Works doesn't even have pipes running out here, and people have to use their own oil lamps or fireplaces to light their homes. The signature feature of this place is the small, crude windmills atop every building, like strangled dandelions twirling slowly in the wind. They provide the few families who live out here with just enough power for the basics, like pumping up water from the sewers and filtering it to make it barely drinkable. The same strong winds that move those turbines also blow the Works' coal dust over here, where it settles on everything. But most people say it's actually the dust of ground-up dreams. It's the harshest district in the city. Not because of violence, but just cruel indifference.

Suddenly we stop between two huge buildings. I see a few people milling around, but I suspect they aren't really people, but vampires. Another thing this place is notorious for: a thriving black market for blood. Victor turns off the ignition, and the quiet is almost deafening. I realize I'm trembling. I thought it was just the rumble of the engine beneath us, but I must be in some sort of shock after the attack.

Victor puts his hands over mine where they're knotted in front of his chest. "We're safe here."

"Yeah. Okay." I untangle myself from around him and slide off the bike, nearly falling to the ground, my legs are so weak. But Victor is there to pull me back up.

"Are you okay?"

"Just . . . just adrenaline."

He touches my cheek. "You didn't get hurt?"

"No. I'm okay. Just shaken. How did they find us? I swear I didn't tell anyone about the theater."

"No one at all? Not even Tegan?"

"No one."

"We'll figure it out. Come on."

He leads me over to a door that is so rusted it blends in with the red brickwork. He opens it onto a hall lined with oil lamps that give the cramped corridor a haunting glow. I follow him inside and he closes the door behind us. I stay in his shadow, never more than a step away, as we move forward.

A light at the end reveals itself to be an entire room. Inside are several couches, like those from Valentine Manor, and old oak tables that people only dream of having now. No windows for obvious reasons: The three vampires within wouldn't want any sun coming in. They immediately rise. I can feel the tension radiating from them, the alertness, the sense of a threat.

They're like Victor, well dressed and well manicured. But one in particular stands out as Old Family, because his jeans and buttoned shirt are crisp and show no sign of wear. His features are the strongest, and his long brown hair is fitted with a single knot of gold ribbon framing the right side of his face.

"We've got a problem," Victor says.

The Old Family vampire runs his gaze over me. "I can see that. Why did you bring her here?"

"I didn't have a choice. Night Watchmen raided the theater, tried to kill us."

"I'm not surprised. I've gathered some of the information you wanted. It's not good, Victor."

As though suddenly remembering his manners, Victor says, "Dawn, this is Richard Carrollton, along with his trusted bodyguards."

"From Los Angeles," I say.

Richard tilts his head. "You've done your homework." He looks at Victor. "What does she know?"

"Nothing."

I jerk my gaze over to Victor. He gives me a look that's riddled with guilt.

"But you can speak freely in front of her. She's going to have to know everything now."

"And just what is everything?" I ask.

"We're about to start a war with my father."

Chapter 23

Stunned, all I can do is stare at Victor as he guides me over to a couch.

"Are you insane?" I ask as he eases me down to the cushion.

"I hope not," he responds, sitting beside me and wrapping his hand around mine, offering comfort and strength. I know I should subtly withdraw mine, but right now I need the physical contact to anchor me.

Richard retakes his seat, but his bodyguards remain standing.

"Richard's been in the city for a while," Victor says. "He's my second in command."

"Second in command of what?" I ask.

"An army I've been assembling. My father, Richard's father . . . all the heads of the families . . . they're from another time, another era, another . . . mind-set. No more bombs are being dropped, but there is no peace. Not really."

"And now that the Thirst has infected the Los Angeles territory, it's only a matter of time before it spreads everywhere," Richard says.

"What's that?" I ask. In all my numerous vampire courses and studies, I've never heard of the Thirst.

"Our dirty little secret," Richard confesses.

"Vampires can feed on other vampires," Victor explains. "That's been under lock and key and was kept out of the VampHu for fear that humans would stop giving blood if they knew."

No kidding. Everyone thinks vampires depend on human blood to survive, and now I'm learning they can feed on one another as well? That they could be self-sustaining?

Richard looks at me keenly. "You're wondering why we need you."

"Drinking from another vampire isn't a permanent solution," Victor says firmly.

They trade sentences back and forth as they explain the Thirst: Under dire circumstances, vampires *can* take the blood of other vampires. It'll get them through the night and give them enough strength until they can find human blood. Once, maybe twice a year and it's fine. The problem comes when they keep feeding on their brethren. Every month. Every week. Every night. The Thirst kicks in and they change. They become addicts, losing all sense of reason and understanding—like rabid dogs. Their fangs grow, their eyes turn black, and all they want is blood. Vampire blood. They've lost the taste for human blood, but it doesn't stop them from devouring any who get in the way.

I remember Victor whispering *thirst* on my balcony. "That vampire that was attacked near the school. You think that's why another vampire was responsible?"

I can see the worry in his eyes. "Yes. I think the beginnings of the Thirst may be taking root here."

"Is there a cure?" I ask.

"A stake through the heart or a field trip into sunlight." Richard attempts to bring a bit of levity to a very serious subject.

"If a cure exists, no one's found it," Victor says. "It's a recent phenomenon. Before the war, there were few vampires and plenty of humans. Blood was plentiful. Now, not so much."

"Which was the problem in Los Angeles," Richard says. "Our blood supply has dwindled as the humans stop donating, but the damn city is so strong, so well defended, that even if I wanted to sneak some vampires in, I couldn't. I've offered to pay blood slaves huge amounts of money, but the stigma of selling blood to vampires lasts a lifetime, and I haven't had many takers."

Richard goes into more detail, telling me that the situation is completely opposite from the one here. The Carrolltons aren't as strong as the Valentines; their grip over the population is weak. As a result, the city is late on blood payments all the time, sometimes going months without delivering at all. And unlike Denver, their walls stretch higher, farther, and are fiercely defended.

"But the inside of the city is rotting like an apple's core," he says. "The Agency there is inept. The people are starving, and so are the vampires on the outside. We have too many damn Lessers."

"So what does that have to do with starting a war with your father?" I ask, trying to draw the connection between the Thirst and family infighting.

"My father, just like Richard's, refuses to give any attention to the seriousness of the problem. The Thirst is like a plague making its way across the country. If it ever reaches Denver in full force, it'll turn the area outside the wall into a giant killing field. Imagine an entire race of vampires driven mad. They'll rip one another apart. And even Old Families won't be safe."

"Are they that powerful? To take on Old Families?"

"In their numbers? Yes. Even a vampire as powerful as my father. The Thirst doesn't play by our rules. Infected vampires don't care about duty or honor. All they care about is where to get their next fix."

"Not only that," Richard chimes in, "they're insane. They've lost all control. No one is safe. Not vampires. Not humans. They can't be reasoned with. They're set on destroying everything. When it comes to monsters, the citizens of this city haven't seen anything yet."

Richard's genuine fear sends a shiver through me.

"So what are you going to do?" I ask.

"I'll try to reason with my father," Victor says. "I've tried in the past, and been harshly punished for questioning him. He still doesn't believe the Thirst exists. He actually thinks it's just a myth, an urban legend spun out of control. If he won't listen this time, I'm prepared to take more drastic measures."

"Such as?"

"I'll ask him to step down."

I scoff. "You might as well ask him to fly to the moon. He'll never give up his throne."

"I don't expect him to," Victor says with regret. "But it's the proper thing to do, before the next step is taken."

I look at him, then back at Richard, seeing the pieces fall together.

"You can't be serious," I say. "Are you really prepared to battle your own father?"

"It's not my first choice, but in a lot of ways, I've been preparing my whole life."

"That's right," Richard says. "And I'll serve as Victor's witness, if that time comes."

When an Old Family vampire ascends the throne through challenging the clan leader, a witness from another family must verify that it was a fair fight. I don't envy Richard the job. Even if his friend were dying, all he could do would be watch. It's the way of the vampires.

"That's quite a burden," I say.

"It's an honor," Richard counters.

"He'll be doing me a great service," Victor says. "Most Old Family vampires refuse to become entangled in other families' affairs. After all, if you're a witness, that means you support the changing of the status quo. Without

Richard backing me, I couldn't do this."

"What if you just staked your father when no one was looking?" I ask. "I mean, who's to argue with you?"

"Every Valentine in the world. They'd all claim they were the rightful heirs. My father has two brothers; they each have several children, and each of them has even more. My uncles and cousins would be vying for control."

"But aren't you the obvious choice?"

"The head of the family is not based on a direct bloodline. It's all about power. With Richard backing me, there will be no question that *I* was the one who destroyed my father, and *I* am the one who will take his throne."

"As much as vampires work in the shadows," Richard says, "we never like to admit that. A witness makes things more *proper*, in our minds."

"What if someone can't find a witness?" I ask.

"Then all they can do is hope for the best. Kill the lord, and then everyone who gets in their way. It rarely works. Old Families don't like when vampires break code."

"If my father won't take the Thirst seriously," Victor says, "then I'll have no choice. I can't stand by and let the entire world face this monstrosity just because a few ancient vampires refuse to recognize its existence."

"Unfortunately, we have an additional problem," Richard says gravely. "I heard through the grapevine that your father contacted your brother a few months ago. Speculation is that he's here in the city. If that's the case, it could explain the attack on you tonight. He might have tipped off the Agency in an effort to get rid of you."

"Why didn't you tell me you had a brother?" I ask Victor.

"He's not really acknowledged. Father hated his other son, called him a bastard child, a freak of nature. I don't know why. He kept him locked up in another manor, far away from us. Eventually, he banished his own child before he was even a teenager. Why my father would reach out to him now, I have no idea. And whether it's tied to all of this, I don't know. But I can't imagine he's just making amends."

"What was his name?"

"I don't even know that. My father refused to speak about him. The only things I gathered were from information I pieced together over time: He was born after me, but he had some sort of mutation. Father wouldn't discuss it, but he blamed the boy's mother. Shortly after the imperfection was discovered, she was killed, I suspect by Valentine himself. My brother, after he was banished, spent his life wandering, never staying in one place for too long."

"So if you saw him, would you recognize him?"

"No. There aren't any paintings or photos of him. I never even met him. I think my father wanted Faith and me to be kept separate from the 'freak,' as he called him." As though unsettled by the direction of the conversation, Victor stands. "I'm going to take Dawn home."

Richard walks us to the door. "How's Faith?" he asks casually, as though it's not important, and yet I sense it is.

"Fine. She'll be on my side soon enough," Victor says.

"Does she ever talk about me?"

I hear the hope in Richard's voice.

"That must've been a hundred years ago," Victor says.

"Ninety-eight. She broke my heart, you know."

"Sorry, Richard, she never mentions you."

"Pity. I look forward to seeing you again, Dawn," Richard says. "You're as . . . intriguing as Victor implied."

I feel myself blush at his words. I follow Victor out, surprised to realize that I never felt at risk in that room, even though I was surrounded by four vampires.

Sometime later, we stop just shy of my building, and Victor cuts the engine on the motorcycle. We disembark and he rolls it behind some brush.

"I'm going up with you," he says. "I want to make sure you get into your apartment safely."

"I'll be fine once I get into the building."

"I'm not going to argue about this. I need to see that you're safe. As a matter of fact . . . it might be time to talk with Rachel, to make sure she has someone watching you at all times."

"What exactly are you thinking of telling her?" I ask.

"Everything. Maybe she'll know something about the attack at the theater tonight. But whatever is going on, I'm sure my father is behind it."

I know Victor's right, but I also know that I'm the one who will be left to deal with Rachel's anger and disappointment. And she *will* be mad when she learns that I've been hanging around not only with a vampire but with Valentine's son.

"Are you sure that's a smart move?" I ask as we walk up the steps to the front door.

"Guess we'll find out."

As we pass the guard, I ask after his family in an effort to distract him from studying Victor too closely. In the elevator, Victor and I are both staring at the numbers changing as we go up. It's the first time we've had a moment to just *be* since we kissed.

"What happened at the movie theater," he says quietly. "It won't happen again."

He's not talking about the attack. He's talking about the kiss.

"You're right," I say. "It—us—is a bad idea. I know that."

"In the next few nights, everything will change, Dawn."

"I know."

The elevator dings and I nearly jump out of my skin.

"Wait," Victor says, and he steps out and glances around the hallway. "Okay."

"What were you going to do if someone was here? Send me back down?" I ask. "Like I'd leave you to fight alone."

"You know, retreat is an honorable defensive maneuver," he says. "Live to fight another day."

"And how often have you retreated?"

He grins. "Never. But that doesn't mean you shouldn't."

Fumbling for my keys, I realize how nervous I am about introducing Victor to Rachel. My keys hit the floor. I bend down to pick them up and my head bumps against the door. It would be incredibly embarrassing, if the door didn't creak open.

"What the hell? We always lock it. . . ."

Before I can stand up, Victor kicks the door wide open with a thunderous noise. I can see straight through the open doors leading to the balcony, the moonlight streaming in, and someone perched on the rails, his hoodie pulled tight around his face. He gives us one look, then jumps.

Victor dashes through the apartment onto the balcony, stops at the railing, and peers down. I come in and flip the first light switch I can get my hand on. The apartment is destroyed. Nothing appears left undisturbed.

And then my gaze lands on a form crumpled beside the couch, blood pooling beneath her head.

"Oh my God! Rachel!"

Chapter 24

Gingerly, Victor lifts her onto the couch while I call for an ambulance. In spite of the vehicle and gasoline shortage, the Agency does make sure that emergency vehicles are available.

Rachel is so still, the gash on the back of her head an obscene crimson in direct contrast to her pale face.

As soon as I hang up with the paramedics, I call Jeff. He must have been nearby, because he beats the ambulance. He's almost as pale as Rachel as he kneels beside her and takes her limp hand. "What happened?"

"Someone broke into the apartment," I say.

"A vampire," Victor clarifies.

I tried to get him to leave before Jeff got here, but he wouldn't. He wouldn't even go into my bedroom to wait in secret.

Jeff looks up at him. "And who are you?"

"Victor."

"A Night Watchman," I say hastily. "We were out together. . . ." I don't want to explain, not now, not until we figure out what's going on. I don't want to put Jeff or Victor in danger.

"Thought you were at a study group." Jeff shakes his head. "Doesn't matter. All that matters is Rachel."

The paramedics arrive then. While they're tending to Rachel, Victor and Jeff flank me as I pore through the entire apartment. It's a disaster, but nothing obvious is missing.

"He was looking for something very specific," Victor says.

"I can't think of what. Any important Agency files are kept at the office, not here," I say.

"Maybe something personal, then," Victor muses. "Some vampires like to know more about who they're stalking before they strike."

A shiver travels up me. No telling what that creep was doing before we got here.

"Stalking?" Jeff asks. "A vamp's been stalking you and you didn't say anything?"

"I didn't know for sure. I saw this guy at school and later in the street. I figured it was just some idiot kid wanting to harass the delegate."

"So that was the guy you saw at school?" Victor asks.

"Yeah." The exact same hoodie with that snake design on the back.

The paramedics are placing Rachel on a stretcher. I

leave both guys behind and rush over. "Is she going to be okay?"

"Looks like she took quite a blow to the head. We can't get her to wake up," a tall, red-haired guy says. "We're taking her to the hospital so the doctors can run some tests. They'll have a better idea of what's going on then."

"I'm going with you."

"I don't think that's a good idea," Jeff says. "There are too many people there—it's too easy for a vampire to sneak in at this time of night. It might even be what your stalker wanted."

"I'll stay with Dawn here," Victor offers, picking up a framed picture of my parents and placing it back on the mantel. "It isn't safe for her to be alone with so much of the night left. You can go with Rachel."

"While I appreciate that," Jeff says, "I don't know you."

"I know him," I say. "I trust him with my life. I *have* trusted him with my life." I squeeze Jeff's hand. "You need to be with Rachel. I'll clean up here so that when she comes home, it'll all be okay."

Jeff nods, looks at Victor again. "A Night Watchman?"

I hear the doubt in his voice.

"Those four vampires killed around the trolley? My work," Victor says.

"Impressive." Jeff nods again and looks at me. "Okay. I'll call you when I know something. Lock up behind me."

He goes out the door. I close it, lock it, bolt it, and press my head to the wood. *Rachel, Rachel, Rachel, please be all right.*

Slowly I turn around. "What's going on, Victor?"

"I wish I knew."

With only two steps, he's wrapped his arms around me, holding me near, comforting me.

"She'll be all right," he whispers into my ear.

"You can't know that."

"And you can't know that she won't."

I lean my head back and look at him. I'm worried about another Valentine in Denver. "Do you think Lord Valentine sent Hoodie to tail me?"

"Possibly."

"Do you think he could be . . . your brother?"

"Son of a bitch," he whispers. He looks toward the balcony. "There was definitely something different about him. I can't explain it."

I can tell he's going into hunter mode.

"If you want to go after him, I understand," I tell him.

"No, I'm not leaving you. Not tonight. Tomorrow night, though, I'll see what I can find out." He touches the sleeve of my shirt. "You have some of Rachel's blood on you." He turns away. "You should probably get cleaned up. I'll take care of the blood in here."

I realize what immense control he has, not to have revealed his fangs while the scent of blood is on the air. For most vampires, it's an automatic response—scent blood, fangs drop.

I don't want to leave him, but I know he's right. I need to change. Otherwise I'll torment him.

When I walk into the bathroom, I immediately jump

at my reflection. It's shattered into a million pieces. The mirror was delivered a single strike to its center, the image forever distorted. My intruder wasn't looking for anything at all, just trying to destroy whatever was in front of him. Including Rachel.

After I clean up and change, I check my phone for messages from Jeff. Nothing. I'll assume no news is good news.

I go into the kitchen to survey the damage done there. If it was glass, he smashed it. He even tore off all the photos I had on the refrigerator hanging by little magnets. The childish drawing of my family is gone. It probably flew under the oven and will take forever to get out, which makes me angrier than any of the other destruction.

"I'm sorry," Victor says, righting a vase that had tipped over but miraculously didn't shatter. "I know this place won't feel the same."

"Why did he do all this?"

Before Victor can answer, my phone rings. It's Jeff.

"Hey," I say. "Give me some good news."

"She's in a coma." I hear the sorrow in his voice. "They don't know when she'll wake up. I'm going to stay with her tonight."

"I'm coming down there."

"No, I don't want you on the street at night. *Rachel* wouldn't want you on the street right now."

As though the apartment is any safer.

"Clive's here," he continues. "He's sending guards to stand watch at your door and around the apartment building. So just stay there."

I nod, realize he can't see me, and say, "Okay."

I hang up and tell Victor what's going on. "So you don't have to stay. I'll have protection."

"I'm not leaving," he insists.

In spite of the circumstances, I experience a fleeting moment of happiness before I turn to tackle the destruction that surrounds us. Victor and I spend the next hour straightening everything up. The entire time, he asks me questions about the things in the apartment, what they mean to me, why I have them. There's an intimacy to what we're doing, an unveiling. It's strange, yet comforting. Almost like we're a normal couple.

When we're finished, it's long after midnight and I'm exhausted.

"You should try to get some sleep," Victor says.

I'm almost too weary to nod. I start walking toward my bedroom, stop, and glance back at him. "I shouldn't ask, but will you hold me while I sleep?"

"For a while."

I'm too tired to even change clothes. I simply slip beneath the covers. Victor lies on top of them, but with his arms around me, it's enough.

The lights are out, but a little moonlight is coming in through the balcony doors. It creates a safe haven for the sharing of secrets.

"Tell me a story. It'll help me go to sleep," I say.

"Once upon a time—"

"No," I interject. "A real story. About you."

"Once upon a time—don't interrupt—there was a

vampire who wanted to touch the sun." He combs his fingers through my hair. "One night he was walking through an alley when he thought he caught a glimpse of the sun wrapped in shadow . . . only to discover it was a girl in need of rescuing. The first time he gazed into her blue eyes, he knew she had the power to destroy him. But he ignored the warnings, because she was the most beautiful creature he'd ever seen."

My breath is uneven. "But he must have seen a lot of girls in four hundred years."

"He had. But none of them appealed to him like she did."

"This vampire and this girl . . . do they get a happily ever after?"

"I don't know. I told you that vampires lack imagination. So I don't know how it ends."

Or maybe he's just too kind to tell me. Because he also told me that things between vampires and humans never end well.

Chapter 25

An hour before sunrise, Victor leaves. The theater wouldn't be safe, so I'm sure he sought refuge with Richard. He said that as soon as the sun set, he would be out trying to discover exactly what was going on, and how his father might be involved.

Surrounded by guards, I head to the hospital. I don't even know if Victor will be able to return to me tonight. I'm being watched as though I'm a precious jewel that the Agency is expecting some thief to snatch away.

Now I'm holding Rachel's hand, listening to the constant beeping of the monitors, a strange symphony of noise. Jeff is out meeting with Night Watchmen and other Agency personnel to see if they can figure out who this guy is. They sent a sketch artist over to work on a composite for the TV stations and newspaper, but all I could really provide was a description of the hoodie. I never saw the vamp's face.

The door swings open and Tegan rushes in, followed by Sin and Michael. Michael's gaze locks with mine, and quite honestly, I'm not sure whether I'm glad to see him. The harsh words we exchanged echo through my mind. So much has happened with Victor since then. I feel guilty, even though Michael was the one who pushed us apart.

"Oh my God! I can't believe it," Tegan says.

Earlier I texted her to let her know I wouldn't be at school and gave her a short version of what happened.

She wraps her arms around me and it feels so good. She leans back and studies me. "Was it that guy in the hoodie?" she asks.

I nod and glance back at Michael, but there's no satisfaction in my words. "I was right. He's a vampire."

"But you first saw him during the day. And it makes no sense," Michael continues. "He didn't drain her."

I was so grateful that she was alive, I didn't even think to question that. "We must have gotten home before he had a chance."

"*We?*" Michael asks.

"Victor and I."

His jaw clenches. "That Night Watchman?"

His attitude irritates and hurts me at the same time. "I don't know why you're mad. You're hanging around with Lila."

"I wasn't. I just . . ." He rubs his hand quickly back and forth over his short hair and looks at Sin, then Tegan.

"Could you guys leave us for a second?"

Sin studies me. "I'm sorry. About what happened."

The way he says it is odd. Like he was responsible.

"If I'd caught the guy the other evening—" he begins.

"It's not your fault," I say quickly. I'm carrying enough guilt for everyone. I should have told Rachel and Jeff about Hoodie, about my suspicions that he might have been a vampire.

"We'll go get you some coffee," Tegan says, pushing Sin toward the door. "Then we'll be back."

The door closes behind them, and Michael releases a deep breath before moving nearer to me. "Maybe I was a little jealous of Sin and Tegan. She never questions him."

"If that's what you want from me, Michael, I can't give it to you. I've lost too many people to sit idly by when I'm worried. I don't want anything to happen to you."

He takes my hand. "I'm sorry. I'm sorry for the way I've been acting. I promise . . . Lila . . . she means nothing to me."

I can't say the same about Victor, especially after everything that happened last night. But Michael is human. He'd never want my blood. He'd never be a monster.

I move into Michael's embrace and welcome his arms folding around me.

The door opens.

"Oh, good, you've made up," Tegan says.

I step away and smile self-consciously. Michael ducks his head, blushes. It's kinda cute.

Tegan hands me the coffee. "So when do they think Rachel will wake up?"

"They have no idea."

"You can stay with me."

"Thanks, but I'll be fine at the apartment. I have a whole pack of guards now."

"You won't be needing them for long," Sin says. "Come on, Michael. Let's see if we can find this creep."

"You don't need to do that. A lot of people are already searching for him," I say.

"We'll take care of him," Michael says, and I know his pride is at stake, so I push down my fear.

"I know you will. Just be careful."

He grins. "Always." Then he leans in and gives me a quick kiss on the lips before he and Sin leave.

With a sigh, Tegan slumps against the wall. "So is everything really going to be okay with you and Michael?"

"I hope so."

"Me, too, because Lila . . . ?" She sticks her finger in her mouth and makes a gagging sound. "Double-dating with her would be a drag."

I grin. "I can imagine."

The door opens and Clive strides in. Before I can even say hello, he's getting down to business. "We just got a message from Valentine. He wants a meeting tonight."

I tighten my jaw. "That's good. Because I want one, too."

That night I don't bother with the stupid Victorian dress. I fasten the chain-mail choker beneath the turtleneck collar of my blue sweater. I slip the stake Victor gave me into my boot. Not that I'd get a chance to use it against Valentine, but it makes me feel safer.

Winston raises his eyebrows at me when I emerge from my apartment building, but all he says is, "Good evening, Miss Montgomery," as he helps me climb into the carriage.

The ride gives me time to think, to put things in order. Victor and Michael, and Rachel. I try to stack them up, make sense of them. But when I arrive at the manor, all of that leaves me.

I march up the steps and bang the knocker. When the servant opens the door, his eyes widen. The way Valentine holds on to the past, it's possible he's never seen a girl in jeans before.

I step inside, but he seems frozen to the spot.

"I'm sure you don't want to keep his lordship waiting," I say.

"Of course not. Follow me, please."

I follow him to the same room. He opens the double doors. "Miss Montgomery, m'lord."

I stride into the room. Valentine slowly sets down his goblet, but unlike his servant, he's not surprised. He's angry.

I'm in no mood for pleasantries. "My mentor, Rachel, was attacked by a vampire. In our apartment. In the city. Are you going to tell me he was a rogue vampire, one you have no control over?"

"You are not properly dressed for a meeting."

"Lord Valentine, now is not the time for games."

"Really, Dawn? I believe they've only begun. Sit."

I'd rather pace, but I drop down into my usual chair.

"Rachel is in a coma."

He picks up his goblet. "She is not my concern."

"VampHu prohibits vampires from coming into walled cities."

"One vampire—"

"It's more than one, and you know it," I snap.

"Watch your manners, child. It is only through my grace that you leave here."

I rein in my temper. He's impossible to deal with. I don't know why I thought I could make him understand that he is responsible for what happened to Rachel. He's responsible for every human who is harmed by a vampire in Denver. It's time for a new approach. Maybe I can use what he wants to reach a bargain.

I can see through the windows that a storm is brewing in the distance, flashes of lightning in far-off clouds. The countryside is bathed in black and blue. Within this huge mansion are inner rooms that the sunlight can't touch, where Valentine remains during the day, but he obviously likes being able to see the night. And why not? He is its king.

"You requested the meeting," I remind him.

"Yes." Valentine swirls his goblet of blood. He seems larger than before, as if he's fed off the night and grown, preparing for his son's rebellion. I remind myself that Victor doesn't want violence, that he'll ask his father to take the Thirst seriously or step down. But looking at this ancient vampire, I realize that seems ever more impossible. Valentine doesn't listen to reason, and he will cede control only when he's no longer breathing. God, how could Victor ever hope to defeat someone as powerful as the Bloody Valentine? An image flashes in my mind: Victor with a stake through his heart, having failed against his father.

Focus. Don't give anything away.

"You should have seen an increase in the amount of blood that was delivered last Friday," I say. The Teen Initiative is making a difference. "And even more so when we deliver this week's allotment. Not double, but we're getting there."

"That's fine," Valentine says, uninterested.

The roaring fire crackles, hitting a weak spot in the wood, and it spits out new light, revealing the lord's face, so comfortable in shadow. Valentine's looking straight into my eyes for the first time. He's reading me. I see it for only a moment, but the feeling seems to last forever.

This revelation takes me by surprise, and I wait for something: for him to speak, for me to, for Victor to rush in and challenge his father. The silence is drawing out, and I don't know what to do. . . .

Then I get control of myself. I've been trained to negotiate. I've been trained to read subtle nuances in vampire body language. What the Agency didn't teach me, my parents instilled in me. I know it's risky, but I'm tired of being afraid. "Does your son enjoy the city?"

He releases a low chuckle. "Victor—"

"Not Victor," I interrupt, knowing it's poor etiquette, but not really caring. "Your other son. The one the Agency doesn't know about."

His gaze hardens. "And yet you seem to know about him."

"It's my job to know everything about you. And even if it wasn't, I would want to know. Someone of your influence and power fascinates me." Vampires use seduction to gain what they want. Maybe I can do the same. Stroke his ego. Lure him into revealing things he wouldn't otherwise.

"That child is banished and forgotten," Valentine says. "His name unspoken for over a hundred years. And it shall remain that way. Forever."

"I see. . . ."

Valentine grows momentarily angry, but then a wicked smile begins to form.

"I assume Victor told you about him."

"I have various sources of information."

"There's no need to lie," he says, nearly chuckling. "In fact, Victor is what I wish to speak about. He fascinates you, doesn't he? I saw it the moment he stepped into this room not long ago. Your eyes refused to leave his, despite my presence." Before I can answer, he continues. "I do worry about him, though. Victor gets these *ideas* in his head." He's speaking slowly and deliberately.

"Ideas, m'lord?" I ask, playing along, trying to stall until I find a way out of this.

"Victor's still a boy in many ways. Always wanting what he can't have. Always thinking he knows best."

"I'm sure, in time, he'll find his way."

"Have you found your way, Dawn? You are the first to stand up to me so brazenly. Now I must decide if that makes you an asset or a threat."

It seems as if the fire has stopped making noise, and the moon's covered by clouds. I think the world's gone silent and dark, and it's just me and the Bloody Valentine and this dance of words.

"I'm a delegate. And I'm very happy serving the city of Denver."

He considers this, swirling his drink before downing it all in one massive gulp.

"I've spent a thousand years reading humans and their lies. Every human lies the same way, and always for the same reason. They lie out of fear of what will happen if the truth is discovered."

My truth will cost me everything, and he knows it. This isn't some scare tactic to get more blood from the Agency; nor is it something to keep me in line. Valentine knows Victor is up to something; he might even know more than that. He might know *everything*. He's an Old Family vampire; he has eyes and ears everywhere. He's avoided the stake for a thousand years by being cautious, by looking behind every shadow and every curtain.

"How often do you see Victor?" Valentine asks.

I can't lie to him. I'm not that good. But maybe . . . maybe I can bend the truth just enough.

"I've seen him only a handful of times."

"And what does he say to you?"

"Nothing of interest."

"Everything is of interest to me, Dawn." This is spoken so quickly that I think this entire conversation has been mapped out, as if he got the script before I did. He knows every twist and turn I'll try to make.

"We speak of the blood supply and other matters concerning the citizens of the city," I say.

"What could he possibly care about the lives of humans?"

"He merely wants to ensure a steady supply of blood to the countryside."

Valentine lets out a small chuckle. "You make him sound soft."

"No, Lord, I didn't mean—"

"Do you think that's what I *wanted* to hear? Are you telling me the truth, Dawn? Or are you humoring me?"

"I have no reason to lie to you, Lord Valentine."

"You have every reason to lie to me. Because I already know the truth, and I know why you're so scared of it. I can hear your heart beating, Dawn. It's faster than it was two minutes ago. I can hear the blood pumping through your veins, faster and faster, even as I speak these words."

I release the breath I've been holding, and it's staggered and choked. Valentine chuckles at that, too.

I fear I've seen my last sunrise when Valentine stands up. He's enormous. I've never seen him out of his chair. What Victor yields in silent power, his father commands in awesome presence. One look at the Bloody Valentine and I hear the screams of millions.

He walks over to me, every step unnervingly quiet. I stay seated, facing forward, like a good schoolgirl, but all the while I'm debating when to make my move. I'm not going to go down easily, not without a fight, not without making him regret he ever set eyes on me. All I have to do is reach inside my boot and grab my stake. He stands behind my chair, and when he speaks his voice vibrates through my chest like a grand orchestra.

"I can make dreams come true, Dawn. I can give you every piece of gold, every suitor, and every star in the sky. You will never want for anything. Servants will tend to your every need. I can make your life an endless ecstasy."

He reaches around me, and his large fingers slowly brush my jawline and run down to the metal collar around my neck.

"I can give you immortality. I can give you eternal beauty, eternal life. I can give you everything you've ever wanted."

He cups my chin like I am a tiny doll.

"I can also make your nightmares come true. You cannot begin to fathom the suffering I am capable of delivering. Not only to you, but to everyone you've ever touched. Rachel. Tegan. Jeff. Michael. I can give them immortality, just to torture them for eternity."

He withdraws his hands, and the only thing I see is the coming storm through the window.

"But there is no need for unpleasantness between us. You just have to acknowledge that your loyalty lies with me, that you and the people of Denver stand to gain the greatest benefit by bowing before me. I know Victor can be very convincing when he gets caught up in his grand dreams. He's had hundreds of years of practice in luring young girls into falling into his hands. But he hasn't been the same since the war. It warped his mind. His dreams will lead only to nightmares."

Another drawn-out silence, a calculated one in which Valentine lets me absorb everything he's said. The dangers of staying quiet, the rewards of exposing Victor's plan. I focus on steadying my pulse.

"So, Dawn . . . what does my son speak to you about?"

I say it before my next heartbeat. "Nothing of interest, sir."

I brace for his massive hands to reach down and strangle me, snapping my neck, or for his fangs to penetrate my skin. But they don't come.

Valentine takes his seat again, and when I finally look over, his eyes are covered in shadow and the entire moment seems like it never happened.

"I believe we are finished for the evening, Miss Montgomery."

"Very well, m'lord."

With as much dignity as possible, I rise and stride from the room.

When I get to my apartment I strip off my clothes, nearly ripping them in two. Then I take the hottest shower of my life. I scrub hard to get Valentine's touch off me. I shudder, thinking about it, and how unsettling his closeness was. I'd grown overconfident, thinking I could play him, could get information from him. Who am I, with only seventeen years of life, to compete with someone who has had more than a thousand?

When I step out of my bathroom wearing flannel pants and a tank top, I discover Victor standing by my bed. The next thing I know his arms are around me, holding me close. I'm inhaling his scent, feeling his warmth.

"I just heard," he says, his voice deep with concern. "I didn't think you were seeing my father until this Sunday, that I'd have a chance to confront him before you ever had to meet with him again."

"He requested that I come out tonight. I thought I could play his game, Victor, but I'm a novice and he's a master. I've never been so scared."

Victor threads his fingers through my hair and tilts my head back so he can gaze deeply into my eyes. "Did he hurt you?"

"No," I reassure him. "No. But he knows you're up to something."

"Are you sure?"

"Yes, I'm sure!" Breaking free, I begin pacing the room. I tell him everything, even the offer Valentine made me to betray Victor.

Victor sits on the bed, a worried scowl on his handsome face. "I'm almost positive he's responsible for the Night Watchmen who attacked us at the theater. Somehow he must have figured out where I was, given them my location."

"You're his son. You think he would try to kill you?"

"If he saw me as a threat—no question." He looks up,

meets my gaze. "We're a bloodthirsty breed, Dawn. My father rules the council that is made up of the heads of the Old Families. It's not because of his impeccable manners."

A chill goes through me. "So what are you going to do?" I ask.

Victor stands up. "I shouldn't be here. I've put you in danger."

I take a step toward him. "No, no. Your father did that when he insisted that I become the delegate."

Reaching out, he trails his fingers along my cheek. "You're the bravest person I've ever known."

It's a cheesy line, but I can't help blushing a little.

"Anyone else would've given me up," he says.

I stare into Victor's eyes and see all the things worth fighting for. A better world for vampires and humans. That's why I didn't give him up.

And maybe another reason motivated me. An emotion I don't want to acknowledge.

"You avoided my question," I remind him. "What are you going to do?"

"Finish our preparations. Confront him tomorrow night."

"I want to go with you."

"No. This is vampire business, Dawn. If you're there, I'm likely to be distracted. I can't afford to show any weakness."

I don't like it, but I understand. "Get word to me as soon as you can, so I know you're okay."

He gives me the smile that I've come to cherish, the one that reveals what's in his heart.

A knocking on the front door startles me.

"Dawn! Dawn!"

And just like that, reality is crashing back in on me, and I know that what I have with Victor would never last.

"It's Michael," I say. "He's going to stay with me tonight. He and I . . . we're . . ." I drop my gaze to the floor. This is so hard. "He's—"

"Human."

With tears stinging my eyes, I lift my gaze to his and nod. "I guess I'm not so brave after all."

He gives me a sad smile. "I've never known a vampire-human relationship that didn't end in tragedy. You're wise to choose Michael."

He turns for the balcony, and I think my heart might shatter.

"Victor, if there's anything I can do to help you in your fight to overthrow your father—"

"You already have, Dawn. You've given me hope that vampires and humans can work together."

He disappears through the balcony doors. I don't follow to make sure he's gone. Instead I rush into the living room just as Michael is crashing through the door, the two bodyguards behind him. I guess Jeff neglected to give them a key.

"What the hell took you so long to answer?" he demands to know.

"Sorry. I was in the shower."

He studies me intently. "You look like you've been crying."

"No. I just got some soap in my eyes."

Looking slightly embarrassed, he glances back at the shattered lock. "Sorry about that."

I release a small laugh. "That's okay. Better to be safe than sorry."

Pulling me into his arms, he holds me tightly and rocks me back and forth. "I never want anything to happen to you."

"The same goes for you."

And I also hope that nothing happens to Victor.

Chapter 26

At school Michael holds my hand as we walk along the hallways. Whenever we pass Lila, she gives me the evil eye, which I ignore. Any other time I might relish those glares from her, but today I'm distracted. I'm thinking about Victor and what will happen tonight. I'm the only human who knows we're on the cusp of a change. . . .

I don't want to think about how it could all end very badly. I have faith in Victor. He will overthrow his father. Life for humans and vampires will get better.

After school, Tegan goes to the hospital with me. Walking into Rachel's room, I see Jeff sitting in the chair, holding her hand. I feel my chest trying to cave, collapsing from the knowledge that I'm responsible for this.

Jeff gets to his feet. "Hey."

He always seemed so tough. Now he looks so vulnerable.

"No change?" I ask.

"None."

I move closer to the bed. Rachel's eyes are closed. I brush her hair aside, wishing her sweet dreams.

"I'm going to get some coffee," Jeff says. "I'll give you some time alone."

But I'm not completely alone after he leaves, since Tegan stays. She takes my hand, squeezes it. "She's gonna be okay."

"Yeah." I lean down and whisper near Rachel's ear, "I'm so sorry, Rachel. If you can hear me, I'm so sorry."

"'Kay."

I release a tiny screech. Tegan jumps back so fast and hard that she nearly takes my arm off with her. I work my hand out of her grasp and shove her toward the door. "Get a doctor or a nurse. Get Jeff."

Then my attention is back on Rachel. Her eyes are fluttering open.

"Rachel?"

She gives a little moan. "What happened?"

"What do you remember?"

"Guy. With a hoodie. Didn't really see him. Came up behind me. I turned. Then lights-out." A corner of her mouth quirks up. "Dreamed Jeff said he loved me."

"Probably not a dream. When he's not working, he's been here."

A doctor and a couple of nurses are suddenly rushing into the room and pushing me out. Jeff and Tegan are racing down the hallway to me.

"Did she really wake up?" Jeff asks.

"Yes. She didn't get a good look at her attacker."

"But she's going to be okay?"

I grin so broadly that my jaw aches. "I think so."

From the balcony, I watch the sun set. I have hope that a time will soon come when it won't signal that the monsters are coming out to play. Maybe I'm too optimistic, but it feels good after so long to have hope.

Michael has an all-night training session. Otherwise he'd be here. I keep the TV turned on, just to have some sound. Rachel will remain in the hospital for another couple of days.

After night descends, I wander back into the living room. My nerves are on edge as I pace. I'm having a difficult time concentrating. I'm wondering when I'll hear from Victor. Tonight? Tomorrow? I'm so tempted to tell Clive that I need to get out there to talk to Valentine about the blood supply, that we had unfinished business from the previous night that *must* be seen to. Any excuse. But I know Victor is right: I'll be more hindrance than help. It's just that waiting is so damned hard.

I hear a knock on the door. Looking through the peephole, I feel my heart jump at the sight of two perfectly dressed strangers. Black suits, long hair tied back, pale skin. They each wear matching lapel pins: a wolf's head in front of a giant V. They're from Valentine.

And they're vampires.

"Dawn Montgomery," one of them calls through

the door. "The great Lord has requested your presence. Immediately."

I really need to learn to watch what I wish for.

I open the door to find my two guards sprawled on the floor. "They'd better not be dead."

"Only sleeping. They'll be fine as long as you come along with us and cause no trouble," the larger one who is obviously in charge replies.

"I have to get dressed," I say.

"There's no need. Or time."

"What is this all about?" I ask.

"We're to bring you to the manor. Everything will be explained there."

What choice do I have? Worse is the knowledge that Victor didn't send them. He wouldn't have left me worrying. He would have had them tell me that Lord Victor Valentine requested my presence. So did Victor confront his father and lose? Or has the confrontation not yet taken place?

"Let me get my things," I say, striving to give the appearance of calm.

"You have all you need." He takes my arm, ending the discussion and confirming my suspicion that Victor didn't send them. He'd never put up with their treating me like this.

They escort me out of the building. A black carriage is waiting for me. It's more luxurious than the one Winston drives, pulled by a team of six horses, each one large and jet-black, as if possessed by a demon and given supernatural strength. The front-desk guard must assume this is simply delegate business as usual, and I try to act natural to perpetuate that belief. Otherwise they might harm him.

The smaller vampire gets into the driver's seat, while the other one assists me into the coach. The inside is much more glamorous than the one I'm used to. With thick red velvet seats, and tiny oil lamps hanging by the windows, it's actually incredibly comfortable. A small cabinet to the left houses wine and glasses, and a bottle of what can only be blood.

The other vampire sits across from me as we begin the journey out of the city. The ride, as I expected, is smooth, like we're gliding on air. I pull out my cell phone to call Clive, or at least Jeff, and let them know what's going on. But as soon as the phone is in my hand, the vampire snatches it from me.

"Hey!" I say, losing all my trained etiquette.

The vampire returns my look with a deadly stare of his own.

"There will be no need for calls," he says. He looks at the device with a certain amount of disgust, marking him as an older vampire.

"Very well," I say. "I will expect my phone back in my hand when I leave the mansion." My manners return in stellar form.

"Of course. *When* you leave."

His tone sends a chill through me.

When we arrive, the vampire in charge escorts me into the house and down an unfamiliar hallway. He stops outside an open door. I peer into the room.

"I'm so glad you could make it tonight, Miss Montgomery."

The Bloody Valentine's voice echoes in the space. I slowly turn my head to the right and see the monster vampire standing on the far side of the room, staring up at a huge painting. He's wearing his full formal attire.

"Please come in," he says.

Despite my fear, I obey. Any other choice is just an illusion.

The room I step into is the strangest I've ever seen. It's an art gallery, small, but at least three stories high. Paintings decorate every inch of space. Big ones, small ones, gorgeous ones and ugly ones. Pencils and pastels. Charcoal and oil. Landscapes and portraits. Hundreds of years of human art swirling upward around me.

"I hate this room," Valentine says, moving from one wall to another. "It's the only place that makes me despise what I am. Not one artist has ever been a vampire. At least, not a good one. We simply can't see the beauty in a hummingbird, or a tree, or especially a rising sun. I don't know why, but we see things so differently."

"I'm sure it's—"

"Don't speak," he says, with a flash of anger I've never seen. It's uncontrolled, a rage just below the surface.

Fear such as I've never known ignites within me. The only reason I don't panic is because I envision Victor storming through the door to rescue me.

"This one is my favorite," Lord Valentine continues

calmly, walking over to a portrait of a young girl. The black background contrasts with her porcelain face. She's beautiful. "Seventeenth-century painting of a servant girl. When I saw this, I demanded the artist take me to her. I was looking for a new companion." Valentine slowly caresses the painting with his massive hands. "When I found her, she was old and ugly. I told her I could have kept her beautiful forever. Do you know what she said to me? 'All is vanity.'"

Valentine shoves his fingers into the painting and rips them downward, tearing the canvas apart. The beautiful girl becomes shredded, dangling down from the frame in pieces.

Silence fills the room until he finally says, "You're not quite as bold as you were before."

I try to respond, but my throat is knotted by the fear that he's completely lost his mind.

"I didn't bring you out here to look at paintings." Valentine pauses. "Every few decades, the Valentine family has a small reunion. My brothers join me here at the manor. And during these reunions, we are each allowed to bring a guest. I've always feared large numbers; one can never know who one can trust in a crowd like that. And trust is an important thing, wouldn't you say, Dawn?"

"Very important, m'lord."

"I'm glad we agree. Because I've decided to trust you, Dawn. So much so that I've brought *you* as my guest."

"M'lord?"

"Yes, I know, a bit unconventional. A human has never been allowed into my inner sanctum quite like this, but I felt that your presence would be welcomed. I hope you'll accept. Everyone is already here; they're waiting for us upstairs."

I swallow hard. Once again, any other choice is just an illusion.

"I would be honored," I say, clinging to formality in the hopes that it will remind him of my delegate status. Hoping, too, that my presence won't be welcomed as dinner.

Valentine gives me a broad smile, and I see his fangs, each one massive in size, glistening.

"Then let's not keep our guests waiting."

He walks toward me, grabs my arm like a vise, and leads me down the hall. And I know by his touch that I'm not his guest; I'm his hostage.

I'm afraid he's not taking me to dinner after all. That he's hauling me into a room to show me Victor's battered and beaten body. That he's going to demonstrate the folly of not giving him total loyalty.

We go up a flight of marbled stairs, down another corridor, and face gigantic double doors. He places one hand on the handle.

"I gave you a chance, Dawn," Valentine says, his grip threatening to break my arm. "I could've given you the earth, the stars, and everything in between. Now you will pay for choosing Victor over me."

He opens the door and shoves me in violently.

The room is cold and dark, lit with just a few poorly placed gas lamps giving off their yellow glow across the stone walls. In the middle is a large, ornate table, thick with aged wood. I immediately recognize one of the four sitting at it.

"Dawn!" Victor shouts, surging to his feet.

I want to rush over to him, because I'm so glad he's alive. But Valentine is beside me, and I'm still very much under his control. Even when he isn't holding me, his vampire speed makes me just as vulnerable as if his hands were already wrapped around my neck.

"Miss Montgomery, I don't believe you've met my brothers, Ransom"—a vampire who very much resembles Valentine stands and bows—"and Seymour." The other male gets to his feet. He's bloated with excess, and I don't want to think about how much human blood it took to get him to that grotesque state. An air of entitlement rolls off both of them in waves. While etiquette demands that they stand until I'm seated, they both return to their chairs, their expressions of disgust telling me that to them I'm nothing beyond a source of blood.

"My daughter, Faith."

She looks to be nearly my age. To say she's beautiful would be like saying the sun glows a tad. I've never seen one before—an Old Family female. Their rarity is reflected in their beauty, as if a huge amount were divided among the very few of them. She has perfect skin, fiery red hair, and an hourglass figure. Her eyes are the same sharp blue as Victor's, but they look more seductive, if that were possible. Her red dress hugs every curve.

She does little more than wiggle her fingers at me,

seemingly bored with my sudden entrance into this room.

"And I believe you've met Richard Carrollton."

I wonder how he knows it. If Richard is wondering the same thing it doesn't show on his face as he steps out of the shadows.

Theatrically, Valentine says, "And allow me to introduce to all of you Dawn Montgomery, delegate, coconspirator, traitor. Curtsy, Dawn."

I don't. I stand there with my shoulders back, my spine straight. I hold Victor's gaze, trying to convince him I'm not afraid, even though my knees are trembling.

"Curtsy!" Valentine shouts, his booming voice echoing off the walls.

Victor gives me a brusque nod. So I do what Valentine asks. I pretend to be meek. I curtsy and say, in my best delegate voice, "It's a pleasure."

Valentine chuckles darkly. "Oh, what games we all play. I know my son tried his hardest not to involve you tonight. And for good reason. He doesn't want you to witness his actions at this final moment."

"This has nothing to do with her," Victor says, taking a step forward.

"It has *everything* to do with her!" Valentine yells. "She had a choice regarding whose side to join: mine or yours. She chose you. That makes her just as guilty as you. Who else? Stand up now! Who else has sided with this bastard son of mine?"

Faith rises, a cool confidence imbuing the move.

"My own daughter," Valentine says, a steely anger in

his voice. "I should have known. You're as disloyal as your mother. Who else?"

Richard steps forward.

"Of course," Valentine says. "When Faith brought you as her guest, I thought it was a joke. Now I see the real purpose. My brothers? Whose side do you stand on?"

Valentine's brothers remain seated, but unlike Faith, they definitely do not give the appearance of being bored. I can see them calculating what all this means to them and how they can best profit by it.

"So this is it?" Valentine says. "Your grand plan to overthrow me?"

"You've gone mad," Victor says. "You no longer reign over the vampires; your own bloodlust rules you while the Lessers starve. When we turned them, we had an obligation to provide for them. Now the Thirst is sweeping east, heading straight for us."

"Ha! The Thirst. An urban legend, believed only by stupid children like yourself."

"It's real! And if you refuse to act against it, I will be forced to act in your stead."

"You may have tricked Dawn into thinking you're something you're not." Valentine's anger flares in his eyes, his fangs slowly extending. "But I've known you for four hundred years. And someday soon, she'll see what you truly are. They always do."

"You're casting around smoke and mirrors, Father, to distract us from the real issue," Victor says. "It is time for you to step down as head of the family."

"Never. Not as long as I draw breath. This is my empire! Forged by my hands. You have no idea what it takes to rule, what I have already set in motion."

"I know you're using my brother to do it."

Valentine chuckles. "I always thought him an aberration, but he is what you are not. Loyal. And he possesses a beautiful evil. More cunning than you could ever hope to be."

I hear the pride in his voice, and it sends a shiver through me. Is that the family trait Valentine would be most proud of passing down the line? Wickedness?

"Destroy me and you will unleash him," Valentine says. "And then it will be as if you released hell itself."

Victor removes a stake from his belt. It's long and metal, perfectly suited for a single, deadly strike to the heart. "You've left me with no choice."

"Make one move and I'll bring an end to your precious Dawn's life," Valentine says, with a finality that stills any movement in the room. Now I see why I'm here. A poker chip. Leverage. Valentine's last hope. "I can snap her neck before you reach me."

"I'll put a stake in your heart before you get to her," Victor says.

"You underestimate me, child. I may be old, but with age comes power."

"She doesn't mean anything to me," Victor says.

I ignore the sting of his words and concentrate instead on his purpose in saying them. He's trying to remove me from harm's way, trying to convince Valentine that I'm useless as a poker chip.

The ancient vampire merely laughs. "Nothing? Nothing at all? Then you won't mind when your brother turns her into what she was always meant to be."

"She's just a human."

"You're wrong. She is so much more."

"She's just a vessel for blood. . . ."

Valentine backhands me across my face. The force sends the world black for a moment, and I fall to the floor as his laugh reverberates through the chamber.

I try to stand up, but the strength of the blow has made me dizzy. Still, I'm able to see Victor's reaction. I've never seen so much hatred on anyone's face. All of it is focused on his father.

"That's right," Valentine says. "Give freedom to your rage. If we're going to fight, I want it to mean more than who takes the throne. I want to know that I raised a son who's willing to kill his father, just as I killed mine."

Valentine pulls a stake from behind his coat.

Richard withdraws his own and looks at Valentine's brothers. "Try to help, and I'll put this through your chest. Understood?"

Father and son are in place. The witness is accounted for. All the pieces are in play. The future of the city, of the Valentine family, of my life, will be decided in the coming seconds. But more, Victor's future will be decided, and in that moment I realize as never before that I want him to have a future. I don't want him to die. And not just because he's the better of the two. But because I care about him more than I realized—with every fiber of my being.

I don't know what happens next; the two Valentines move too fast for human eyes to catch. It's nothing but blurs and grunts, them stopping in frame for one second, only to continue on. The entire scene plays out as though lit by a strobe light, quick flashes of still life: Victor with his stake in hand; Valentine dodging it; Victor chasing; Valentine feinting.

I'm frozen in fear. It could end at any moment, with Victor falling to the floor, dead. Regrets slam into me. There is so much I never told him. How much I admire about him: the way he watches over the vampires in the city. The way he watched over me. How much I want the world he envisions: vampires and humans working together.

It's difficult to believe that a short while ago I would have celebrated his death. One fewer vampire in the world. Now I would grieve with the same fierceness that I mourned the loss of my parents and my brother.

I want to help Victor, but I know the best way to do that is to stay as still as possible, not to be a distraction. All his energy and focus have to be on defeating Valentine.

I glance over at the other vampires. They have no problem translating the rapid movements before them. Valentine's brothers are smiling, their eyes gleaming at the violence they're witnessing, even thriving on it.

But Richard is more concerned, studying every sharp movement. His eyes dart back and forth, following as his best friend fights for his life.

I see a flash of Victor's blue suit, and I've never wanted

anything more than for him to win.

Please. Please, Victor. I know you can do this.

Suddenly everything stills. Except for heavy breathing, silence descends. Everyone is held captive by the sight in front of us. On the floor, the monstrous Valentine huddles over his smaller son. Both as motionless as statues. Unable to breathe. Unable to move.

Then Valentine's body slumps over and falls to the floor. Victor's stake is buried deeply in his father's chest. The Bloody Valentine's heart beats no more. That tiny spot of darkness in the world seems to have been made bright for now.

I see Victor's chest rise and fall with the rhythm of his breaths, deep and full. I want to hold him, but I'm scared that he has too much anger still, too much ferocity. He needs a moment's pause. Slowly he brings himself to his feet, standing tall.

I can see the determination in his eyes. I was right. This isn't over.

"After my uncles have seen to Father, take them to the dungeon," he says in a forceful voice that leaves no room for argument.

"You can't—" one begins, but he cuts him off.

"You are either with me or with my father. Both paths have consequences. The funeral will be at dawn. At that time you can give me your answer."

His uncles struggle to carry the behemoth that was Valentine, as Richard and Faith escort them from the room. I'm glad. I'm glad that it's finally just Victor and me.

"Victor," I say.

A moment passes before he turns toward me. There aren't tears in his eyes, but an infinite sadness that is even deeper.

I can't stand the distance any longer. I cross over to him, reach up, cradle his face, and tilt his head toward me so he looks me in the eyes. He needs to see me. He needs to know that I'm here for him. What he did . . . it doesn't change what he is. But it has changed what I feel for him. From the moment we met, he's tried to show me that he's not a monster. Tonight he proved it. He didn't want to kill his father. He was forced into the confrontation.

I could have lost him and he'd never have known that I'd fallen for him. Hard. My feelings snuck up on me, one kindness, one revelation at a time. The vampires took everything from me, but I'm looking into the eyes of one who has the power to give me back a reason to live, who can heal my gaping hole of sorrow.

I don't know how to put any of that into words. So I just wrap my arms around him, welcome his arms coming around me. Then he pulls me in tighter, and I end up being the one to shed tears.

"I thought I was going to lose you," I whisper. "Victor, I was so scared that I was going to lose you."

"You'll never lose me, Dawn. Since I met you, for the first time in my life, I truly understand what I'm fighting for. You are every sunrise that I will never see."

He lifts my chin and lowers his mouth to mine. The kiss is so gentle, made sweeter by the knowledge that we've both survived. That we're on the cusp of a change. My heart swells with emotions I don't quite understand. They're almost frightening in their intensity. For the first time, I don't think of Victor as a vampire, but simply as someone I love. Our tongues dance together and I press myself nearer, wondering if I'll ever be able to get as close to him as I want, as I need.

For this one moment, he is all that matters.

Chapter 27

I feel something warm and wet seeping through my sweater, just below where my heart is thudding. Pulling back, I glance down. Victor's blue shirt is glistening, soaked in blood.

"Victor, you're hurt."

His hold on me weakens and he stumbles back a step. "My father was right. I underestimated him."

"What do you need? Tell me and I'll do it."

"I need to rest, that's all. Help me to my bedroom; it isn't far."

But his wound is worse than he let on, and it quickly drains his strength. We struggle laboriously to climb a flight of stairs. When we reach the top, he groans as though the last step was almost too much. With me holding him up, he staggers to a large wooden door. I turn the knob and shove the door open with enough force to cause it to slam against the wall. His bedroom. The only thing I notice is how dark it is. I make out the large four-poster bed and help him stretch out on it.

"Don't die on me," I urge. "I think I'm finally glad you're in my life."

"It's not as bad as it looks."

I turn on the gas lamp next to the bed, giving me a better view of how the wound's progressed. The blood seeps from the open gash. I rip off a section of the sheet and press it against his side. "You're in agony. You need blood, Victor."

And the only blood here is mine.

"I'll be fine, Dawn. I just need to rest."

I sit on the edge of the bed. "What can I do?"

"You've already done it. Just by staying with me. Tonight you've seen vampires for what we are: violent, bloodthirsty creatures of the night. I killed my own father, just as he killed his. Bloody hands run through our family. No matter what I do, they'll never be clean."

"You're not like him."

"You once assured me I was. What if you're right?"

"I wasn't. Not then. I am now. You're not like him. I saw that tonight." I shake my head. "No, I knew it long before tonight. What I feel for you . . . it's almost frightening."

"My father made a mistake in bringing you here tonight. He thought your presence would distract me, but it made me realize I would gladly sacrifice my immortality for you." He touches my cheek and then skims his fingers along my throat. "You will be in my life such a short time, but it will be worth it."

"Lounging around already, brother?" Faith asks.

I jump back as though I were caught doing something wrong.

Faith glides over to the bed, Richard at her side.

"He's been hurt," I say, stunned by how uncaring she acts.

Faith glances at the wound in Victor's side. "Nothing a little blood won't cure," she says, and her eyes move toward me. Her fangs come out just a little as she laughs softly. Then she inhales deeply, and her eyes grow hungry. "A-negative. It goes so well with steak."

"Faith," Victor warns.

"You're right. O-negative is better. It goes with anything."

"Enough." Victor's tone is firm, and I realize he has stepped fully into Valentine's shoes. He is the new lord and ruler. "Are our uncles settled?"

Richard leans against one of the bedposts. "Coffins nailed shut."

My eyes widen in disbelief.

"He's trying to be witty," Faith explains, rolling her eyes.

"You like my wit," Richard says.

"Not really." She spins on her heel and heads for the door. "Come on, Dawn. Let's see if we can find you something to wear."

"Why?" I ask.

"Not very observant, are you?"

I follow her gaze to the blood on my sweater. I look back at Victor one more time to make sure he's okay.

"Go with her," he urges. "I need to talk with Richard. After you've changed, Faith will show you to a bedroom so you can get some sleep. I know it's been a very trying night for everyone."

"All right."

Outside the room, Faith gives me the once-over. I know what she sees. I'm shorter than she is, not as voluptuous. "Probably a skirt with a stretchy waist would be best," she says.

Not to mention stretchy hips. And a top whose limits wouldn't be tested as much as they are when she wears it.

She leads me down the hallway to a bedroom that is seduction painted on four walls. Red in every shade imaginable fills the entire place. She crosses over to a double set of doors and flings them open dramatically to reveal a walk-in closet that's larger than my bedroom.

"Oh my God." I stare in amazement.

"I know, it's pathetic. My big closet is in Europe," she says as she wanders inside, touching silks, satins, cottons. "I admit, clothes are my sin, and I've had quite a few years to collect them."

"How many, exactly?"

She grabs a hanger. "Hmm. Nearly two hundred." She tosses a silky flowing skirt my way. "That should work."

Before it hits the floor I snatch it and run my hands over it. The material is incredibly soft, satin against my fingers.

She collects a couple of tops and a few other things. "Come on."

I follow her into a marble bathroom, where the red motif continues. Even the marble is red.

"Vampire blood is hell to get out. Just throw your clothes in the corner and I'll burn them."

She leaves me alone. I'm surprised to discover running water that's actually warm. Maybe they have a few modern conveniences. I remove my clothes and toss them into the corner. I'm okay with her burning them. I could never wear them again without thinking of tonight. It's a memory I'm anxious to have fade.

After I quickly wash up, I sort through the items she brought in. I find a pair of red silk panties. Not what I usually wear, but I suspect Faith doesn't own anything else. I slip them on, not wanting to admit how sexy they make me feel. I kinda hate to cover them with the skirt. But I do. Then I pull a red top over my head. It's sexy, too, draping off one shoulder, creating a flattering frame for my tattoo.

When I step out of the bathroom, Faith is lounging on the bed. She glances up from the book she's reading. "I suppose it'll do," she says.

I'll take that as a compliment from her.

I run my fingers self-consciously through my dark hair. I'd left it loose after brushing it.

"At the end of the hallway is a set of double doors," she says. "They lead into Father's old bedchamber. I wouldn't recommend sleeping there, but otherwise, take any room you want."

I lick my lips. "Uh, I'm sorry for your loss."

She stares at me blankly for a minute. "Oh. Father, you mean." She shrugs. "Old Family so seldom die. . . . I'm not quite sure . . . what I'm supposed to feel. We aren't burdened with the emotions that humans are."

"Not even love?"

Ignoring the question, she thumbs through the book. I see the cover. It's a romance novel.

"What about Richard?" I suddenly ask.

Faith lets out a groan. "That's a night I'll regret for an eternity."

"I think he cares about you. The night I met him he asked about you," I hasten to explain.

"You're so innocent."

She says it like an insult. I bite back a retort. I don't need to defend myself, to claim that I'm not innocent at all—not with my history. But I'm not really in the mood to deal with her. I'd rather be with Victor. "Thanks for everything."

"Don't mention it."

When I step into the hallway, Richard is standing there. "How is she?" he asks.

"Cold, unemotional."

His eyes are fastened on the door. "She's probably confused."

He takes a step toward her bedroom.

"I don't think—"

He stops, looks back at me. I can't explain why I don't want to see him hurt. Perhaps because he's Victor's friend, and I've learned to trust Victor's assessments. "I think she wants to be alone."

He gives me a small smile that says he knows I'm trying to protect him and he appreciates it. "I'll be fine."

He disappears into her room, no longer my problem.

I walk down the hallway to Victor's room. The door is open, an invitation. I peer inside. He's in bed, beneath the covers. His suit is gone. He's wearing a simple cotton T-shirt.

Slowly he opens his eyes. "Dawn."

I move farther into the room. "How are you feeling?"

"Exhausted. Healing takes so much out of us." His brow furrows. "Faith was supposed to take you to a bedroom."

"I'm staying in here."

"No."

"Yes. We can argue if you want, but you're weak and I'll win."

He flashes a quick smile. It's probably the sweetest surrender I've ever seen.

I turn the gas lamp down until it's just a hum, the glow disappearing from around Victor, leaving half his body in shadow. I crawl onto the bed and nestle up against his good side. He brings his arm around me.

"I can't even believe I'm going to say this," he says, "but you're probably the best medicine for me."

I know that so much more has to be done to ensure Victor's ascension is complete, and I'm aware that he may have a very dangerous brother out there to deal with, but at this moment, as incredible as it seems, I'm actually happy.

"This is where I want to be."

He pulls me in even closer. "What about Michael?"

"I have to let him go. It'll be hard—I've known him for-ever—but it's not fair to him. Even if things with you and me . . . don't work out." Humans and vampires. When has it ever worked? "Michael deserves someone who can give him her whole heart. The Teen Initiative party is Saturday night. I'll say good-bye to him then."

"In four hundred years, I've never felt for anyone what I feel for you. No matter what happens, remember that."

And I know that he understands as well as I do that things between us will never be simple. We may never have a happy ending.

Chapter 28

Shortly before dawn Victor's stirring wakes me up. He touches my cheek and I wish we could stay here all day.

"How are you feeling?" I ask.

"The wound is almost healed," he says. "Most of my strength is back. While I hate to kick you out of my bed, I need a few moments alone to prepare for the funeral."

Reluctantly, I leave the room, close the door, and wait in the hallway. When he joins me, he's wearing a silk suit. In black.

I wonder if I should change into something more somber. As though reading my mind, he says, "You look great."

As we walk through the manor, he holds my hand, but when we step outside into the predawn darkness, he releases it. I understand that he has to be strong in front of the others. They, particularly his uncles, can't see that he needs anyone. Especially a human.

A short distance away from the house, on a raised platform, is a plain pine coffin, no lid in sight. As Victor and I near it, I see that Valentine rests inside. Faith is fiddling with his cravat, straightening it.

With a guilty yet sorrowful look, she meets my gaze. "Father always took such pride in his appearance."

"Which is the reason he drank so much blood," Ransom said.

"To retain the appearance of youth," Seymour added.

Their voices are flat, unemotional. No sorrow, no grief. I have the impression that they feel nothing at all for their brother. At least Victor isn't as cold and wooden as they are. I saw the regret in his eyes. He did what he had to do, but he didn't enjoy it.

Faith moves away from the coffin to stand near Richard. He's armed with a stake in each hand, and one more is threaded through his belt.

"What did you decide?" Victor asks his uncles. "Are you with me . . . or will you be joining my father?"

"My allegiance is to you, nephew," Seymour says, and gracelessly drops to one knee.

Ransom glances around. I wonder if he's thinking about trying to make a run for it. Then he, too, kneels. "As is mine."

I wish I could trust them. But now that Victor is head of the most powerful vampire family, they have to resent it somewhat.

"I accept your fealty," Victor says, but he watches his uncles closely, too, as though he wants to sneak into their minds and read their thoughts as well. "You'll begin your journeys back home tonight."

The brothers stand.

All gazes veer to the coffin, to Valentine, and I'm wondering if they expect him to rise from the dead. For a moment, silence surrounds us. Respectful. That's when I notice the servants, Lessers, standing a short distance away, including the two who picked me up last night. Will they easily accept Victor's ascension?

"It's time," Victor says quietly.

Everyone turns toward the house, and I realize the first fingers of the sun are stretching up beyond the horizon.

Victor places his hand on my shoulder. "I have one more thing to ask of you, Dawn, something only you can do."

"Anything." Though it's hard to imagine what that could be.

"When the sun rises, my father will become ash. It's important that you watch it happen. Let there be no question in anyone's mind that the Bloody Valentine's reign has ended."

As much as I hated Lord Valentine, seeing him burn is . . . unsettling. But I've come this far. "I'll stay here while you go in."

"Thank you, Dawn. It's no different from cremation. There won't be any pain; there won't be any screaming. He's dead; this is just the final step. His soul is gone, and soon his body will follow."

The coffin waits, holding the massive former lord. If his eyes were open, he'd be able to watch the sun rise.

"Join us in the study when it's done." Gently, he touches my cheek.

As he walks back to the manor, the sun begins chasing away the shadows. I want to yell at Victor to quicken his pace, but he continues on with an unhurried stride, as though anything faster would be undignified, or maybe he thinks he now commands the sun.

When he's safely inside, I release the breath I've been holding and spin back around—to perform my duty as the final witness. I'm standing far enough back that I can't actually see Valentine, only the pine box that is now his resting place. The sun is rising higher, higher, lighting the sky, warming the earth. I feel it touching my face, so comforting.

Suddenly there's a *whoosh* and flames shoot up from inside the coffin. I hadn't expected them to be so beautiful. Orange, blue, red, yellow. I can feel their heat. I can hear the crackling as the pine box catches fire. It burns swiftly, along with the wooden platform upon which it was resting.

Until nothing is left except ash.

A cool breeze gently lifts it and carries it away. I wonder if it's the same breeze that carried the remains of my parents from me when their coach stopped burning.

As I turn to leave, the sun glints off something in the dirt. I walk over and kneel down. Resting beside his unburned fangs is the massive ring that once wrapped around Valentine's finger. The family crest is imprinted deep into its gold. Cradling it in my palm, I can feel the history.

I spin on my heel and return to the house, where a new Lord Valentine awaits me.

The study is large, but full of so many couches and chairs it feels cramped. The fireplace is oversize and crackles with fresh wood. The gas lamps are ornate with brass, and book-shelves line every wall, stretching up farther than I can reach, filled with volume upon volume. It makes our city library look pitiful.

Victor is alone, sitting on the largest sofa next to a low table. He appears powerful, and yet not at all in the same fearsome manner as his father. I walk over and hold out the ring.

"I believe this is yours."

I see the weight of the symbolism settling over him.

"I couldn't bring myself to take it from him," he says.

"You didn't. The sun did."

"You're right." He takes it and places it on his right fore-finger. He turns it one way and then the other, as though he's not quite comfortable with it yet.

I sit beside him and wrap my hand around his. "What now?"

"Do you know how to drive a car?"

I give a small laugh at the unexpectedness of the ques-tion. "Actually, yes. Jeff taught me. He said I never knew when I might need the skill."

"He's wise. I'll give you the keys to my car so you can return to the city. Your absence has no doubt been discovered by now, and people will be worrying. We don't want the Agency sending Night Watchmen out here."

"Right." Reality is beginning to intrude on our fairy tale.

"The uncles have retired for the day," Faith says as she and Richard stroll into the room. Despite Richard's clear devotion to her, she seems utterly indifferent to him. Maybe she has too much of Valentine in her. "One of the bodyguards wanted me to give you this."

She hands me my cell phone. I notice that she isn't as disgusted by it as the others.

She and Richard take chairs across from us.

"What are your plans now, m'lord?" Richard asks.

"To start with, do away with all that 'm'lord' crap."

Richard grins. "It *is* rather archaic. But I was referring to the more pressing issue. This brother of yours. Do you really think he's as dangerous as your father indicated?"

"It's impossible to know. Father was a master of exaggeration."

"I've already had your loyalists and mine ferreting out information on him, but it's like he's a ghost. I can't find anyone who knows anything."

"We don't even know what he looks like," Faith says, and for the first time I think I catch a glimpse of someone who is not as uncaring as the aura she projects. I think Tegan would have a field day crawling around in Faith's psyche.

"Have you given any more thought to my suggestion that he could be Hoodie?" I ask.

"What's a hoodie?" Faith asks.

"Not what, who. Someone who's been following Dawn," Victor says, before turning his attention to me. "It's possible. Father obviously figured out that you were my ally, so whatever mission he set my brother on could involve you as well. It would explain why the guy was searching your apartment, trying to get a better understanding of you."

"Not sure that helps us much," Richard says. "We still don't know what he looks like."

"He wears a distinctive hoodie with a snake on the back," I offer.

"Which he can easily remove."

"True."

"But it's a place to start," Victor says.

"Or it could be a waste of our resources, a wild-goose chase," Richard points out.

"Which is why you're my second in command." He nudges me. "He's very good at strategic thinking."

"Except when it comes to love, apparently," Richard murmurs beneath his breath.

"Well, there's little we can do until nightfall," Victor says. "For the time being, I want to keep Father's death quiet. This other son will remain leashed as long as he thinks Father is alive. He may even come here looking to meet with him. It'll give us an advantage. Clive will need to know, of course. Dawn, you can fill him in. And I want Night Watchmen with you at all times."

He looks at Richard and Faith. "I need a few minutes alone with Dawn."

Richard stands. "Once again, it's been a pleasure."

Faith rolls her eyes at him before turning to me. "I understand that the increase in the blood supply is because of your Teen Initiative, and that there's going to be a party. Based on the unflattering clothes you were wearing last night . . . well, I picked a couple of things out of my closet as a thank-you. They're in a bag by the front door. Take them on your way out."

Before I can respond, she's swept out of the room, Richard chuckling at her heels.

"She likes you," Victor says.

I stare at him, dumbfounded. "You're kidding. That's her liking someone?"

"You have to understand that it's not easy for us to reveal our emotions. They're seen as a vulnerability." Twisting around, he faces me squarely and takes my hands. "Which brings me to what I need to say to you. While you were sleeping last night, I did a lot of thinking. My father clearly saw that you're my weakness. I have other enemies who will as well. You'll always be in danger if you're with me."

"I don't care."

"But I do." He skims his hand over my cheek. "You belong with Michael, Dawn. Vampires and humans—we never work out long-term."

"We could try."

"That's one of the things I love about you. When you believe in something you fight for it. But this is a battle

that's larger than the two of us. One where you must sacrifice for the greater good. You're as dangerous to me as
my enemies are, because whenever you're close, my desires
cloud everything else. We can't be in each other's lives. Too
many people are depending on us. I'm sorry, but this has
to be good-bye."

I feel something hard biting into my palm and realize he's placed the car keys there and wrapped my fingers
around them.

"Drive safely," he says.

He rises and walks from the room, leaving me alone. I
think I can actually hear my heart breaking. Once again
because of a vampire.

Chapter 29

"What the hell is going on?" Clive bellows as soon as I enter his office. "Last I heard you were seen leaving the city in one of Valentine's carriages. I almost sent an entire squad of Night Watchmen out there after you!"

"You might want to sit down," I say, afraid Clive will collapse when I tell him. Unfortunately, that only makes him more anxious.

"Dawn, I want to know everything, and I want to know it now!"

Everything. I can't tell him everything. Not the personal stuff between me and Victor. Not how much I care for him or that we kissed or that I really wish there was a way for us to be together. But I can tell him the political ramifications of all that's happened. "Okay, then. Valentine is dead. His son Victor has taken the throne."

I hit all the highlights that involve Valentine, from the moment I met Victor on the trolley until I drove his car into the parking garage here.

"An ascension," he whispers when I'm finished. "I can't believe it. I was hoping to retire without ever seeing one. They're messy, complicated affairs."

"This one won't be."

"You're putting a lot of faith in this Victor fellow."

"Because he's earned it."

Clive opens a drawer, removes a bottle, and pours some clear liquid into a glass. I don't think it's water. He downs it in one long swallow.

"We can't tell anyone yet, Clive. There's still the matter of Valentine's other son. Do you know anything at all about him? Have the Night Watchmen reported anything?"

"They've found a couple more vampires with their throats torn out, but other than that and the same small-scale abductions, it's business as usual." He studies me. "I'll increase the number of guards protecting you. Maybe you shouldn't go to this damn Teen Initiative party."

"No, I have to. It was my idea. I have to see it through. Besides, I'm not going to cower in my apartment. That would give Valentine a victory from the grave."

"You know, I thought he was nuts when he requested you as a delegate. Now I'm beginning to think he underestimated you. Maybe we all did."

I can't help but smile. "I think that may be the sweetest thing you've ever said to me."

"Go on. Get out of here, before you give me an ulcer."

I turn toward the door.

"Dawn?"

Stopping, I glance back.

"I know you don't want to hear it," Clive says, "but your parents would be proud of you."

I feel the tears sting my eyes, because for the first time I believe I have earned their pride in me. I'm doing what I can to bring about a world in which vampires and humans are truly equal. But more, for the first time I want them to be proud of me. I always resented that they gave so much to the city, felt that my mother loved me less because she gave up so much to be with my father. I'm understanding their devotion to their jobs and each other a little better.

Although I doubt they'd be as pleased about my feelings for a vampire. But I do finally understand why my mother served at my father's side. Because I would give anything right now to be with Victor.

Chapter 30

"Don't you look beautiful!" Rachel comments, sitting on the couch in our living room and watching me twirl. They released her from the hospital just this afternoon.

Beautiful is not a word I ever really associated with myself. But then, since her brush with death, Rachel is seeing everything as beautiful. So I don't put a lot of faith in her words.

I spin around once more so she can see my new outfit. New to me, anyway. It could be a hundred years old for all I know—a red silk dress that flows around me and whispers against my calves when I move.

It's been two days since Faith gave me this gift. Two days of thinking about this party. Two nights of thinking about Victor. So far his ascension has not made the news. Clive agreed to keep things quiet until Victor has secured his place among the vampires.

"I wish you felt up to going with me tonight," I say.

"I'm not exactly a teen anymore." She rubs her brow. "And I still have this headache. I don't know why it won't go away."

"So what are you going to do while I'm out having a good time?"

"Jeff's coming over and we're going to talk."

"Oh, yeah, I'm sure that's what you're going to do. Talk." I wiggle my eyebrows at her.

"Seriously."

I grin. "Whatever."

A knock sounds on the door. I open it and smile up at Michael. It didn't seem right to cancel on him so close to the event. But while I'm not looking forward to it, after tonight I'm going to tell him everything. Even if Victor was serious about not wanting to be together, it's not fair to Michael for me to be with him when I have strong feelings for someone else. But for tonight, I'm determined to be a good date. "Hey, come on in."

"You look great," he says.

"Thanks."

"What's with all the guards?"

"Rachel's home now, and with the party tonight, since I'll be out after dark, the Agency just felt that we should have additional protection."

"But you'll be with me."

"I know. I told them that." I can see that his pride is at stake. But it bothers me a little that he needs so much reassurance. And that he believes so blindly that he's a match for all the monsters in the night. He's never seen an all-out vampire battle like the one I witnessed between Victor and his father. He has no idea of a vampire's true capabilities. "But you know Clive. He just wants to take extra precautions."

"Okay." But I'm not sure he's convinced.

He walks over to the couch. "Hey, Rachel. How are you feeling?"

"Not as bad as I did. But you guys had better go before the sun sets. Once it does, they're locking the doors at the Daylight. We don't want to be responsible for any kids wandering the streets after dusk."

"Sure you'll be okay?" I ask.

"I'll be fine."

"Okay, then, see you later."

Michael and I step into the hallway, and four hooded Night Watchmen immediately fall in around us.

"Four?" Michael whispers. "Are you sure there's nothing going on that I need to know about?"

I decide to tell him a little. He needs to understand the dangers, to be on alert. "There's been some speculation that Hoodie is one of Valentine's sons."

"Shit. An Old Family vampire in the city?"

"We're not sure, so keep it to yourself. We don't want to cause a panic. Especially tonight."

"Right."

But as we step into the elevator, I can see that he'd really like a shot at taking down an Old Family vampire.

Outside, the city is so quiet, like a weight is bearing down on it, smothering all the sounds. The early evening feels thick and unending. The wind picks up and stops, but carries only silence with it.

"There's a strangeness on the air," Michael says quietly.

"Yeah. I can sense it, too."

We climb into the limo. Tonight we're traveling in style, and as Michael runs his hands along the seats, I consider letting him drive the Mustang before I return it to Victor. He'd love that. Course, I'd have to explain where I got it, but then, I've decided to tell him everything. He deserves to know.

Michael slips his arm around me and we do our best to ignore the two guards facing us, trying to pretend everything is normal. Just for a few hours.

When we get to the Daylight Grill, we discover the place is completely packed, the busiest I've ever seen it. The bartender has a huge grin on his face as he serves lemonade after lemonade after lemonade. And as I see the kids, and how much they're already enjoying themselves, I realize this could be the start of something major. Maybe the key to getting regular blood donations really does lie in the youth. We are the future, after all.

"Dawn, this is awesome!" Tegan shouts as she and Sin join us.

Michael draws me in against his side. "That's a rocking band."

It's the same one that was at the other party, out near the wall what feels like eons ago. Only I don't want to be the lead female singer anymore. I'm content with my position as delegate.

"You should say a few words," Sin tells me.

"You think so?"

"Absolutely," Michael says, and he takes it upon himself to lead me to the stage.

The band stops and the singer ushers me over. She hands me the mic. "Love your ink," she says.

I laugh a little. "Thanks. Love yours, too."

I step forward. The last of the sunlight is streaming through the windows. I clear my throat. "Hello. I'm Dawn Montgomery. Denver's delegate. Your delegate."

I expect a few boos and hisses, but instead I get applause and cheers. When it gets quiet, I say, "I want to thank you for donating your blood. You're helping to keep the citizens safe, and we want to keep you safe in return. We have a dozen Night Watchmen here tonight. And now that the sun is setting, we're locking the doors." Rachel had choreographed this moment. I signal to a Night Watchman, and he chains and padlocks the front door.

The sun sets and the lights on Day Street come on. Other Night Watchmen hang black drapes over the windows in order to give the place a more "party" atmosphere. The effect is perfect, bringing the tone down just a little, embracing the darkness, creating pockets of privacy where couples can escape for some time alone.

Everyone claps.

"Now let's party until dawn!" I shout, then hand the mic back to the singer and step off the stage.

Michael is waiting for me, and his smile makes me feel guilty.

"That was great," he says.

"Thanks."

Sin nudges Michael's shoulder. "Let's go get drinks. Lemonade for everyone?"

Tegan grins up at him. "*Special* lemonade."

There wasn't supposed to be any alcohol served, but I can tell the bartender is taking the opportunity to cash in on some bribes, and the special lemonade is flowing from the taps. And if that's not enough, kids have brought their own flasks, and are unabashedly emptying the contents into whatever drink they have in hand.

"You got it," Sin says.

Michael gives me one last squeeze before heading to the bar with Sin.

"I am so glad things are working out with you and Michael," Tegan yells in my ear.

I tell her the truth—albeit not the full version, not yet. "He's a great guy."

"Still, I wish Victor could be here," Tegan says with a wink. "Guess he needs to be patrolling the streets."

"Yeah." Only he's not. He's at the manor.

"What the hell does that bitch think she's doing?" Tegan suddenly asks, and I hear the anger in her voice.

I look in the direction she's pointing and see Lila wedged between Michael and the bar, her hand pressed to his chest like it was that day I saw them in front of his locker.

"I mean, really, what is she doing here?" Tegan asks.

"You know she didn't donate blood."

"Her daddy probably bribed someone for a ticket."

"Get her ass out of here."

"Can't. Once the doors are locked, they're supposed to stay that way until the sun comes up. We don't want to provide an opportunity for a vampire to sneak in."

"That is just so wrong." She pushes me. "You'd better go set her straight about who Michael will be dancing with tonight."

Only I think that maybe I should just leave them alone. If he likes her, maybe she can be there for him when I'm not. Hurting Michael is going to be the hardest thing I've ever done. I don't want to do it, but I know that it's not fair to him if I don't.

"Hey, what's wrong?" Tegan asks.

"Just a lot of Agency stuff on my mind."

"Don't even think about the Agency tonight."

"A little hard to do when this whole party is because of the Agency."

"What you need is to dance. Go get your man."

"Okay. Yeah." But as I'm working my way through the crowd, halfway to the bar someone knocks into me and spills lemonade on the front of my dress. So I detour to the restroom. The hallway is way in the back, far from any windows, and the lightbulbs haven't been changed in a long time. Their dying glow barely provides enough visibility. The collection of noises—music, laughter, stomping feet—is muffled here, but the excitement still carries through. I wish Rachel could be here, could see how well everything turned out.

The bathroom is bright and clean. I'm the only one in it as I snatch up a towel and soak up the lemonade. The dress is ruined. Just as I know my relationship with Michael will be when I tell him everything. I wish we could still stay friends, but knowing his pride, I think it's probably unlikely. It makes me sad, and tonight there should be no sadness.

Calming my nerves, I'm determined not to ruin the night for Michael. It'll be my parting gift to him. I head back into the hallway.

As the door closes behind me, taking the little illumination with it, I realize that something has happened to the lights in the hallway. Where before they were dim, now they are nonexistent. The only light is coming from the end of the hall, where the party is in full swing. I start toward it when an arm shoots out and stops my progress.

"Dawn."

The voice is low, almost ominous, but I recognize it and press a hand to my chest to calm my thudding heart. "God, Sin, I didn't even see you there. You startled me."

"Did I? I'm sorry."

His voice has taken on a strange scratchy quality. I have the image of smoke coming out of his mouth as he speaks. Almost like he's been dying since he was born. There's a creepiness to him that has never been there before, too, as though the darkness is shifting him into something else.

With his palm against the wall in front of me, he leans in, and in the dim light I can see him smile.

"Dawn Montgomery," he says, "the delegate who never wanted to be. Following in your parents' sainted footsteps."

I tried for Tegan's and Michael's sakes to warm up to Sin, but now he's making me angry. Yes, I never wanted to be a delegate, but I have since embraced my duties, and I don't like him mocking my parents. "Shut up, Sin. You don't know anything about my family."

I shove him, but he doesn't budge.

"I know your poor brother died while you hid in a closet. What were his last words to you? 'Don't be afraid of the dark'?"

I can't find my breath. It's impossible for him to know that; I've never told anyone Brady's final words. Not Rachel, not Michael, not Tegan. They've been burned into my mind alone.

"But his words were little comfort, I'm sure. Are you still afraid of the dark?" he asks.

My chest feels leaden. Why is he saying these things? Where did he learn them? I want to tell him to get the hell out of my way. But all I can manage is . . .

"How . . . how could you . . ."

"Know that? Poor Dawn. Still that little girl trapped in a closet."

"What kind of game are you playing here?"

"I can hear your blood rushing through your veins. So fast. So strong. So . . . tempting."

I try ducking past him, but he moves his arm down and swiftly brings his other one up to trap me with unnatural strength.

"Let me go," I say, keeping my voice strong despite the sudden fear coursing through me.

"But I haven't thanked you yet," he says.

"For what?"

"For the death of Lord Valentine."

How could he know that? It's still a secret.

"What are you talking about?"

"It's a pity I didn't get to kill him myself. How I *hated* him."

I laugh. "You've never even met him. Do you have any idea who the Bloody Valentine is?"

Sin smiles. There's something very, very off about it.

"Do *you* have any idea who *I* am?"

Tension crackles in the air.

"From the moment I was born, I've been known only as Sin. My father wasn't very kind when he named me. You see, I was a bastard child. A mistake. A freak accident, he said. He beat it into me every day and every night. He said I was evil incarnate. I was a *monster* in his eyes. Ironic when you consider that he is—excuse me, was—the greatest monster of all."

"Your father?"

"Murdoch Valentine."

My heart slams against my ribs. "No, no, he can't be—"

"But he is. Or was, I should say."

He lowers his head to my neck and I hear him inhaling deeply, can imagine his nostrils flaring as he's scenting me. When he straightens, a pair of awful fangs appear in his mouth.

"That's not possible," I say. "You . . . I've seen you walk in the sun."

"So you have. I'm the first vampire in history to be born a Day Walker. The sun has no power over me. Imagine what I could do with an army of Day Walkers following me. Worshipping me. I can rule not only the humans but the vampires."

"You're the son Valentine sent for?" Valentine's dangerous weapon. Locked up with a score of teenagers. And me.

"Yes. He thought I would do his bidding where Victor would not. His plan was to take over Denver from the inside. I've slowly been turning Night Watchmen to our cause, making them into the ultimate beings. You see, whoever receives my blood receives my gift as well. They are vampires, but are no longer cursed to walk only in the night and fear the sun."

I struggle against his grip, but I might as well be caught in a bear trap.

"Tonight is perfect," he continues nonchalantly, like we're talking about the music. "This stupid little party couldn't have been any better suited for me. An entire gathering of idiotic and impressionable teenagers. It's just what I need to begin the next step. Victor took care of our father. And soon, my *special project* will take care of Victor."

"Special project?" I manage to get out. "What are you talking about?"

"You call him Hoodie."

A vampire who appeared when the sun was out. I assumed he was hiding in the shadows, under the dark clouds. But he didn't need to. Like Sin, Hoodie isn't afraid of the sun.

Oh, God. And Victor doesn't know. He doesn't know that Hoodie is after him. He doesn't know that even during the day he won't be safe from him. I have no way to warn him.

"If my Night Watchmen, who can walk in the sun, are my children, then Hoodie is . . . my favorite creation. He's perfection."

I'm about to scream, but as if he can sense it, his hand comes up and presses against my jaw and neck. It won't keep me from crying out, but the message is clear: Scream and I'm dead. Still, I can fight with words.

"You need an Old Family witness to make a legitimate claim to the Valentine throne."

He laughs. "Do you really think that's my goal? Something as pathetic and paltry as that?"

"Why come here, then? Why help your father after he banished you?"

"Anything that caused strife in the family was in my best interest. I hear Father wounded Victor greatly in their battle. And Victor, being the noble idiot that he is, didn't drink from you to restore himself." Sin trails his finger along my unwounded neck. "So Victor is, at this very moment, weakened. And I want Victor dead."

"He's had plenty of time to recover. He'll be a formidable foe."

"I think he kept from you how badly wounded he truly was."

"I won't let you hurt him."

"Such devotion. I can't wait until it's directed my way."

"Never," I ground out. "You'll never be anything to me."

"You're so wrong, Dawn. I'll be everything."

"I'll die first."

Sin remains completely calm. "You aren't seeing the whole picture yet, Dawn. You don't understand how well you fit into it."

He leans in again and smells my neck. I cringe in disgust.

"Victor's death will serve me well, but not yours. You're very, very special. In time, you'll see just how special you are."

"Why not kill Victor yourself then, huh? Why do you need to send a lackey to do it?"

"I'm needed elsewhere tonight. But rest assured, before the coming dawn, he'll be dead."

Sin lowers his hands and gingerly places them on my shoulders, like a friend helping a mourner standing over the grave of a loved one.

"Poor Dawn. You think everything's been taken away. But you have so much more to lose." With a quick movement, he presses me against the wall, and I expect to feel his fangs burying themselves into my neck despite his earlier words. But instead, he leans close to me and whispers, "By the way, your brother tasted delicious."

"Wh . . . wh . . . wh . . ."

He lets me go and I fall to the floor. I feel like I might sink all the way through it, past the basement and sewers, farther and farther until I hit the earth itself and then go through that. I'll fade away, disappear forever.

Somewhere in the back of my mind I'm aware of his striding away. And then the darkness of the hallway engulfs me again and it seems to last an eternity. My brother's final words play over and over like a mantra that'll protect me. But it's tainted now, corrupted by the image of Sin feeding on him.

I was looking at the thing that killed Brady. And I've never felt more powerless.

"Dawn!"

I come back to the real world, and Michael is holding me. "Dawn, are you okay?" he asks.

I nod.

"Talk to me. Say something," Michael urges.

"Don't be afraid of the dark. . . ."

"What?"

I shake my head violently, feeling the shock wear off. My surroundings become familiar. I clutch Michael's shirt. "Sin. He's a vampire."

"Did you hit your head or something? He and I do half our workouts in the sun—"

"He's a Day Walker."

"A what?"

"He can walk in the sun!"

"Dawn, I know you haven't always gotten along with Sin, but I think you've gone a little far this time."

"No." I struggle to my feet. "We have to stop him. We have to get help." I pull out my cell phone. No signal.

"Can you get a signal?" I ask frantically.

He checks his phone. "No. That's weird. It's usually not a problem this close to the tower."

Unless Sin had it disabled.

I grab Michael's hand and start dragging him toward the party. The music suddenly stops. I hear a few cheers. Then Sin. "Thank you, thank you."

"He's taken the stage," I say, quickening my step.

"Dawn, you're overreacting."

I stop and face him. "Michael, trust me, please."

He shrugs and doesn't argue as I push on. When we finally get into the main room, I look toward the stage. I was right. Sin stands tall above everyone else.

He isn't the same anymore, and I feel so stupid for ever being tricked. His mannerisms have changed, now reflecting the centuries-old vampire within. He's shed his teenager image and put on the appearance of someone older, someone wiser, but with his fangs once again hidden from view, no one in the audience knows they're looking at an Old Family vampire.

I glance around at the Watchmen standing near the doors and at the edge of the room. Will they help or have they been compromised? Are they Sin's Watchmen?

"Could I have Tegan up onstage, please?" Sin asks, and she quickly hops up to join him. She beams with excitement, and my heart is going a thousand miles a minute.

"We've gotta get her off of there," I say.

"Dawn, this is insane—" Michael begins, and I know he doesn't believe me. Why should he? Sin's greatest weapon is his charisma.

"As I'm sure you are all aware, the blood you donated has already been distributed and consumed by the vampires on the outside," Sin says.

Some in the audience boo and hiss.

"I know, I know," Sin says. "It's a losing battle, isn't it? You give and give and give. And you'll have to give forever, won't you?"

Silence sweeps through the room. Sin's voice has taken a turn for the serious, and people are paying attention to this sudden, and strange, spectacle. I turn to Michael and see that even he's mesmerized.

"You're young now. Maybe too young to realize how long a lifetime of blood giving is. But there is a way out. A way I'm willing to offer everyone in this room."

Sin snaps his fingers. As two Night Watchmen begin walking toward the stage, parting the crowd with ease, my worst fears are realized. He controls them.

I start pushing my way through the crush of bodies. They won't budge, almost in a trance as Sin speaks. But I fight to get through. Maybe if I can reach the stage myself, I can distract Sin. Maybe . . . maybe I can destroy him.

"These gentlemen took my offer months ago. They were smart; they understood that a life of giving is no life at all. The age of altruism has passed. The age of greed is upon us. The barren sands that surround this world, created by the falling bombs of your tiny species, can no longer render beautiful flowers."

The Night Watchmen arrive onstage. They unravel

their black masks, and then smile. Their fangs, razor sharp, catch the light, leaving no question as to what they are. I'm so close now, and when I glance at Tegan, her eyes reveal her terror.

The audience gasps, threatens to get out of control, but Sin's voice brings calm.

"Those who know me have seen me walk in the sun. They have seen me soak up its rays, bathe in its glory. These men, these vampires, these Lessers, enjoy the same fruits. I can give you immortality as a vampire, without asking you to forsake the sun. No one can do that except me."

Sin opens his mouth, grabs Tegan with one arm, and plunges his immense fangs into her neck. Her scream is high-pitched and brutal, one that I already know will haunt me forever.

I try to rush forward, but the crowd's panic carries me farther from the stage as I stare in horror.

He drinks from Tegan and there's nothing I can do. He pulls his fangs out and a line of blood and saliva runs from the open wounds. When he drops her, she falls to the ground like a rag doll.

Wrenching out a knife, he slits his wrist and holds it up to reveal the blood flowing. It's an offering to everyone here, the nectar of a new god.

"Who's next?" he asks.

That's when all hell breaks loose.

Chapter 31

Around the room, the other Night Watchmen have pulled off their masks and revealed their fangs. More screams sound as they attack.

The mob threatens to crush me in its wake. My immediate fear is of being knocked down; I know that if I hit the ground, they'll trample me, and I'll never have a chance to get back to my feet, to fight this monster before us. Valentine's monster.

Shoulders and elbows batter into me, and I nearly lose my balance, but a familiar hand settles on the small of my back.

"Come on!" Michael yells.

Without any regard for the others around us, he pushes them roughly away, holding on to me as he bulldozes his way through.

People rush to the door, maybe hoping that their combined weight will break the hinges or warp them enough that they can pass through. But not only is the padlock holding the door tight, it's strong—meant to hold back vampire attacks from the outside. Nobody wagered on their already being inside.

Sin's devilish laugh rings out across the crowd, louder even than the mob of stomping feet. The evil travels from him straight through my bones.

"I can't leave Tegan!" I shout, looking back and seeing her petite body still lying on the stage. Whether Sin has fed her his blood yet or not, I don't know.

"It's too fucking late for her, Dawn."

Michael drags me with him, and even though my heart rebels, my mind knows he's right. We have to get out of here; we have to get help.

We rush around the outskirts of the crowd, Michael's hand wrapped tightly around mine, until we get to a distant window. While everyone has pushed to the front, we've gone to the back of the room. Michael rips the makeshift curtains from the window. He quickly picks up a chair and throws it, the glass exploding onto the sidewalk. We leap through the opening.

We race down the street. I hear shouts. Screams. Sirens. Even sporadic gunfire. Sin's plan obviously involved more than the Daylight. Maybe the madness erupted there, but it's spreading like a virus. I check my cell phone again, desperate for a signal. I need to alert the Agency, Jeff, Victor—

Michael suddenly stops short, and I slam into his back.

"Why'd you—" But then I clearly see what's arrested his attention.

In the middle of the deserted street ahead of us stands Hoodie.

"Don't fight him," I plead. "He's connected with Sin, somehow."

"You picked the wrong night to mess with us!" Michael shouts, pulling a stake from his belt.

"Michael, please!"

But my words are lost on him as he charges in. Hoodie doesn't even look at his approaching attacker. His gaze is fixed on me. Though his face is still covered by what seems like a constant shadow, I can feel him staring. And I think that will be his doom. His obsession with me has blinded him to everything else. Especially Michael.

But as Michael lunges with the stake, Hoodie grabs his arm, and I hear Michael's wrist break, followed by his scream of agony. Hoodie delivers a devastating strike to Michael's chest, and I hear more bones crack, robbing Michael of his breath. With a backhanded slap, he sends Michael to the ground like a child who's stepped out of line.

And then he comes for me. Slowly stalking up the street like he has all the time in the world.

I can't leave Michael. But I can't get to him either, and even if I could, I can't lift him up and drag him away. So I pull my own stake from my boot. Hoodie's gaze has never left mine. And as I prepare to defend myself, out of the corner of my eye I see Michael getting up. Even injured, he's so fast, so powerful. With his uninjured hand, he brings his stake down on Hoodie, the metal going cleanly into Hoodie's back. Hoodie releases a pain-filled grunt.

But then he throws his elbow backward, catching Michael squarely in the nose. Michael staggers and drops to one knee.

"Run," Michael calls to me, as Hoodie turns his attention to him.

I just shake my head, my voice knotted in my throat.

"Run!" he repeats.

"I . . . I can't." Too many people have risked everything to protect me.

Michael lunges at his opponent, trying to distract him, even though he must know he's outmatched. He's not hoping to win; that's impossible. Michael is just hoping to buy me time.

"Dawn, run!"

His desperate command snaps me out of my trance, and I haul ass. Not so much to escape, but to draw Hoodie away from Michael. He wants me. I know he'll follow me. And I'm right. I turn down the first alley I see, knowing I can't match his speed, but hoping I can lose him in the brick maze.

But he's there. Every turn I take, every corridor I run down. Like a nightmare, I can't escape him. He's in front of me, then behind, and then I seem to lose him altogether, until he appears in the corner of my eye as a fleeting image. But always there is that constant stare from under the darkened hood.

I'm out of breath. I'm sweating. I slip on pieces of garbage. I keep slamming into walls and shouldering doors, trying to open them, only to find they're locked.

And my stalker dogs me patiently. He knows time is on his side. This labyrinth is too large, too confusing.

The dead end catches me off guard, and I have nowhere left to run. I rest my back against the wall. I put my head down, pulling in the air. When I look up, he's there, waiting for me.

"We have unfinished business, Dawn," he says, his voice like a scratched childhood record, familiar but destroyed.

No matter how fast I ran, no matter which direction I took, it was always going to end here. I feel stupid because he knew that, didn't he?

"I won't go down easily," I say, gripping my stake.

"Don't fight me."

He moves toward me with his hands up, signaling that he means no harm. Yeah, right. I pretend to relax, taking a deep breath with each step he takes.

Breathe in. Breathe out. Breathe in. So close. Almost now.

I've been through too much for it to end here.

Once he's within arm's reach, I strike with the stake. But he sees it coming. He just throws me over his shoulder and onto the ground. The precious air I'd recovered leaves me again.

"I didn't want to do it this way," he says from above me. "This isn't how I planned our reunion."

Reunion?

He pulls a syringe out of his pocket and uncaps it. I raise my arm to defend myself, but he simply takes it and twists my palm up. He injects the needle into the muscle of my biceps and presses down the plunger.

As blackness hovers at the edge of my vision, I see something. A flower. On the back of his hand. Made by coal dust trapped deep under the skin. Untouched by the years of aging he should've experienced. The little flower I used to stare at while he sat beside me and brought color to the black-and-white images in my coloring book.

I barely get out his name before the darkened abyss swallows me.

"Brady . . ."

Chapter 32

If there's still chaos in the city, it's died down. Then again, we're so far from the center, it's impossible to tell exactly what's happened since Sin revealed his true self at the Daylight Grill. Eighteen stories up, we don't even have the view of the Agency building; we're on the wrong side of town. They used to call where we are Greene Tower. We used to call it home.

I'm sitting against the living room wall, in the place I watched television with my family, in the place I now burn photos of them. To my right, the gigantic hole, where I perched with Victor a few nights ago, gives me a perfect image of the night sky. The moon is so bright, so many stars are twinkling, that even this place glows. Or maybe that's just the residue of my childhood memories.

Across from me, leaning against the wall, is the one I

used to call my brother, who I used to call Brady.

But he isn't Brady anymore. His hood is back and I can see his face now. It's skeletally thin, like he just stepped out of a night shift at the Works. Even after all these years, it seems like the coal dust never washed off his face. It certainly didn't leave his eyes. They're pitch-black. Nothing human left in them. Why does he look like that? And why are his teeth so monstrous? It isn't one pair of fangs; it's an entire row. More demon than vampire.

In his hands, he's looking at a piece of paper with creases running along it showing how neatly folded it once was. I did that when I brought it to our new apartment. The drawing of my family I put on the refrigerator all those years ago. The drawing I still had when Brady broke in and attacked Rachel. The only thing he took. The only picture I had with all of us together. Drawn in thick, sketchy crayon.

"Why didn't you let us know you were alive?" I ask.

"Look at what I am!"

"You're still my brother."

"No! Sin changed me." His head twitches. "I was dying. He dragged me off, drank my blood until my heart was practically dry, each pump—so loud, so hard. It hurt. I was so scared, Dawn. You don't understand how scared I was of dying. And all he did was slash his wrist, let the blood hit the floor, and then walk away. He knew exactly what I would do. He's smart like that. So I licked his blood. Off the ground. But vampire blood won't save us. I died . . . and then I woke up. Like this. I changed . . . into this."

"But, Brady, you don't look like—"

He lets out a primal scream, then punches the wall behind him, his fist going straight through it into the neighbor's living room.

"Into this!"

He grabs a patch of his hair and tries to tear it out, but it won't budge, so he punches the wall again.

"Brady, stop! You're scaring me." He is frightening me, but maybe if I sound like the Dawn he knew, the scared little girl, I can reach the part of him that's still human. I can't believe he's the one who's been stalking me. My own brother was my bogeyman. In some ways, it makes it so much worse. Once he protected me, and now he's this *thing* that I barely recognize. I don't know what he's capable of. If Sin created him, he has to be filled with evil. It hurts seeing him like this.

"I couldn't do it, Dawn," he says, suddenly composed again, as if he hadn't just ripped the wall apart. "I just couldn't do it. Not after Mom and Dad. They'd be so ashamed of me if I did it. They'd be so ashamed if they saw me."

"What couldn't you do?" *Please tell me that you couldn't kill Victor.*

He screams again, and I press my back harder against the wall, as if I can retreat through it, get back inside that closet until this all goes away. He grabs a rotting kitchen chair and throws it out the huge hole in the wall, where it crashes far, far below.

"I just couldn't do it," he says, laughing at his own inside joke. "I wanted to. God, did I want to! I wanted to know what it tasted like. I had to know. I had to know why they wanted us so badly. Why they needed our blood. Why we had to be scared every night!"

He slams his foot into the wall, and I see bits of the ceiling flake off and fall down on him. It's as if his sanity is currency, and once he runs out, he has to destroy something to get it back.

The shock of seeing my brother like this is unbearable. A part of me always thought he might've been alive. But why is he like *this*? Losing his grip on reality, rambling and repeating himself, twitching like he has some neurological disease.

And then I realize what's happened to him. I'm not sure when, or for how long he's been suffering this way. But there's no question *why* he has rows of fangs, why his eyes are blackened, why he's a stranger in his own body, why he disarmed Michael so easily.

The Thirst.

"You couldn't feed on humans, could you?" I ask.

"Never. I never did, Dawn. I want you to know that. I never did. All those vampires, for all those years, I stalked them on the outside. Killing and drinking them. I didn't want to do that either; I wanted to stop. But it was too late. It's all I can think about. It's all-consuming. But it'll end tonight. It'll end very, very soon. When Victor comes for you."

My eyes go wide. I'm the bait. No, he can't be that cruel, to use me in that way.

"I've been watching you," he says, answering me before

I can ask. "Someone had to, after Mom and Dad died. I've been protecting you. That vampire at Dawson Elementary. He wanted your blood. I wouldn't let him have it. Or any of the others. When they got too close, I took care of them."

By ripping out their throats.

"Only one is left. Old Family Victor. And when he comes here, I'm going to kill him. Then I'm going to drink his blood. And I'll be cured, Dawn. I'll become human, and then we can be a family again. I can get my job back at the Works, and I can come home every night and we can watch TV together, and we can—"

"That won't cure you, Brady. There's no cure for what you have."

"No! He told me! He said it would cure me."

"Who told you that?"

"Sin!"

"Sin?" His favorite creation. His perfection.

My brother nods. "He slit his wrist and bled onto the ground. His blood is like gold. It costs him so much to give away even a little to another. So he has to be very select in who he turns. He has to turn the right people for his army. Because of him, I can walk in the sun. But because I feed off of vampires, I've become this! I . . . I thought that Sin would hate me for that. I had taken his gift of day walking and become a monster. But he didn't hate me. He gave me a special mission. He told me . . . he told me that Victor wanted to hurt you. He said I could protect you by killing him, and then drink his Old Family blood. And it would cure me."

Sin. He took Brady and now he's trying to take Victor. Only he won't do it himself. He must not be as strong as his half brother. Letting Victor kill his father, then letting this perverted version of my once-loved brother kill Victor. Is that Sin's weakness? Does his ability to walk in the sun come at the cost of the strength and speed gifted to every other vampire? He may have power that exceeds humans', but he could still be weaker than other vamps.

"Sin lied to you," I say. "There's no cure for the Thirst! He's just using you as a pawn in his game."

"No!" He digs his nails into the wall, brings them down, scoring it, paper and plaster crumbling onto the floor. He makes fists and pounds the wall like an upset child. "He told me the truth! He had to; it's the final escape from this . . . this torture!"

Oh, Brady. The only reason you're like this is because you couldn't harm another human, couldn't drink their blood. If you had taken their lives, you would've saved your own sanity.

My heart is heavy with sadness. But it's heavier with the guilt I'll soon have to swallow. Because there's no cure for the Thirst, except the stake.

"*Victor's* no good," he snarls. "He's using you. My precious little sister. So innocent. So naive. No one's good enough for you."

"I'm not a little girl anymore!"

Though to him, I am. To Brady, who heard my screams as he fought, I must still be trapped, still need his protection. Has he played that night out over and over again in this room? Has he found a way to change things? Has he found a way to be redeemed? That's why the final confrontation has to be here. Victor, not Sin, will be the vampire who stole his life eight years ago, but this time Brady will win. In his mind, when he drinks Victor's blood, he'll be cured.

"He won't come," I say. "Victor doesn't know I'm here."

"Of course I do."

I jerk my head around.

Victor's standing in the doorway. I instantly regret seeing him. Brady would never kill me, but it's too dangerous for Victor to be here. Brady is beyond reason, and he thinks Victor's blood offers an escape from his torment.

"I had a feeling Father's other son would be creating havoc tonight," he says to me, not even acknowledging Brady. "Richard, Faith, and I came to the city as soon as the sun set, trying to figure out where he would strike."

"It's Sin. He's a Day Walker."

"That explains why he feels like a ghost. Vampires can usually sense when another one is near, but when I met him"—he shakes his head—"I couldn't read him. I didn't give him much thought because I had other things on my mind."

"Why would your father not embrace him?"

"He must have feared his power."

"It's my power you need to fear!" Brady shouts.

"Victor, this is my brother. Brady."

"Not anymore." And with that regretful phrase, Victor pronounces my brother's death sentence.

"I wish you didn't have to do this," I say, speaking to

them both, although I know there's no salvation for Brady.

"Don't worry," Brady says. "It'll all be over very soon."

"You have no idea who I am." Victor's fists curl, his forearms surprisingly large for his slender body.

"Old Family, always thinking you're the best."

"I'm so sorry, Dawn." Victor pulls out a metal stake from behind his back.

"Me too," Brady says, opening his gaping jaw, revealing the razor-wire fangs.

Victor makes the first move, kicking a chair so hard it flies at Brady, who smashes it with his fists. But it was just a distraction, and Victor is on him. I expect the sound of metal piercing flesh and bone, for Brady's eyes to go wide, and then years of torment to end violently, tragically. But all I hear is the clash of bodies, no one gaining the advantage over the other. It's fast and brutal. It isn't like Victor's fight with his father, which seemed oddly beautiful, a choreographed ballet of blurred motions, as if they'd been dueling for a hundred years and now it was displayed. In front of me is the raw, animalistic need for one to destroy the other.

And me, scared, backed against the wall. I want to help, but I'd just get in the way.

One of their ribs cracks; I can hear it echo in the small apartment. One of them gasps as all the air leaves him.

Victor sinks his stake into Brady's thigh, but it doesn't even faze him. Victor extracts it and tries to slam it into his opponent's heart, but Brady dodges somehow, then locks Victor's arm under his own.

With strength I didn't think possible, my brother lifts Victor up and throws him, like he would an oversize pillow, through our living room wall into the neighboring apartment. Wood and plaster rain down as Victor slides across the floor.

"Stop it, Brady!" I shout, but I might as well be on the moon.

Brady reaches down and picks up Victor's stake, which has fallen to the floor. He stalks over to the Old Family vampire and brings the stake down toward Victor's heart.

Victor reacts just in time, deflecting the blow. The metal penetrates his chest, but is off the mark. The vampire's heart still beats.

Brady, ripping the stake out, cocks his head back, revealing the rows of deadly fangs. I force myself to my feet, wave off the dizziness from whatever Brady injected into me, and rush across the room as my brother, whose screams haunted me for eight years, clamps down on Victor's shoulder, his grotesque fangs cleanly piercing the skin, blood spurting in a sickening arch.

"Brady, no!" I slam into him, wrap my arms around him, struggle to pull him—

With one arm, he flings me away as though I'm nothing. I hit the floor hard, am disoriented, but I can see Victor's eyes. He's tired, worn-out, on the verge of surrendering.

Look at me, Victor. You have to fight.

Brady's teeth grind into his shoulder, and Victor is beyond feeling pain. He's slipping away.

"Victor!" I shout, all the emotions I've ever felt for him

coming up in this singular moment.

He closes his eyes, and when they open, it's like nothing I've ever seen in him. An all-consuming rage has taken over. He grits his teeth, his fangs longer than before. He grips Brady by the shoulders and pushes him away, tearing his own shoulder flesh as Brady refuses to release him.

Victor punches him across the face so hard one of Brady's many fangs flies out, covered in the blood that was once Victor's. The Old Family vampire delivers another well-timed strike to his opponent's jaw, and then sends Brady flying with a kick. My brother crashes through the coffee table in front of me. His mouth is dripping with red. He shakes his head and stands up just in time for Victor to jump on him, stake at the ready, placed right above Brady's heart.

I watch the scene unfold. Seconds pass, but they might as well be years. Eight years. Alone in that closet. Scared to come out. Scared to help. Scared to do anything but cry.

Stupid girl. Stupid, stupid girl.

I couldn't have saved you then, Brady. But I can save you now.

I crawl over to Victor, who can't overcome Brady's strength alone. Each has his hands wrapped around the stake, one pressing down, the other pushing up, the tip resting just on the surface of the skin, not yet piercing it.

I put my hands over Victor's. I feel his blood rushing through them, thumping with his heart. I afford Brady only one look, because it's all I can endure—knowing what I have to do. His black eyes see the betrayal. But can he understand that I'm doing this for him? Somewhere deep inside his infected brain, is there a part that says, *Please, Dawn, end this agony?*

The only reason he has the Thirst is because he could never harm a human. He hates what he's become—the shattered mirror in my apartment makes sense now. And with that thought racing through my mind, I shed one final tear for him, for my parents, for this unfair world.

"I love you, Brady," I whisper, with tears in my eyes. "Don't be afraid of the dark."

Then I press down with all my weight. It's quick. He doesn't even scream. He simply stops struggling. Then goes still. Forever.

Leaning over, I press a kiss to his forehead and pray that he's now at peace.

I know my struggles aren't over. My hands are covered in blood. Victor's blood, still pouring from his shoulder. And worse, escaping from his chest.

He's moved away from Brady, and his eyes have returned to the ones that enter my dreams. Only now they're sad.

"Victor," I say. He doesn't respond, just stares off into the night, his back resting against the couch. "Victor."

"I'm so sorry, Dawn." His voice is weak. He pulls his hand away from his chest and the blood flows out. I rush over to him, kneel down, and put my palm over his chest. The blood is warm, and I can feel his heart slowing, sputtering, struggling.

"Victor . . . why won't the bleeding stop?"

"I'll be fine. The wound in my heart is deep, but it'll heal. In time."

"How much time?" I know vampires can heal in a matter of minutes, maybe an hour if the damage is severe. But if his heart has been punctured, what then? Even with the stake removed, it still bleeds.

"Don't worry. . . ."

"Victor! How long!"

"A day. Maybe more." As he says it he coughs and grits his teeth, pure agony resonating through him.

"We don't have that long," I say. "Sin might still be out there; he might be looking for us. He might be looking for you."

"Then let him find me. At least I'll have . . . these last moments with you."

"Don't say that. Come on, we can get you out of here."

I try to lift him up, but he weighs too much, and I know that we'll never get him to a safe place fast enough.

"I wish this could've ended differently," Victor says.

"It isn't your fault."

"It's always been my fault. Everything around you. I created this."

He's losing his grip on the world. His head moves lazily in circles.

"Victor, you have to drink from me. My blood can heal you." I move forward, working my dress down so my neck is exposed clearly.

"No! I won't do that to you, Dawn."

"You'll . . . you'll die. If Sin doesn't find you, the sun will."

"Better me than you. I need too much blood to heal this

wound. And the only way to save you . . . You'd hate being a vampire."

It won't end here. Not like this. I grab a piece of sharpened wood, splintered off of the table when Brady shattered it. I press it against my neck. I don't know where the artery is, but if I can get it deep enough at all . . .

"Don't," he says, trying to swat my makeshift instrument away, but he's so weak now he can barely lift his arm.

"Victor, I can't let you go. I won't let you go. Not because you're important to the city, but because you're important to me."

"Dawn . . ." He breathes my name like a soliloquy.

"Take my blood."

"I won't be able to stop. To save you, I'd have to turn you."

"You aren't a monster, Victor. I trust you."

I put down the stake, lean in, and nestle my face against Victor's good shoulder, placing the throbbing pulse in my neck within easy reach of his fangs. "It's okay," I whisper into his ear. "I love you."

He cups my face and turns me toward him. I look into his eyes as he kisses me, and then close my own. It's the sweetest kiss I've ever known, made better by the struggle that brought us here.

He draws away, but I keep my eyes closed. He gently turns my head, exposing my neck, and plunges his fangs into my skin.

I gasp as they penetrate. It hurts. Tears spring to my eyes, not from the pain, but from the relief, the satisfaction.

I've offered him the essence of my body and he's taking it. I expected to feel guilty, to see images of my parents and their sacrifice, or the Agency and everything I'm supposed to stand for. But I don't see anything. I just feel Victor's warmth as he drinks my blood. I feel his hand steady against the back of my head, his fingers laced through my hair. He brings me in closer.

"It's okay," I whisper, softer than before.

His other hand wraps me close so I can't escape, even if I wanted to. But I don't. I want to be here forever.

"It's . . ." I try to tell him it's okay. But I'm losing focus. Losing life.

The world's getting dark. His hands tighten, squeezing me until it hurts, clamping my head until I want to break free.

He's strong again. But he can't stop. He told me this would happen. And my last thought, just before everything goes away, is that maybe he was right.

Victor, you are a monster.

And soon I'll be one, too.

Dying to know what happens next?
Read on for a sneak peek of

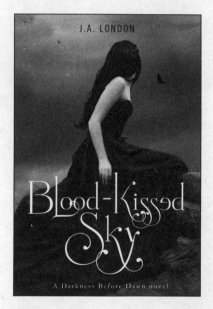

Chapter 1

Death isn't what I thought it would be. It's an acute awareness, a consciousness. A chill that seeps deep into my bones. Most surprising of all, though, is that it's not ethereal. It's solid, substantial—hard stone, narrow ledges, steep drops.

The black sky is laced with stars. A high moon visible over the snow-capped peaks cloaks everything in cascading blues and grays.

I've been wandering aimlessly through this mountainous maze for what seems like forever.

Ever since Victor killed me.

Victor Valentine. Vampire. How could I have fallen for him—knowing what he was?

How could I have willingly given him my blood—knowing it would mean my death as a human?

How could I have accepted becoming a monster—knowing it was a life I would detest?

He warned me: Once he tasted my blood, he wouldn't be able to stop. He would drain me. I would die. So here I am, waiting for him to bring me back as a creature of the night like him.

Did he change his mind? Did he decide that I would hate him too much if he turned me? Or is the metamorphosis from human to vampire a slow process that seems to take an eternity?

I begin to hear a soft lyrical sound. Almost as if this place is singing to me. A voice suddenly echoes from within the stone.

"Find me."

"Victor?" I rasp, desperate to be with him again, but it's not his voice summoning me.

"Find me."

I don't want to answer. I don't want to search. I'm suddenly afraid. More afraid than I've ever been.

"Find me!"

Air fills my lungs and I feel as though a cord is attached to my spine, yanking me backward. . . .

My eyes spring open to stark, white surroundings. Where am I?

"Someone, get Dr. Icarus! She's awake!"

Through a dense fog of confusion, I watch as a petite woman in light blue scrubs comes over and begins adjusting dials, checking a bag that is dripping fluid into my arm. Then she leans over and smiles at me. "Hello, sweetie. Welcome back."

Does she know I was in the land of the dead?

"Where's Victor?" I croak. I can hear the beeps on the heart monitor going faster. "Why isn't he here?"

"Easy, sweetie. The only Victor I know is the new Lord Valentine, and you sure wouldn't want him to be in this room."

He's alive! Thank God. I was afraid my blood hadn't been enough. But if it was, then why am I here? Why didn't he kill me? Turn me? I had accepted that I would become a vampire when I offered him my blood. I had felt a sense of relief that the battle was behind me, that the differences between us would no longer separate us.

If I wasn't in the land of the dead, then where was I? I have to find Victor, discover exactly what happened. Why am I in this cold room and not in his warm arms? I try to sit up, and she gently pushes me back down.

"Relax, you're not going anywhere in your condition."

I force my breathing to even out, my muscles to go limp. She's not the one with the answers. But who is?

A door creaks open. She steps away, and another face hovers over me. It's not as kind. It looks to be all business. Maybe that's the reason his hair deserted him. He wasn't any fun.

"Miss Montgomery? Miss Montgomery, can you hear me? I'm Dr. Icarus. You're at Mercy Hospital. Do you know why you're here?"

Should I know? I give my head a slight shake and pain

ricochets through it.

Everything is so fuzzy, so distant. Their voices echo along with my own. I feel like I'm in a dream. Before—that strange world in the mountains—seems more real. Now it's like all my memories are running away, heading toward the dark corners of my mind, and I can't snag the one I need. I don't know how I got here.

"I was . . ." I start, but instinct keeps me from finishing. I was with Victor in a crumbling apartment building. He was dying. He fought my brother—Brady. Oh, God, Brady. A sharp pain pierces my chest as though a stake was thrust into my heart. All these years I thought he was dead. I thought vampires had killed him—but they chose a worse fate for him. They turned him. No, not they. Sin. Sin, who attended our school. Sin, who dated my best friend, Tegan Romano. Sin, who earned our trust and then betrayed us all. He stood alone as a new breed of vampire—a Daywalker. How could we have known he thirsted for our blood? By the time he showed his fangs, it was far, far too late.

He sent Brady to kill Victor. He almost succeeded, but my love for Victor was stronger than Sin could ever comprehend. I rub my neck, remembering the pain of Victor's fangs sinking into my flesh, but I can't feel any healing wound or scars.

"It's strange," the doctor says, observing my movements, "you arrived a few heartbeats away from death with deep puncture wounds in your neck. I've never seen anything like that. Most vampire bites take days to mend and scar tissue develops. Even your tattoo is completely intact."

I have a crucifix inked on either side of my neck. Even though they don't ward off vampires. My brother had them as well, which was the reason I had the ink work done. In honor of him—when I thought vampires killed him.

"How did I get here?" I ask.

"A week ago some guy dropped you off in the ER and took off once he saw us tending to you."

Victor couldn't risk exposing himself as a vampire, or what he had done to me. If anyone thought he'd attacked the city's delegate, he'd have a difficult time convincing people he wasn't like his father, Murdoch Valentine. Murdoch was Denver's overlord until Victor overthrew him.

"We gave you blood transfusions, but you went into a mild coma," the doctor continues, interrupting my thoughts. "No doubt it was your body's defense mechanism kicking in so you could recover from the ordeal. It's a miracle you're alive. Can you tell me what happened?"

"Strangest dream," I say.

"You want to tell me about it?" the doctor asks, turning to his charts.

"I don't really remember anything. Just that it seemed . . . real. I mean, right now, this all seems like the dream."

"But you don't remember anything from it?"

It was so vivid while I was in it, but trying to recall the images now . . . it's like my mind is fighting me. "My head hurts."

"I'll get you something for that, but I can't medicate you too much; we need to make sure your body is stabilized."

The door opens. My guardian, Rachel Goodwin, enters. She is always put-together in dark blue suits, with her brown hair clipped up neatly. But right now she's wearing jeans and one of my fading T-shirts. She looks as though she hasn't touched a brush or makeup in a week. As soon as our eyes meet, she drops whatever she's carrying, hurries across the room, and hugs me hard.

"Oh my God," she says. "I go out for a few seconds to grab a bag of chips from the vending machine, and you wake up."

I squeeze back, so very glad to see her. Like me, she works for the Agency—which is responsible for protecting the city—serving as my mentor, guiding me in my role as the city's delegate to our vampire overlord.

"Tegan," I whisper hoarsely, tears stinging my eyes. "Do you know what happened to Tegan?" She's been my best friend forever, and the last time I saw her she was in a crumpled heap on the floor after Sin plunged his fangs into her neck. Did he kill her? Did he turn her?

"She's fine," Rachel assures me. Releasing her hold on me, she tucks my hair behind my ears.

"What about Sin? Did we get him? Tell me he's dead."

Sadly she shakes her head. "Not yet."

"Do we have any leads? What are we doing to find him?"

"Shh. You don't need to be worrying about that yet."

How can I not worry about it? Sin may be Victor's half brother, but they're nothing alike. Victor sees a future with humans and vampires together, while Sin sees . . . I haven't a clue. His plans are still unfolding, which makes him all the more dangerous, especially to those who know him.

Like Tegan. Poor Tegan. She loved him. "I need to see Tegan, Rachel. I need to see her."

"I know, I know. I'll call her." She pulls out her cell phone.

"She's not ready for visitors yet," the doctor explains, but Rachel just holds up a warning finger to cut him off and then dials anyway.

Half an hour later, the doctor and nurse have left and I'm surrounded by some of the most important people in my life. Even with all these blankets over me, I feel exposed. I've never much enjoyed being the center of attention. Right now I feel like Dorothy awakening after her trip to Oz. Only I didn't follow the yellow brick road. Victor took me down a rabbit hole into the darkness of the vampire world.

Rachel gives me another hug that almost strangles me. Jeff gently pulls her away.

"I'm glad you're awake, kiddo." He pats my shoulder. He's a bodyguard, watching over Rachel and me when we move about the city on official Agency business. Although lately he has been hanging around even when we had no business, and I'm pretty sure his relationship with Rachel has moved beyond simply professional.

"We all are," Clive Anderson says, his voice weary but still commanding authority.

He's the director of the Agency. My boss. I already know that my report to Clive will leave out a lot of details—mainly those that involve Victor and how much I've come to care for him.

"The Night Watchmen that Sin turned—at least tell me that you got them."

The Night Watchmen are the most respected group in the city, dealing with any vampires who breach our wall. Somehow Sin infiltrated them and did the unthinkable: he turned some of them into vampires. He corrupted the incorruptible.

"We called a special meeting of the Night Watchmen," Clive says. He explains that they locked the doors, and brought out buckets of blood. The Daywalkers couldn't stop their fangs from dropping and those who hadn't been turned staked them. It was quite a carnage. "We're confident we got them all. We haven't had a Daywalker attack since."

"But that's just the Night Watchmen. What if there are others Sin turned?"

"Then we'll be facing an absolute nightmare come to life. We'll be at war all over again. Only this time, the enemy can walk in the sun."

"But you shouldn't concern yourself with that right now," Rachel says, knowing that I could discuss this issue with Clive for hours. "We weren't able to contain the news that a Daywalker exists. Too many kids at the party saw Sin at school. But at this point, we have no proof that the turned Night Watchmen were in fact Daywalkers. Still, we've increased the guards on patrol, the Night Watchmen are working day shifts. We're doing what we can. You just need to get well."

I look past her to Tegan. She's petite with short blond hair that frames her pixie face and makes her startling green eyes stand out. They used to be so vibrant and bright. Now they're dull, and it's all Sin's fault. She's studying the floor as though she's searching for a crack she can slip through.

"Can I have a moment alone with Tegan?" I ask.

"Sure," Rachel says, squeezing my hand before ushering out Jeff and Clive. When the door snaps closed in their wake, Tegan gives a startled jump.

"Tegan?"

Finally, she looks at me. Tears are welling in her eyes.

"I could really use a hug," I say, knowing she needs one a lot more than I do.

She rushes across the room and wraps her arms around me.

"I didn't know Sin was a vampire," she whispers brokenly near my ear. "Oh, God, I'm so sorry."

I hold her close, rocking her slightly, like she's the patient instead of me. She has a set of small, neat stitches on her neck. Why don't I? What if Victor did turn me? What if I am a vampire? They heal quickly; they don't scar.

"No one knew what he was," I reassure her. I hate what he did to her. I need to get out of here, find him, and make him pay.

"I should have known," she insists.

"There was no way to know."

"I loved him, Dawn, I loved him, and now I hate him."

I rub her back. "I know. I know it hurts."

She breaks out of my embrace and paces the room. "I

just feel so stupid. How could I have not known?"

"No one knew. Not even Victor. Vampires can sense other vampires, but not Sin. No one knew what Sin was."

She stops with her shoulders slumped in defeat. I hate seeing her like this. She's always been ready for any adventure, grabbing all the fun she can from life. I'm afraid Sin has stolen that spontaneity and joy from her.

"I thought he was the one, you know?" she says in a low, self-effacing voice. "I've never been in love before and I thought . . . I thought he was everything. He bit me, Dawn." She jerks her head up and I see the first sign of fire and life in her eyes. "He sank his fangs into me—without even asking! I mean, how rude is that!"

"Very rude," I reassure her.

She dries her eyes, gives a few little sniffs. "Yeah, well, I plan to sink my stake into his heart without asking."

"I'll help you do it."

She gives me a quick smile before she furrows her brow. "I wasn't the only one with a vampire in my life. Victor is the new Lord Valentine. Why didn't you tell me what he was?"

I hear the edge of betrayal in her voice. Michael and Tegan had met Victor, but they'd thought he was a Night Watchman. And I hadn't corrected them. "I was afraid it would put you in danger."

"You told me you liked him, but how could you if he's a vamp?"

"It's complicated."

"Do you love him?"

I groan. "I don't know. I care for him deeply, but we're not a couple, if that's what you're asking. Humans and vampires never work out."

"You got that right," she mutters.

I know Tegan is struggling with everything she went through. In some ways, what she endured was worse than what I did. Vampires have been screwing with me for as long as I can remember. Even when I began to care for Victor, I was wary. I didn't commit my heart completely.

Tegan thought she was falling for a human.

"I hope he's dead," she says quietly.

I know she's talking about Sin. "I hope so, too."

The door opens and the nurse strides in. "Sorry, visiting time is over."

"One more minute," I plead.

"Nope. You've got a lot of recovering to do."

I give Tegan another hard hug. "It's going to be okay."

"I'll try to sneak back in when she's not looking," she whispers.

My heart lifts at a shadow of the old Tegan.

The nurse flaps her hands at Tegan like she's a bird that needs to be shooed away. "Now go on."

When I'm finally alone, I feel exhausted, but my mind is racing with so many questions that I can't sleep. I can't stand being in the bed. I throw back the blankets, sit up, and swing my legs over the side. I ease my feet to the floor and when I stand my knees buckle. I catch myself by bracing one arm on the bed and grabbing the IV stand with the other hand.

I can't believe how weak I am, but I'm also determined. Using the stand for support, I shuffle toward the window. The sun's rays stream into the small room and I pause on the edge of them. I've never been afraid of the sun. So why am I now? It used to illuminate my world, make it seem worth fighting for. But now . . .

Oh, God. Did it happen? Did Victor turn me? Is the vampire instinct to fear the light already in my blood?

I hold out my hand and tentatively ease it forward, exploring the empty space in front of me, unsure of where the sunbeams truly begin. It feels like I'm pushing toward an invisible Venus fly trap, one that may snap close, or one that may let me pass.

I watch the light highlight the tips of my fingernails. No burning.

I expose more. Up to my knuckles. No stinging.

Finally I plunge my whole hand into the light rays, letting the golden glow wash over me. It feels wonderful.

I step fully into the sun and press my cheek and body against the glass of the window. Closing my eyes, I absorb the warmth. When I offered Victor my blood, I was certain that I would never again watch a sunrise, would never again experience its perfect illumination.

Yet here I am in a hospital with morning sunlight filtering gently through the window. I have to admit I'm slightly disappointed.

No longer property of
Long Beach Public Library

Loved *Darkness Before Dawn?*

Then don't miss the Dark Guardian series from Rachel Hawthorne, part of the team behind J. A. London.

HARPER TEEN

An Imprint of HarperCollinsPublishers

www.epicreads.com

JOIN
THE COMMUNITY AT

Epic Reads
Your World. Your Books.

FIND
the latest
books

DISCUSS
what's on
your reading
wish list

CREATE
your own book
news and
activities to share
with friends

ACCESS
exclusive
contests and
videos

Don't miss out on any upcoming
EPIC READS!

Visit the site and browse the
categories to find out more.

www.epicreads.com

HARPER TEEN
An Imprint of HarperCollinsPublishers